THE ALBANNACH

THE ALBANNACH

By
FIONN MAC COLLA

" Is ann aig deireadh an latha is fheàrr
na Domhnullaich "

SOUVENIR PRESS

First published 1932
Reprint by Reprographia 1971

and published 1984 by
Souvenir Press (Educational & Academic) Ltd.
43 Great Russell Street, London WC1B 3PA
and simultaneously in Canada

*The publisher acknowledges
the financial assistance of The
Scottish Arts Council in the production
of this volume*

ISBN 0 285 62644 2 casebound
ISBN 0 285 62674 4 paperback

Printed in Great Britain by
Photobooks (Bristol) Ltd.

FOREWORD

The first thing to understand about *The Albannach* is that its first appearance (in 1932) initiated a trend. The trend later became so well established and familiar – the 'Novelist of the Highlands', and so forth – that the book is practically bound to read now like just one more example of a *genre* which in fact it initiated. It was the first novel to treat life in the Gaidhealtachd in a realistic manner. That life had of course been previously written about in an *authentic* manner. The works of Neil Munro for instance are irradiated and suffused with the unique flavour of Gaelic life in a way which is totally authentic and beyond praise. But they are otherwise marred by a treatment exempt from circumstance, by the pushing back of the events to former and distant ages, in other words by romanticisation – a course forced upon Munro by his refusal to come to grips with the realities of the situation of the Gael in his day. That was the responsibility which I accepted in *The Albannach.* With it the modern Gael, as he was in his actual conditions, for the first time stepped on to the stage – one reason why Hugh MacDiarmid called the book on its first publication 'the most radical product yet of the whole Scottish Renaissance movement'.

In assessing it certain things have to be kept in mind. I sat down to write it at twenty-three, which was not necessarily a handicap. It is possible that more maturity might have improved the book in specific ways. But the matter couldn't wait. For I was extremely angry – as I still am, in the same context. But I was also as to my official status a foreign missionary of the Church of Scotland. That last fact is crucial, because the attempt was made at the time, as I have little doubt it will be made again, to evade the issues presented in the book by the simple, time-honoured method of suggesting that it was a 'Roman Catholic' (and therefore treacherous and dishonest) attack upon Presbyterianism. It was nothing of the sort. It was certainly intended as a radical criticism of the life-negating and culture-destroying 'religion' being imposed on the Gael, but it was a criticism I felt entitled to make, with all the more fierceness and anger, as being myself at that time 'one of the family'.

But in the course of my studies, and as a teacher of the History of Cultures, it could not have failed to come to my knowledge and awareness that the Catholic or as it was historically, simply the Christian Church had all along maintained a quite different doctrine of Man. One which, had it remained in the ascendant, would have prevented the destruction of the Gael and the eventual elimination from the human scene of the last remnants of the Scottish nation, which we are at present witnessing.

There are two attitudes, the one that human nature is in its essence good, the other that human nature is absolutely, radically and irredeemably evil. Those are not two forms or aspects of the same 'religion'; they are totally exclusive one of the other. The first is Christian, the second is not. It was the second which in the sixteenth century, under the name of 'Reformed Christianity', took total command in Scotland.

There has been in short a misunderstanding. Reformation Protestantism was not Christianity or even a form of Christianity, but its almost complete antithesis. Its affiliations are not with Christianity in its historic form, unceasingly at war with the very spirit that produced such life-negating doctrines, but with Communism of the present day. Communism is another system which negates man, and does not respect his freedom. Communism deifies not man but the Social Collectivity, regarded as the totality of those who are indoctrinated with Communism. Instead of bringing man freedom Communism *liberates negating wills into membership of a Dictatorship of Negators.* Normally establishing itself by the indiscriminate slaughter of inaccordant elements, where slaughter is no longer advisable or possible Communism perpetuates itself by declaring the isolation and social death of irreconcilables; as also of course by its total control over the minds of the young so that every succeeding generation may be indoctrinated – something which is sometimes called 'zeal for education'.

The essential thing about the 'Reformers' was that they formed precisely such a take-over Group – *their specific doctrines were nothing more than a sort of accident of the times.* They and their successors were those who withheld their *Amen* from man's greatness and the glory of all that *is:* a sort of Congregation of Resentful Mediocrities of the Spirit, who replied to human creativity and greatness and all the glory of *being* with a fierce *Anathema, let it be accursed.*

For of course if the nature of man is totally and

radically corrupt and evil, it followed as an ineluctable corollary that everything that emerges from that nature and is an expression of it, such as the whole creative life of man – such as specifically the entire body of the poetry, music and literature of the Gael – was in itself evil and therefore as a first priority requiring to be stamped out. Living in the Gaidhealtachd I witnessed that stamping-out actually going on, and the remains of the enormous deposit of Gaelic culture surviving only in furtive and surreptitious fashion, put socially beyond the pale by the hard and hating negations of the dominant 'religion'. *The Albannach* was the resulting angry protest.

Murdo Anderson in the book, the protagonist of my own attitude in the complex context of human life – which I had not then, of course, completely worked out intellectually, as I tried to do later in 'And the Cock Crew', and more completely still in 'At the Sign of the Clenched Fist' – Murdo Anderson has a soul open to poetry, music, the visual beauty of the world, in a word, to Life, and reacts violently against the stifling prohibitions and negations which he finds ruling his native community in the north-west highlands. For a time it seems he is to escape – by means of his considerable intellectuality, through Glasgow University. But mere escape would have settled nothing, life has to be met head-on – as is meant to be shown by Roderick Urquhart, who does qualify and ultimately gets an important post – in England; but is never inwardly at ease because of an obscure, ineradicable sense that he has lost touch with his roots, and whom we last see positively snarling with a sense of frustration at what he now senses as his exclusion through his own act from a revitalised life in his native community and culture – he had, he was obscurely realising, 'backed the wrong horse'... So Murdo, by force of circumstances, has to return to his original community, where he is obviously going to be compelled to live out the rest of his life. He reacts at first with self-protective numbness, then with active despair, and eventually contemplates – and intends – suicide. At this point he perceives he has an alternative, the only course other than suicide open to one in his position unable to escape out of a Nay-saying community – to choose to make a personal change-over to Yea-saying to life and the glory of all that *is.* Leading his life thereafter quite simply in the light of that Affirmation, or, to put it otherwise, basing his life thereafter on an unspeakable Permanence on which he had seen that he could rest his heart. At the end we are supposed to see a society, all but dead from continuous Nay-saying to the glory of life, beginning to be regenerated through the spreading influence of a single individual who had freely chosen to render an unimpeded, emphatic Yea to all *being* simply as *being.* It is not without significance that the book more or less leaves him playing the pipes. The First Cause or Unmoved First Mover – we must forget the infinitely subjective and question-begging term 'God', and for a thousand years! – the Ground of all Being or Creative Absolute – or as some moderns are calling it, the Ultimate Reference – is in *piobaireachd,* as it never was in Calvinist theology – which, I repeat again and again, was nothing more in essence than a rationalisation, making use of terms picked from here and there out of the Bible, of a purely subjective and largely subconscious impulse to be free of the necessity of obeisance to whatever was experienced as *overshadowing.*

Certain specific points – at the time of writing *The Albannach* I had met only one Catholic priest, and he was the prototype of Father O'Reilly. (He was the only character in the book – with the exception of two minor characters who appear momentarily – who was drawn from life). He was in fact a Scot, but as he was very much alive at the time I made him Irish and called him O'Reilly. (His photograph in old age is to be seen opposite page 193 in Sir Compton MacKenzie's seventh Octave of his 'Life and Times'). But in making him Irish I did no injustice to either Scotland or Ireland – and fulfilled indeed a certain symbolic intention. It is true that since writing the book I have come to know a great many Catholics, and I can see the point of the suggestion someone made to me that the typical Irish priest was more likely to be 'a lantern-jawed puritan'. It depends what one means by typical. I have long been aware that in both the Scottish and Irish Catholic communities there is a discernible element of the immanent spirit of Jansenism, which was a sort of puritanism within Catholicism, which lingers on although the tenets were long since anathematised. Father O'Reilly, however, was the typical *Catholic* priest, his spirit unclouded by Jansenist or any other negations, the keynote of whose personality was joy and affirmation. W.B. Yeats was talking sound theology when he said: 'The good are always the merry, save by an evil chance'.

The point of view, whose function is to impose unity on the work, is from inside the hero's perception throughout: we are supposed to apprehend the state of his consciousness at any moment by seeing things as he was seeing them. This is important as I have been accused, among other things, of seriously maintaining that a million people in Glasgow have pendant ears! If people and the world appear distorted it is meant to be an indication of the state of the observing soul. Normally, however, and in general, Murdo's vision of the world is that of the affirming or Yea-saying consciousness. For my part I have always seen people, particularly perhaps against the background of the natural scenery of Scotland, not as pleasing or unpleasing, but as *real*, and therefore wonderful – adventitious drops at noses irrespective. Has anyone bandy legs? – he can be assured of my hallelujah. Not because bandy legs are pleasing, but because *his* are *real*.

In the midst of the current preoccupation with sex I have hinted perhaps more broadly than enough at the conflicts and disasters that may be caused in personalities and lives by the equating of sex with sin, and purity with ignorance.

On that subject, it was never intended to be suggested that the lay missionaries of the Free Presbyterian Church are particularly characterised by lechery. To suppose so would be to miss part of the allegoric intention.

Finally, the exigencies of the method used in reproducing this edition require that a few misprints, misplacing of accents, etc. which found their way into the original edition, remain.

Dun-Eideann September 1971 Fionn Mac Colla

I

EASTWARD the great bens flamed and burned —Sgùrr Ard, Beinn Bhreac and Càrn Mór glowing dark red at the roots of them and rearing in air high tops a vivid scarlet against a sky grey-blue like the cushat's wing.

Aloft hung a great dome of pink and gold.

Westward the huge bulk of Guala Mhór heaved up black as night over still, black waters, right in the face of the sun that was shooting long tongues of copper fire into a sky bloody like a memory of heroic wars.

The islands—Eilean Sona, Long I, Eilean Ron and Tanera—floated black on a Minch of polished brass that took fire where it met the sky far to the west, just where you could see the Outer Isles on a clear day if you were on the hill.

The great stillness that lay over the world was not broken by so much as the beating of a wing, —and if a bird had started up anywhere in Alba you would certainly have heard the echo of its wing-beating on such a night. But if you looked long enough at the pink waterfall high up on Sgùrr Ard you would think at last that you could hear its distant tinkle.

Now and then, however, a sound would

break through the stillness—the barking of a dog among the crofts or a shout of laughter from the town, where the men would be gossiping in the street at this hour of the week, and drunk enough to have forgotten any word of English.

No breeze from hill or sea shook tree branches on this night; only the willows down by the bridge quivered in their own breathings as is their custom; but the great pine woods over by Torr stood up so still and silent that if you had never seen them lashing the air in the black mouth of winter you would have thought they could never move at all.

It was as if Alba was waiting once again for the birth of a man, and all the mighty bens stood listening for the first cry of the babe that was to be a poet.

In those moments Murdo Anderson, standing out in the roadway with a flush on his dark cheeks and a bright eye for all the lights and shadows between the two horizons, seemed to feel all the poems that were ever written—now it would be far sailings on summer seas, deep as high heaven and a deeper blue, with silver tinklings where the running after-wave lipped on white beaches; now, with a quickening of the pulses, it would be the pale moonlight shining on the face of a maiden, she looking out from a high window, that looks on a garden, and all the air filled with the perfume of flowers; now, with a catch in the throat, it was the long thoughts, the deep nameless ones, that we will all be having now and then at such a time when we are young and the world still to conquer, and that the best of us can sometimes recapture in the eddies of a life half-lived; these are the poems that have never been written, because the man is not yet born that can put words on them.

At the moment Murdo had crossed over into that other world which overlays this one, and which most men find so difficult to enter because there is no space or time in it, and you have first to be able to see that God and the Devil are really the same, and be prepared to partner an apostle, or maybe Christ, when God feels like putting a reel on the pipes. You have almost to be an Albannach, or perhaps an Eireannach, to feel readily at home in it, but it is only there that you have no problem, because since God is merely the Devil with clothes on, or the other way about, you can see that there really are no problems.

However, you can never stay there long according to this world's counting, and another shout of laughter from the men who would be standing round Mexico's big window brought Murdo back through a door of sound to the world our bodies know. He filled his lungs with the golden silence and the thought came to him, as it had often come in the past few years, that the only life for him must be the clean and pure one. It was clear enough to him now—and he wondered he had never seen it so before—that a man must have no dealings with the flesh that will always be dragging like glaur at his heels. (He forgot that he had seen the same thing just as clearly many times before, and as often made the same resolve.) Thoughts of the monasteries of the Catholics came to him, as he imagined them; places where the coolness and calm of long stone corridors soaked through into hearts and stilled the pulse, and where high stone walls shut out the world. You could look out then on glimpses of the life outbye and see men swayed about by impulses and affections that here had no kingdom. Brother Murdo was pacing slowly a long path between beds of white flowers, and the stones were cool to his sandalled feet. But as he advanced beyond the shadow the stones became warm and the flowers caught a tinge of pink. He walked right through the thick wall and was immediately amid a riot of huge red flowers breast high. Long willowy trees beckoned with broad succulent leaves, swaying slowly to a warm air that came thick through the nostrils like milk; and the stones were hot under the feet of Murdo Anderson. A gleam of white that flashed among tree stems brought him back with a start to the road and the high black shoulder of Guala Mhór. With a stamp of the foot he turned to watch the shadow creeping up the long column of pink smoke from Beitidh Mhór's chimney. The cailleach would doubtless be at the cooking of the Sabbath's meal.

The old green door flew open with a rasping on its hinges and Murdo bent suddenly to the two pails at his feet, with never a look over his shoulder, for he knew by the prickling in the back of his neck that his father would be standing in the doorway there behind him.

" How much longer are you to take with that water ? Are you to be standing there till the morn so that you can break the Lord's day after an' all as you would like ? Murdo ! We're waiting on you this half an hour for the reading. Bring in them pails and be quick about it ! "

Murdo was too wise by many sore ears to venture on reply. With a glance at black bens and summits now turning to pink, and with an eye to the promise of fine weather in the west, he picked up the pails of water and turned bent shoulders towards the gleam of lamplight from the still open door. . . . Really life was not worth living when a fellow was always to be come down on like this. It would be better to go away somewhere. And the place was not worth living in, anyway—nothing but moors and crofts and bare rocks and that perpetual musty smell of cloth and wool and boots and stuff in the shop. How could a fellow settle to anything here ? Yes, he would get away somewhere and show them he wasn't to be ordered about and bullied like this, somewhere where the folk didn't wear black clothes on the Sabbath, and lit their pipes with pages from the Book of Genesis. . . .

" Are you coming, Murdo ? Do ye know

ye're keeping your faather out of his bed and him working hard all the day to put the food in your mouth ? "

" Aye, I'm coming."

" Well, mind your feet on them boots there an' don't be spilling water all over the place. Look at ye! Ye're spilling water all over this kitchen floor, an' me just after cleaning it all up for the morn. Ye'll just be taking a clout to that now. Ye'd drive a body wrong in their head with your clìobaireachd."

" Do you hear your mother speaking to you, Murdo ? Can't you speak when ye're spoken to ? "

" Well, I'm just bringing the cloth as soon as I'll put this water down "—with a protest in the words.

" Well, matà, be quicker about it and don't be always speaking back."

Murdo went through to the little back place and dumped the pails down on the stone floor, with an extra clatter for his father's benefit. Then he picked up a cloth with a red border and returning to the kitchen wiped the splashes of water from the stones, with a swish to the cloth that sent spots flying and brought his mother's eye on him again.

" What are you doing there ye—ye amadan ? Can you no see that's the best dishclout in the house ye're taking to the floor ? What's the use to your faather him scraping and scraping and you taking the best dishclouts to the floor ? Yes, an' I'd like to know what you've been up to all this time you're supposed to be going to the well!"

"I was just looking at the sunset."

"Looking at the sunset, a chreutair! Looking at the sunset! Here's your faather no better than a slave the way he's working and you, ye sgalag, won't do a hand's turn. Ye should be ashamed of yourself, if you've any shame left in you. Going to the Univarsity this year an' ye can do nothing to help your faather for looking at the sunset! But that's what's wrong with ye! 'Worshipping the crayter more than the creator,' that's what's wrong with ye! If it's not the one thing it'll be the other you're at. Yesterday it was singing vain songs in Iain Beag's workshop. Last week your faather goes over to Achgarve to Mary Bheag's Janet's wedding an' yonder's Murdo with an arm round a bag of pipes an' him blowing, yess, plowing like a—like a—like a whale, an' all the folk watching ye an' all. A fine like thing that for your faather's son! 'John the Elder's son's a piper,' they'll be saying. Och, it's myself can hear them saying it! Janet Ruairidh an' Mina Bhàn'll have it round the town like it was in the *North Star* itself, an' old Beitidh Mhór here will put it round the crofts. The One-I'll-no-name is in that woman, her tongue's aye clapping like a townful o' bells that she should have bitten out with shame when her man went over the bridge thirty years ago an' him full of Macinlay's whisky. But she'll get what's coming to her yet, that cailleach! An' who learned ye the pipes what-effer? O Murdo, sure am I it wasn't your old mother!"

Murdo, through much practice, could put up with his mother long enough when she was at the scolding, giving her head a toss now and again in a way she had and shaking wisps out of the business on the top of her head, where she contrived to gather most of her hair, that was getting grey and thin; but the pathetic was always more than he could be doing with, and the idea of his mother giving him a lesson in piping, strutting up and down on the roadway, swinging her old behind and getting purple in the face, while her big red fingers with the joints swollen with the rheumatics fumbled about on the chanter—that was too much, and for the life of him he could not keep the lips over his teeth.

Up jumps John the Elder in a fine rage.

"Would ye be laughing at your mother?" says he, making one stride of it round the table and knocking the big Bible with a thud to the floor. "Take ben that clout and come back here at once! I'll be having something to say to ye myself, you rascal."

Murdo was not sure which he was to take ben, so took them both, as well as a singing head would let him. With the door between him and the kitchen, and trembling with rage, he rolled the best clout in the house into a ball, spat at it, and swung an arm, and the Devil was in his hand if it did not go splash into the

Sabbath water. Half ashamed in an instant for his years, he fished it out with a crook of the finger and dropped it into the white sink Hector Matheson had put in last week and his mother had been telling the neighbourhood about ever since. Then he came back to the kitchen, where his father's face was still red with the anger that always made his pale eyes look squint, and from the rush of blood to the head that always came on him when he bent his back to pick something off the floor.

"Dean suidhe," said he, a wee thing short in the breath, "I'll have something to say to you in a minute, but first"—with a swing of the arm that was meant to resemble Mr. John MacIver—"let us turn to our defoshuns."

Murdo could never for the life of him remember where the reading was at nights, but it was always a mild surprise to him that they were not nearer the end of the book. However, after he had wondered with the half of a wandering mind how it was that the Gaelic was kept for worship and the house of God, and it only used at other times by the crofters and the men in Mexico's back room—and by an elder from the town now and then when the bottle was far down—he started, under his black brows, to study the faces of his father and mother, and they with their noses in their Books.

It was a queer thing he could never put a finger of his mind on what that relationship meant. It was long since his mind had been travelling highways and hillpaths of its own that never led him within sight of the road his parents were on. It was doubtful if he would recognise it indeed if he happened to put an eye on it, although it stuck in his head that it was "cumhang," strait and narrow, with some mention of golden gates at the far end of it. But the question of destinations was troubling him much these days and he preferred to let the golden gates go for the moment. At any rate from this hillpath his mind was on he could never get an angle on his parents that would let him see them as he felt he ought to, but always he would be seeing them as you might see two people from Mars, or it might be animals of another species, say two stirks looking over a fence. And that happened most when he was near to them, as at these times. He suddenly had a very queer sensation that would come on him now and again, as if while he still sat where he was he was looking at them from a position behind his head, with some eye of a mind that was still his although it had no memory of experience and recorded no emotion. At such times the two faces before him, strange-looking, as if seen for the first time, seemed to grow bigger, and he could see with a distinctness that startled him (that is the mind that still recorded emotions) the fleshy bags on his father's cheeks, the thick neck with a pulse bobbing in it, the veins, blue and red, that showed on the thick nose, with red hairs sticking out at the nostrils darker than the other tufts that grew in the ears, and the big red moustache that covered the mouth, drooping down at the ends over his chin—a thing that, taken with the bald skull and colourless eyes, always put the thought of a walrus in his mind. Funny thing, that big red moustache greying at the ends and covering the mouth. He had never seen the mouth. Food went in under the big moustache—bits of potato and meat and bread, and, with a sucking noise, broth or tea—and various smacking and squelching noises came out from under it; but for all he had tried he had never seen more than a lower lip, and that blue. His mother, for all the fine unselfish talk of her, really bullied his father badly (though he had a fine masterless swagger to carry it off) and he felt that if he could only see the mouth under the moustache the explanation would be open before him.

And then there was his mother with the thin, grey-streaked hair gathered up in that affair on the top of her head, with the tuft or two that would always be sticking out of it. Just now the black brows were bent on the Book, and her reading spectacles balanced far down on a reverent nose. He used to keep a watchful eye on the black fringe on her upper lip whenever there would be anything in the chapter about the Philistines or any of those clans the Lord was always smiting, because whenever He did the hairs used to bristle and she gave a toss of her head and a flap of the loose skin between the chin and the scraggy neck of her as if to say, " Sin a bhalaich! Well done, God! That'll learn them! " The same look as used to be on her when she heard of some bit of ill fortune befalling Janet Ruairidh or Mina Bhàn.

What would his father look like when he was dead ? He wouldn't take long to go to pieces. He looked a bit " high " already sometimes, if he had been lifting something. Blue and swollen like the bodies Iain Beag had seen in France, with the bellies of them blown out like so many balloons, and they letting gassy groans out of them. There was the day he was out on the shore, and he a child, and put his foot on something that gave. He remembered he scraped the sand away and discovered a white swollen something with blue patches on it. He could not for the life of him think what this was and what must he do but out with his pocket-knife and stick it into the thing. And then off he was running as if the Black Thief his black self was at the heels of him, and as sick as the dog daft old Danny Mór had not put enough sand over. He could not look at his meat for a whole day without retching, and his ears burning for the green apples he never stole out of the schoolhouse garden. . . . Look at that long fellow oozing out of the left nostril and hanging down, head wagging, ripples of vermiculate laughter running up him before he popped in again—and that bunch among the red ear-tuft—God, funny thing they all looked so happy. . . .

But meantime David had exhorted his soul for the last time to praise the Lord.

Now Murdo was on his knees, staring right into the seat of his father's trousers. . . . You would think when a man was speaking to his Maker he would take up some kind of a dignified position that would give Him some satisfaction in having made him, instead of getting down on all fours like a beast of the field and sticking a fat behind up in the air. The seat of the trousers was well polished, and the behind quivered now and again when there was mention of " them of other beliefs that know not Thy truth," and Murdo knew well enough that John the Elder was thinking at the moment of Roderick Gunn and the big glass window he had put in in his shop on the street. And Roderick Gunn of course was U.F. You might near as well be a Papanach itself when John the Elder had his mood on him. Dhia! Would it not be the funny thing to see a whole congregation without trousers on—just their black jackets and Bibles and long, sour faces, and below that the image of their Creator! Probably red-haired men would look funniest of all. But if you were in the back seat and a whole congregation of trouserless Seceders in front of you—on their knees they would need to be, to get the right expression of humour, or of holiness, on their " Sabbath faces "! Ach, a chreutair, Mr. John MacIver would need to stop opening a pig's eye on the young girls in the way he had in the middle of a prayer, because anyone that lifted a head would be able to see him, and him standing in front yonder.

But John the Elder got up from his knees and Murdo prepared himself for what was coming, ashamed already of the thoughts that had been running through his head.

He could not imagine what it was he had been doing this time. It might be any one of all the things he did or said between the beginning and end of a day, for every one of them, he well knew, was just the wrong thing. It was his misfortune never to be able to do the right thing in any single instance. Yet every one of the things he did was right enough in itself (with maybe one exception) and he had no feeling that he was wrong in any one of them (except maybe that one) and yet somehow he had only to come in the door to feel that he was hiding something that to be right he should be ashamed of.

Sometimes when he was in the house for a while he would almost come to their way of looking at things; and then a breath of clean air through an opened door would remind him of another world of values, and of the fact that he had only to step outside to see that this wrong was really right.

It was a strange and unnatural thing that a half-inch of wood should divide two moral codes like this, and two scales of value, too, two whole philosophies. Inside at times he would come to see some beauty and desirability in the idea of a town of golden streets and even pulses

—not difficult to see that when a man was forever struggling against an insistent, weakening flesh—but he had only to step outside on any day of rain or sunshine between the two ends of a year, and with fair luck he could shut the door on two thousand years of history and be back with bounding pulses in a day when the next world was a vague something of no importance, while the other world where God threw off clothes and danced was easy to enter, given any sea-squall or sun-struck ben top or mist effect on high moorland to open the door.

Sometimes on such an occasion he found himself loving the flesh that indoors clogged him and rising to heights of fair imaginings on wing-flights of desires that indoors were shorn of their pinions and dragged him down in choking waters, like a lump of lead at the feet.

But at such times nineteen years of life rose up in clamorous protest and frightened him into a mental return to his father's house.

John the Elder had reverently put aside the Bibles, with a fondling stroke of a hairy hand to the backs of them in a complacent way Murdo noticed he always had when he had got the Almighty on his side against Roderick Gunn and the others upbye who were drawing trade to a blaze of windows the folk would gather round on the wettest of nights, when, with a scrug to the bonnet and the hitch of a collar over red ears, they would scurry by the solitary lamp that only reminded them by contrast of glowing peats and a swept floor.

With a downward pull on the left side of his moustache, and a cough to throw the spittle from his throat, he was preparing for one of those lectures that always (for all he had been getting them off and on as far back as he could mind) jangled a sense naturally acute in Murdo of proportion and restraint.

The whole thing was so obvious. It stuck out as plain as Càrn Mór under snow. It was that his father made him an unwilling audience when he was at his favourite trick of imitating Mr. John MacIver—swelling out with the righteous indignation that was on him, and he sticking for the words now and then when that, or a spittle, got in his throat, or he was not very sure what the indignation was about—while his mother stood by with her features composed to Paul's requirements in a wife, but giving yon occasional toss to her head that set neck-skin flapping as it were in silent applause.

And it was always the same thing anyway. The offence might vary, and indeed was sometimes uncertain—a heresy implied in folded arms or a crossed leg maybe, a mere excuse—but the phrase was always the same.

" And now, Murdo "—this with a large wave to a big hand, as if to take in the table, the big box bed with the blue and red-spotted counterpane and the yellow side curtains, and half a side of whitewashed wall—" And now, Murdo "—as one would say—" And now, friends "—" we come to another milestone in your career. I would have thought that by now you would have learned to walk in the right path and to forsake the ways of the ungodly. But there is no end to the ways the Evil One will be taking in order to capture the careless soul. With some it will be the one thing and with others the other—yes, with others the other. With Uilleam Gunn it is the bottle, and with Murdo Alec it is—it iss—yess, yess, it will be other things." And John the Elder with a red face shot a glance at his wife who was at the moment looking at the floor. Having nearly made a bad slip he would now cover it up by getting angry, and Murdo knew by the Gaelic blas on his words that he was already annoyed and excited. "Now with yourself it's neffer twice the same thing," says he in a half shout. "Ass if it wassn't enough to have one fice itself it must be two or three or a dossen you have. One time it's bad books under the pillow, another time you're at the singing of fain songs, and now indeed it's the piping itself! And all this comes of the bad company you'll be keeping, yess, it's led astray you are by the keeping of baad company, and that's one of the Tefil's fayforite wayss of destroying the soul. I don't know what you'll get that you'll be foreffer in Iain Beag's shop but it's no goot you'll be getting whateffer for the folk that will be gathering there on nights iss not the company I would be choossing for a son of mine. But this iss going to stop, I'm telling you! We are instructed in the Scriptures to bring up our children in the noorture and admoneeshon of the

Lort and that's what myself will be doing from now on. It's too soft altogether I've been on you in the past, but if kindness itself will not do we can be taking other wayss"—and much more to the same effect, till Murdo felt stifled and the blood drummed at his temples. "Now be off with you to your bed, and before you sleep—and it's the hardened conscience you must have if you can sleep at all—see that you won't be forgetting your prayers."

And John the Elder, having got to the end of his oration and his breath, and purpling a bit in the face, gave a gesture of dismissal and pointed a hairy hand at the door.

2

Murdo dropped a latch on the lamplight and felt his way up wooden stairs that creaked on every third step. He put a forefinger under the latch of his bedroom door and slipped in, closing it behind him. It had no lock. He then walked across three yards of creaking floor and sat down on the bed, with his feet on what had been Lachie's skin when John the Elder still had a few sheep on the hill.

In front of him the window looked right into the eye of the west and he could see about nine square feet of sky lighted still with the faint pale streaks that in this region at such a time of the year stand sentry over the western sea until the yellow light above the bens relieves them. A star winked high up in the right-hand corner of the window, and now and then Alba stirred in her sleep and gave a long, contented sigh. Some of her warm, moist breath found its way in through the window, which Murdo kept open all the year, so that the pagan night air might refresh two thousand years of stuffiness. His father slept with his mother in the room below, with the window shut tight on Isaiah and the Apostle Paul and all the prohibitions. It was stuffy even to think of it.

It would be difficult to describe the disordered thoughts that were tumbling through his mind at the moment as he sat on the bed edge in the dark room, staring out through the window; but the prevailing emotion was shame.

It was always so after one of these performances. The thing was so ridiculous in itself, and yet he could never help taking it seriously after the first five minutes. It was not that the performance ever made him ashamed of the offence, or even came near convincing him there was any offence in it, because it never did, but each time his father went into one of his passions he lost at one stroke all the self-respect he had managed to summon up since the last one. Thin-skinned, that was the word the English had for it. He felt like an over-sensitive Gulliver tied down by the Lilliputians. No, that was not all. He was fundamentally a coward. He made up his mind every time to stand up as befitted his years against this petty tyranny, and every time he failed to say a word, or if he managed to get anything past his teeth it always sounded defiant and loud where it should have been quiet and dignified and restrained, while he always collapsed miserably at the purple-faced blustering his feeble attempt at protest called forth. It was no good. He must realise that he was a hopeless coward. His father's coarse horse-energy was too much for him every time.

Tears of self-pity and humiliation started to his eyes, and the star shot out long rays all the colours of the rainbow.

Why, at any rate, should he be so different from everybody else? It was the same at school. Murdo MacKenzie and Roderick Urquhart could sit down with equal application to any of the tasks set in class, with no repugnance and apparently no particular enthusiasm, but when anything was being done that made no appeal to *his* imagination something like a shutter slammed down in his mind, and with his eyes still on his book he would be careering along the hill-roads or watching the green breakers seething round the black rocks at Cove. And it was no use fighting against it. On the other hand a snatch of an old song would bring tears smarting to his eyes, and two lines of Greek would at times give him an airy enlargement of consciousness, as of fleece-white clouds patterning a blue sky, or of open squares of pillars marble-white under a clear moon. But even in this he was conscious of a difference between him and his fellows, a difference he thought he could trace very easily to its source. There was no telling why in this particular he should be different from every boy in the school, but it was no doubt due to the fact that he was the nasty coward he was, with a flabby will that had never gotten a grip on the reins.

He blushed in the dark at the thought of it.

He might feel surer of himself in the morning if he would get into bed now and sleep, he thought several times, but when he got into this train of thought after a bad bout with the one downstairs the utter hopelessness of the whole thing, if you considered the weakness of this will of his, that, it seemed, would never be any tougher in the fibre, the hopelessness of it came over him like dark waters on the head of a drowning man, and he could not keep the same purpose even for the five seconds necessary to start the simplest action, just sat where he was, raging impotently round the inside of his skull and no sooner decided on doing something, however small, than he was back again revolving the same thoughts.

If the high hills had not been keeping the cool east winds from him he might have felt better, but here he was hemmed in and suffocated by the four walls of the house, and more particularly by the walls of his own skull—and in any case the east winds could not penetrate that. And there was a worse barrier than those, all the more effective in that it was intangible. You could break through a stone wall (if it was merely a stone wall and did not stand for something else, some authority you had not the will to break) but you could not break through this because it was of the consistency of jelly and simply gave to your hand and came back to its position the moment you took your hand away. It was composed of wills, such as his father's and his mother's and his teachers', and of the opinions of a whole district, and of innumerable pointing fingers and whispering mouths and smug respectabilities. That was where Gulliver came in again, for through it all you felt the whole thing was petty and contemptible. It was strange that he would often feel insignificant and ineffective in the company of the most ordinary person, and at the same time, and as part of the same feeling as it were, seem to be looking down on him from disdainful heights. He often felt like that with the teachers themselves, even with Mr. Matheson, who was dignity itself and had got such a surprise when he was made head master that he had never been able to forget it for a moment since. But these feelings he was careful to keep to himself.

For the moment he was able to convince himself of his superiority over the whole petty tribe, forever crawling about on their bellies and grubbing in the dirt, and the filth of their own making, under the very shadow of bens that would now be flaming red, now smiling in the face of a tender sky, now with the black gloom on their brows brooding over dead days and a gone race that you could not somehow believe had fathered these. He alone of them all had the grace to lift his eyes. The muscles tightened about his neck and wrists and the chest expanded at the thought.

But right on the heels of that came another thought that brought relaxing, for he was bound to realise that when the morrow came and he was mixing again with the folks at the sacrament of Achgarve it would be with the old sense of shame on him, because for all their pettiness he sank at times much lower.

A creaking of the bed downstairs brought him back to the scene just ended, when he had played so poor a part, and knew he would again were it repeated—and there he was back where he had been before.

But not exactly. The creaking, by some association he might have seen clearly enough if he had had time to think about it, brought to his mind in a flash the picture of Strongorm woods on a summer evening, and Murdo Alec as he had come on him that time with Mina MacIver. And that set him off on another and familiar tack which he felt he was almost justified in indulging as compensation for the humiliation he had just gone through, as also because it did after all cut away the weight of weakness and ineffectiveness and make him feel for the time that he was still able to exert some energy in one direction at least. There was consolation in that.

He got hurriedly to his feet and began to

unbutton his clothes without troubling to light the lamp. That done, he jumped into the bed. . . .

It was hours before he slept after that. The night had somehow got terribly hot and stuffy. He tossed from side to side and went over the whole train of thought again from the beginning, only now he went quicker and quicker and more impotently round the inside of his head, and was so much the more conscious of being the weakling he was that now and again he unconsciously drew the blankets over his face for very shame and then as quickly drew them down again and stretched out his arms because of the heat.

This went on till he knew the light must be springing up behind the hills because the air suddenly came cool to his nostrils, with a taste of wet earth on it.

He could see the cobwebs where the rafters met the roof; and the hens had begun their busy clucking right under the window.

3

When Murdo awoke it was already full day. Banks of cloud covered the western sky and blocked up the window space, but the sun must be shining none the less because from where he sprawled lazily and blinked sleepy eyes he could see a sparrow right out on the end of a spray-tip, chirruping loudly and fluffing gold-red feathers in a ray of sunlight. The hens were still making a great clucking and scratching down below, and the old cock with a tremendous flapping of wings flopped on to the top of the dyke and after a pause to arrange himself began to crow.

That brought his mother out fussing and shaking a shocked apron—the blue one with the white dots it would be—to drive the protesting creatures from the front of the house. The silly creatures had not enough sense to preserve a decent silence on such a day, but must be pattering about making cheerful noises even on the day the Lord had set apart for quietness and thoughts of death.

The sparrow flew away at the first sign of the commotion and Murdo lazily watched the spray swinging up and down and changing from green to yellow as it bobbed in and out of the sunlight.

At the eighteenth swing it came to rest. He stretched himself and rolled out of bed with a chuckle. The events of last night were forgotten, and after all the world was still an infant on a morning like this.

He pattered round the floor on bare feet (and they not over clean since his father put a stop to the sinful enjoyment of swimming) with his shirt tails flapping round bare legs and humming "Mo chailin dìleas donn" to himself softly enough not to be heard downstairs, while he rattled at drawers swollen in the grooves and pulled out his Sabbath clothes, sad-coloured things with an ancient and reverent cut to them at neck and waist. He stuffed his shirt tails into the seat of his trousers, slipped the braces jauntily over his shoulders, and having a feeling that he was a bit late fastened the buttons while he creaked his way downstairs.

The door stood open and there was nobody in the kitchen. His father would be in the byre and probably the Lord knew where his mother would be. However, the dishes were set out on a table more than usually white after last night's scrubbing, also a loaf and the large bread-knife, while the kettle swung on its chain over red peats, puffing steam at lid and spout.

He clattered through to the back place and struck into a port-a-bial while he splashed about with his head in a pail. A step on the gravel outside, however, put a sudden end on the port in the middle of a note, and with a vigorous scrub from a towel he scrambled upstairs again.

He was just struggling into a collar and looking at the red scratches on his neck made by the rough points of the towel, which must have been new from the wrapper, when his father's heavy step sounded below and his voice came up from the stair foot. Murdo was at his old capers again, lying in in the mornings, lazy rascal that he was. This was set apart as a day of rest, but the Word of God said nothing about a day of laziness. Breakfast was on the table.

Murdo gave a grunt in his throat because he knew that otherwise these pieces of information would be repeated, at the same time giving some vicious tugs on his tie, popping out his tongue at himself each time in a way that made him grin at his own reflection and sent him downstairs in a good humour.

His father and mother were already in their places when he got down, and lifted impatient eyebrows at him as he entered and took his place facing the fire across the table. His mother was for starting off on him again right away,—What did he mean by coming down late again ? He should have been up seeing to the cow for his faather. And what sort of a grin was that to have on his face on the morning of the Sabbath day ? And what did he mean by not shaving off that beard last night ? He knew very well this was no morning to be paying attention to the needs of the body. He would just need to go to Achgarve now with the beard on him. And what would the folk be saying about her letting her son to the sacraments with a beard on his chin like a kitchen besom ? That might be well enough for the crofters, but the son of John the Elder had to think of the respectable position of his faather, if indeed he would ever be thinking about anything at all but himself.

She got no further than that, however, because John the Elder looked at her with a reproachful eye, and with a " Let us ask God's blessing " bent a bald and reverent head.

There was more to it than the blessing, however, and by the time his father had got half through the list of the sins the place was namely for, Murdo was squinting up, and, still in a good humour, thinking that his mother would be none the worse of a shave herself on Saturday night, or any night.

They had finished their breakfast, put the dishes in the sink to await to-morrow's washing, and were on their knees and ten minutes through the Elder's prayer when there was a great rattling on the road outside, and a loud knock on the door.

They got to their feet, the Elder plainly not pleased because he had not been able to put mention on " them of other beliefs."

" Ye'll better be taking your coat, Murdo. For all it looks fine enough you can never be telling if it won't be pouring before night," said his mother in a way she had of mentioning common things, and she with her knees but half straightened after the prayer.

If his father had had the smallest bit in the world of the artist in him he would see the anti-climax in that and feel it like a cold hand on his neck, thought Murdo, as he took his coat off the peg, picked his Bible off the table and made for the door.

Outside a gentle breeze had lifted, with summer in its breath, and was at the moment chasing the cloud-banks over the western horizon. The sun was very warm and already high in the sky. Not a cloud was to be seen anywhere in the heavens, except one little fleecy thing like a lamb strayed from the flocks that was wandering about in the east knocking its silly head against the bens.

Right in the middle of the road stood the affair that had caused the rattling, with "John MacDonald, Merchant," painted in white on the side. John MacDonald himself stood at the snout of it with one leg crossed over the other and a hand on a battered mudguard that had never been straightened out since he ran into the bridge the very day he brought the thing home.

Five years ago it had still been a gig he had and he used to stand in just the same position at the horse's head, with a hand on the shaft end, while he waited for his customers. He had bought the thing second-hand from a man in Dingwall, and although that was five years ago now he had never got out of the habit of standing at the snout of it as if it were liable at any moment to give one of its snorts and gallop off.

While still in his youth John MacDonald had been for a time in the service of Lord Lovat, in some menial capacity, and for the past twenty years no name but "Lovat" had been given to him. It was the custom in the place to be giving names like that.

Murdo nodded to Lovat and strutted round the end of the van. Seven or eight white faces stared at him in silence out of it. Black clothes and white, sour faces turning down at the corners of the mouths and glowering, glowering at him, with reproach in the eyes.

He gave one look and then skipped round to the other side of the van and fairly doubled up with silent laughter so that the Bible fell out of his oxter on to the road.

What in the world would come into his head when he looked inside, what but that here was a cartload of apes coming back from the hospital, glowering out reproachfully because of the glands they had left behind in a bottle! Take eight gibbering monkeys; remove their "glands"—eight silent Seceders! That was how the contrast struck him between the outside and the inside of the van and he was still chuckling when he straightened his back after picking up the Bible.

A yellow head was sticking out from the driver's seat, and Rory MacIver with the very devil of mischief in the eyes of him said, "Caught you, my lad! Ye'd better be getting inside. Here's your damned Elder of a father and the old hen too, and she clucking."

His mother was just heaving herself into the van when Murdo got round.

Nobody had said a word. They all sat on the narrow seats, with their lips pursed up, and stared across at each other. Lovat went round to the front of the car and turned a handle once or twice. The thing gave two or three snorts and started shaking and ráttling. The folk had difficulty in keeping the right expression from being shaken off the faces of them, and Mina Bhàn looked round with a white face and fear on her clearly. Lovat got in in his slow way, tied up the door and cast an eye back to see if they were all in. Then he worked about with his levers, grasped the wheel in his two hands as if it were a pair of reins, and with a final snort and a spout of black smoke from the pipe that stuck out behind, they were off.

Murdo asked nothing better than this.

For a while he was still laughing to himself and had to cough once or twice to cover it up, and once Rory MacIver glanced round at him from his seat beside Lovat with a look of such holiness on his face that he spluttered.

Now he was looking out from his seat at the back end of the car with an appraising eye for the bens and rocks and trees as they leapt into sight, rotated slowly and finally disappeared.

For the whole hour of the journey he was never without a song or a port at the back of his mouth, and last night was not even a memory.

They went past Achbay, Camuslong and Mellonree, with lazy smoke in the chimneys and no sign of life at all but a flutter of curtains here and there where some wife would be peeping out, and finally they passed the first houses of Achgarve, with folk in dark clothes carrying Bibles out at the doors. The car swerved aside and rattled to a stop on the bare patch behind MacKinnon Bros.' shop.

It was hot in the churchyard that day.

There was a big company from both sides of the loch and Mr. MacAulay had come from Dingwall, all the way, to assist Mr. MacIver.

That meant a service of about three hours, and the sun beating down like a furnace on the people in their thick clothes crowded around on the grass and on the gravestones, sweating.

Sweat stood out on noses and faces and fairly blobbed on the bald heads of the old men when they took off their caps for the prayers. The folk were all feeling heavy. Even old Alasdair Fraser from Mellonree, with a great reputation for holiness, was nodding by the time Mr. MacAulay was through his first prayer.

The bens quivered in the heat and the high-up trees danced in its rising ripples. A poor little panting of cool air came up from the loch now and then but only played about for a moment, and when it passed the air was loud again with heavy breathing from many noses. After a while this breathing was so loud that you wondered you could hear Mr. MacAulay's quavering voice above it, and were almost certain the dead bodies down below were joining in and breathing in chorus. From your seat on the grass you could easily imagine the ground was moving with the heave of their rotting lungs, and the very worms in them breathing too.

For a time Murdo sat and read his Bible. There were certainly fine bits in it, and the way the Gaelic had them put a taste on the tongue. There were the Psalms for instance. Then there were the Gospels, with a simple way of putting things that would almost bring a wetness to the eyes. Then again it was queer at this late day in time to read the letter of the Great Apostle to a people in Asia who spoke the Gaelic and whose kin were reading the words at the very moment in this out-flung corner.

Then his back got sore and he shifted his position and let his eye wander over the bens and the loch and the white houses of Sand and Badachro shining through the heat-mist at the far side of it. Life must have been good here in the old days. The folks were a lusty race in those old times, with a song never far from the lips and feet ever itching to be at the dancing. And the fine piping there must have been! But then the dark days came, with a new kind of religion that changed old ways, stopped the song on the lip, and let the wind out of the pipes with a squealing of drones. Then the folks began going abroad till none were left but the old people and bairns.

His mind wandered again. He began idly fluttering the pages of his Bible. Finally from sheer boredom he set to picking out and studying with a stirring of the blood choice passages such as the ongoings of Noah and Judah and the way of David and Amnon with Bathsheba and Tamar. By the time Mr. MacAulay had finished he had been for quite ten minutes a ruler in Israel with wives and concubines to last over every night in the year.

At these times Mr. John MacIver always ate meat in the house of his colleague Mr. Donald MacIver, Seceding minister in Achgarve, and as befitted his position of Elder so did John

Anderson and his folks. Mr. MacAulay from Dingwall would naturally be there too.

Murdo was just standing on a fallen stone, stretching his back and his legs and preparing to go towards the house, with no great stomach for the dreich business, when Rory MacIver came up. He had a mop of yellow hair and a big mouth nothing on earth could take the grin off. He had the advantage of a year over Murdo, and had it too by an inch in the head and maybe two across the shoulders.

" Well, Murdo, you're not as cheerful as you were upbye yonder. Now what in the world would put a laugh like yon on you ? "

Murdo explained; and could tell by the way Rory laughed that he had seen no great amount of humour in the thing. If he had told him he had stuck a pin into Mina Bhàn, now, not all the sacraments ever held in Achgarve would have kept Rory from letting out a guffaw. But that was it, you see. It was his misfortune that not only was there none in the district to go all the way with him in the thoughts that came to him, but he could not even be getting them to laugh at the same things. His mind swung in circles on a different plane altogether. He was certainly a queer fellow by their standards, and it depended entirely on his mood whether he was pleased or not to be so. . . .

It was a sombre company in Mr. MacIver's house.

The ministers, the missionary, and the elder sat round an empty grate, the ministers with their Sabbath tails turned up at the back, and were for the most part silent. Now and then one or the other would make a remark about the service or the congregation, and grunts would come from the others. It was pretty sure, however, that their thoughts were of the needs of their bellies. You could almost be sure of that by the fact that all the remarks were made in the Gaelic, that will always come readier to the tongue of a hungry man.

Murdo and Rory sat beside the window on a black sofa covered with a white lace which, however, did not keep the hairs from going through your trousers and pricking you. The window had two pots of flowers in it. It was open two inches at the top. The wall-paper was grey, with big blotches of red flowers all over it. There were long, red stains of damp at the side against the gable. The women were whispering together in the kitchen and bringing in the cold food for the dinner—some kind of beef.

Mr. MacAulay's blessing was mercifully short. The sun fairly took the strength out of you. Then they all started shoving bits of beef and potatoes into their mouths—You would think holy men would show a proper disdain for mere victuals destined to rot in the belly and finally pass out of the body again.

Mr. Donald MacIver's beard bobbed up and down as he chewed. He was ruddy and healthy-looking from spending most of his time in the open air. The hands that clutched the knife and fork were not the soft hands of the student.

He knew very well the feel of a big fellow at the end of a line.

Mr. John MacIver's gaze never left his plate. The little pig's eyes of him glittered and fairly popped as he gobbled off his knife. There was sweat on his nose.

John the Elder was eagerly pushing food under his walrus tusks of a moustache and sweat stood out on his bald head.

The air was filled with the noise of chewing, only broken when John the Elder paused to suck a morsel off a moustache-end.

With the dead-white skin of Mr. John MacIver and the little eyes of him to give it countenance you were reminded of nothing so much as pigs.

Annie MacIver was like her father without the same deadness of the skin. She had just that plumpness and bigness about the breasts to add a beat to the pulse of a man naturally somewhat slim himself.

The room was stuffy. Outside there was a breeze lifting, for the tree-tops nodded now and again. You could see the ripples breaking along the loch side, and, far out, the blue of a quiet Minch.

After the dinner Murdo found it long sitting on the sofa watching the hours crawl by and as soon as he could reasonably make the evening service an excuse he and Rory were out in the open air. They were able to take a little turn on the road without seeming too clearly to be taking a walk. A yard or two beyond the last house they turned and came back. Mr. John MacIver was standing in the road outside MacKinnon Bros.' shop talking to a young girl from Sand, a pretty girl. He was looking at her neck. There was the same look in his eyes as when he was at his meat, and now and then he was running the tip of his tongue slowly along his lips.

"I was sorry to hear about your father," he was saying as they passed, and he looking at her neck.

As soon as they were likely to be out of ear-shot of his father Rory dug his elbow in Murdo's ribs.

"Did you see the old bastard talking to Mary Campbell?" said he, with a chuckle. "There's some juice in the old stick yet. I'm sure it wasn't for him they were taking the glands off your monkeys, eh, Murdo? But she's a pretty girl, no doubt of it, and a fine leg on her. It's just the pity she doesn't live a bit further north."

Murdo smiled and said nothing. He was thinking how white that girl's neck had been.

The evening service dragged slowly past after that. The company was not as big as it had been in the morning. Some of the folks who came a distance had already gone off to their homes. Mr. MacAulay had had to return to Dingwall and so to Mr. John MacIver fell the honour of giving the sermon. He spoke for a full hour and a quarter, and the folk said they had never heard the like of the powerful way he dealt with the lusts of the flesh and the seven-times-heated fire that awaits whore-mongers and adulterers.

Old Alasdair Fraser shook hands with Murdo afterwards and asked him how he liked the sermon. Murdo said in the English, " It would certainly give the strangers a fine idea of the kind of man our missionary is—that is, them that would have sense enough to understand it."

Old Alasdair said, " Yes, yes, a bhalaich, you have the right of it there right enough. It's not many will have the sense nowadays to be understanding a good sermon." He added, " O dhuine, dhuine! man, man! " to himself as it were, and from force of habit turned an eye up to the weather. One big yellow tooth showed in his mouth as it hung open and a long slaver ran down his beard.

4

The day of the sacraments of Achgarve might be memorable in that year for the extreme heat of it, but did not stand alone of its kind. It was the beginning of a period when the warm days went past in procession, each one in every way like its fellow. Each morning the sun came up behind the bens in a cool air of the dawning. The world stirred, and the first breath of her stirring rose white over all the land so that anyone whose business took him abroad waded in it to the knees. This mist gathered thick in the glens where it surged and billowed like milk before beginning to ooze and clamber up the mountain-sides. When it reached the top the wind up there tore bits of it away and sent them chasing each other across the sky. And long before the last of them had hurried out of sight the air had warmed already and the sun beat down on a world of waking men. Smoke came thick from the roofs of crofts and the town chimneys and here and there a door would be set ajar to let out air heavy with a night's dreams, or a man would come out yawning and giving a hitch to his belt.

For long days the sun beat down out of a blue sky on brown moors and long patches of field where a thin corn was yellowing. The bens quivered in a tremble of rising air and for long periods no sound would be heard but the beat of that trembling on the ear.

Up in the street the heat was thrown back from the walls, walls that the westering sun bloodied at evening when the men lounged at corners in a slow hum of conversation. Flies in a fatigue of heat crawled up to one another on the insides of windows and crawled away again. In the warm nights down by the bridge end the midges in their millions swayed up and down in a long column so that you dared not stop to lean over and watch the water, with a mere trickling at the stony shallows and a plopping of fish in the pools.

At first the folk had been pleased at the weather, and when two of them met on the roads you would always hear a hearty "It's a fine day that's in it!" and then "A fine day, indeed!" But the crops had not had time to fill with sap and as the days went by and no showers came the folks began to be uneasy. You would see a man now and then leaning on a dyke and staring at the short stalks growing sparsely among the stones, and the poor heads of them already far on in the ripening. Then he would wag his head and walk away; or maybe he would call out to the man on the next croft, "It's a poor crop we'll be having the year if there won't be more rain in it!" And the other would reply, "Aye, man, it'll hardly be worth the cutting, I'm thinking. And the potatoes are like to be small too for want of the wet that doesn't look like coming yet."

The folk in the street, with their shops, were of course indifferent at first, though they would talk sympathetically enough to the folk from the crofts just for something to say, or in the way of business; but by the end they too were looking for the showers. Business was not so good these days that they could afford to lose even the difference in custom between a good crop and a bad one, what with the competition and the way folk were getting stuff direct from Glasgow by the *Claymore*.

The only ones who were not caring how long the weather lasted were the children. They put in long days at the laughing, running about on the braes with bare legs browned and scratched, or down on the shore splashing about in the water and fairly shrieking with joy. What did it matter if school would be opening soon; it was not every day you could bathe your body in water warm enough to be comfortable and then sit on a rock till the sun dried the wet off you. And it was a great delight just to take your clothes off so that the others would see you running about naked; you could compare your body with theirs and count each other's birth-marks.

During those weeks things went with Murdo just as usual.

The shop with its smell from the wool and woollen stuff that crowded the shelves, and the boots with their thick, studded soles that swung from hooks in the ceiling affected him with a kind of suffocation if he had to be in it long. He was jarred also by the way things were piled on the shelves and in the window with no regard to the colours of them.

One day, or maybe only half a day, nothing would be impossible. He could look forward with confidence in himself to a welcoming future. He went about with a song in his mouth or in his head, and there were no limits to the queer fancies you could have if only you got out on the hill with yourself or down by the sea, with no sound to break in on your thoughts but only the pounding of waves which in itself is a door to the elsewhere. You could tramp roads that led to no place on this particular earth and climb hills and crags in your own head just as long as no inharmonious noise from this world or no accusing memory thrusting up into consciousness broke the thin wall of mood and let in the thinner air of the world as we think it is. Then the next day (or the other half of the same one it might be) he would be down in the depths so that it was impossible for him to get off the actual at all. He was again a coward and a poltroon and could face a future that held innumerable meetings with people, all self-possessed, with no sort of confidence. Confidence is not an attribute of worms and in those black moods he crawled in imagination before the innumerable people he met there in all sorts of circumstances disadvantàgeous to his own chances of preserving dignity. At those times and when in the circumstances, imagined or real, he shrank and shrank till all there was of him was gathered inside his skull and caused such a fullness there that it threatened to burst along the sutures. It was a black world at such times, very aged and very Hebrew. Indeed the time was about twilight, you felt that, the twilight of a short and silly day. The night would no doubt be dark and hot, and when the dawn came it would be the breaking of a blacker darkness on the black of night, with a scorching air black-hot and no cool breathings at the dawning. You would arise unslept with muscles lax as now to burn in the black fires of shame.

The moods might have an uncountable number of gradations according to the circumstances, and now and then there would be a merging of them—a fatigue that was in some way pleasant or an elevation that came with pain in the feet of it—but in general there were but the two of them. Now up, now down.

His mother was still the scold, and if anything John the Elder was oftener at the preaching than before. It always seemed to be the most unsuitable time also, that he would choose, just the time when it would have the worst possible effect upon Murdo. Chiefly it was after the reading at night that was his head time. He seemed to get worked up to it then.

Now that was just exactly the worst time as far as Murdo was concerned. It was a strange thing that if his imagination had been running on the usual lines during the reading or the prayer, on the aspect of the dead body and so on, more particularly as far as his parents were concerned, he always rose from his knees in some way repentant and feeling a sort of kindness towards his father. It was just that moment that John the Elder would choose for the preaching and naturally that sent him down into depths the greater for the contrast with his repentance, all the more so as the fresh light of day had gone with its heartening and left an open field to Hebrew stuffiness that only indoors and in lamplight had an entirely unchallenged influence.

Then after it was all over you had no choice but take your gloom to bed with you, and that was a dangerous bedfellow.

It happened that on a certain evening Murdo walked along the south road towards Torr.

He had been up in the heights all the morning in the shop, humming away to himself and smiling at the odd fancies that came to him, and when anyone came in he flashed a wit that in its Gaelic sharpness surprised himself. Old Beitidh Mhór hobbled in from her hovel next door. Her mutch was dirty and the drop at her long nose quivered dangerously as she mumbled toothless gums, but he would be a nimble fellow indeed that could get the better of her in the matter of words. She had the full of her head of old tales and sayings and in her youth they said there had not been the beat of her in the parish at the singing and the dancing. She could keep going at the puirt-a-bial yet and put her own words to it too in a way you would never have believed if you had not seen it yourself.

To-day Murdo's sallies put a thin, dry cackle of laughter on her.

" You have the Gaelic, a laochain," she said at last. " It's long since I heard the like of you to-day. It's poor Gaelic the young folks have now, when they have it at all, and words of the Beurla sticking out all over it like pimples on a lass's face, as if we hadn't good enough words in the Gaelic itself for anything a man would be wanting to say. It did my turn whatever, and in the old days we were alive."

But that was in the morning. Since then the way things had come about had brought the worst of black moods on him again, and by the time he was able to slip away there was no creature whose company he could have put up with for a moment with the touchiness that was on him. The evening was fine, however, with a cool air of the sea blowing, and after a time its calm settled on him and the black mood toned to a quiet sadness that while it held no thread of forward-looking hope was yet not unpleasant, like a last note of music left hanging in the air, after the hand that struck it will never strike another.

There was once a man from these parts that was namely for the lasses. A jaunty, lusty lad he was, and a way with him nothing feminine could resist. Let him but appear upon the scene and there would follow a rustling of petticoats, for the silly creatures could deny him nothing.

Now whether it was he had tired of the fare at home and was seeking tastier morsels abroad, or whether he just happened to be coming round that way, we are not told, but the tale has it that one day the Devil came home and found our fine fellow kissing his wife.

It was a difficult moment for the lad and he did not stop to argue, but took his heels for it out of that place and made for home with the One-I'll-not-name snorting at the back of him.

They ran for seven days and seven nights and the Devil must have had the worse of that running, for by the time he got to the top of Càrn Mór our hero had put a good ten miles between them and was making for home where he had a nut that would save him could he but put his hand on it. However, he never got his hand on that nut for the Black One wrenched a great rock out of the ground and threw it after him with all the breath he had left. It came down on the top of the head of the worthy man and put a sudden end on his cantrips.

And if you want proof that the tale is true you can see the hole to this day on the top of Càrn Mór where the rock was wrenched away, while the rock itself is still lying as it fell and the Torr road makes a turn round it where it joins the main road to the south.

Murdo stopped in his daunder when he came to this point. A mile of pleasant evening had put him in some sort of humour with himself by this. He put his hands in the pockets of his old trousers and with a half-humorous cock of the head surveyed the old rock slowly from top to bottom for all the world as if he had never put an eye on it before—a great lump of an old rock about seven feet high at the top of it where some earth had gathered and a scanty grass was withering, and the flat places on the front of it like a parish register with the names generations of boys had scrabbled there with old nails.

"Well, now, that was a mighty throw right enough," thought he half aloud, nodding his head to himself, "and sorry am I for the lad yon landed on the head of. The way it struck him it must have shut him up like a telescope. He'll be spread out under there like a bit of bannock, with his jaw between his two feet and his teeth sticking out the top of his skull."

The air had been warm and still for a time, but now a little breath of wind from the west found its way round the edges of Guala Mhór and touched the back of his neck like a cool finger.

He turned round to scan the west and saw that the sun was preparing to drop behind the high, jutting angle of Guala Mhór, with haste on her to be over the horizon and letting the Islesmen to their beds. A great black shadow was creeping up the face of the Guala itself, but north and south the moors and machairs were turning a lighter brown and the chimneys of the town were reddening. The little wind there was down there was slowly marshalling the clouds that lay low in the west, darkening on their undersides, but high up there must have been a lusty breeze, for a string of little clouds shot through with light went scudding at a great height across the sky.

We're going to have another fine sunset, thought Murdo, and I'll be getting a better view of it from the higher ground nearer Torr. And that decided him which road to take.

He turned and began to stride round the bend of the road. His hands were still in his pockets and his eyes were on the ground as he bent to the slight ascent when suddenly a foot appeared right in front of him, almost under his nose as it were, and he noticed the little fuff and spurt of dust as a woman's shoe came down smartly on the roadway. He straightened himself with a jerk only just in time to get his balance and avoid banging right into Annie MacIver, who stopped in her tracks and let a squeak out of her.

The foot had come crashing through the wall of his thoughts as well as missing his nose by inches, he was in a fine quaking inside, and it was quite three seconds before a snigger from the girl reminded him to shut his mouth.

" Oh, Murdo, what a fright you gave me! " says she in the English, with another snigger that was meant to be insinuating and friendly.

Murdo grunted and looked aside. He scowled at the letters "J.McK." scratched on the rock face, long, straggling, ill-formed letters. Some John MacKenzie most likely. There were dozens of them in the district. Must have been a fool whoever he was. Looked like the straggling hand of an idiot. Now what the hell let this female meet him just at this place and time? And how the hell, hell, hell was he going to get past her? She was looming up in front of him there like a black dream. Would he make a rush for it? He was still shaking inside from the shock he had got, shaking quite ridiculously, like a woman. That was to be expected of course, since the evening naturally followed the afternoon and no great distance between them. Here he had been standing for a good three seconds as if he had met a bochdan itself. Looking like the very devil of a fool, no doubt, with his mouth sagging open. That was all her fault.

"Are you no' speaking to me, Murdo?"—with another friendly little snuggling snigger.

Damn those friendly little snuggling sniggers! There was a tang of the familiar about them, as if they were in place of all that needs no saying between old friends. They seemed to put a wall between the two of them and the rest of the world, a wall of friendly little snuggling sniggers. You felt as if you were caught in a trap, with these cosy little noises. What right had the woman to be pretending there was anything between them, an understanding of some kind? He had hardly even spoken to her.

Meanwhile he had evidently said "Oh, yes, I'm speaking to you right enough," or something like that, for she made no sign of moving but began at the chattering.

"Oh, Murdo, I'm just after visiting on Cathie MacKenzie. She was on our class at the school, you'll remember, and I couldn't be going away without saying good-bye to her, you know. You'll have heard I got a place in Inverness. I'm off with the mail-car tomorrow. A good place too it is. Grace MacDonald heard about it and wrote me a letter. It's with the Rev. Mr. Morrison. There was a lot after it I'm hearing but father wrote him himself and of course there was no trouble after that," and so on, and so on.

Murdo was not listening. He was looking from side to side, getting hotter and more self-conscious, and haste on him to be off. She was just plump just now; she would be fat later on. Something gross about the whole breed of them. Something gross and fat about her as of sweat and rutting bitches. It was an insult to her poor little thin drudge of a mother to be so fat, and she after bearing thirteen of them. Like a murderer waving the bloody knife and boasting about the deed. And of course she would be mincing and mumbling away at the Beurla. One of these stupid asses that thought any kind of mangled English was more respectable than the good mouth-filling Gaelic that would have given a kind of dignity to even their conversation, that would only be fatuous in any other language on earth.

" It's terrible the dust there is on the roads just now, Murdo. Don't you think so? Just *look* at my shoes! "

Murdo had no objection whatever to looking at her *shoes*. He turned to look down, but it was not her shoes he saw. She was wearing a blouse cut low at the neck, and as she bent down to look at the shoe on the left foot, turning it up at the inside, Murdo found himself looking right down between her two breasts. The blood rushed to his head and a giddiness passed like a hand across the back of his brain. Faint blue veins under the white skin ran down into the cleft between the plump and swelling breasts.

She looked up quickly and caught the direction of his eyes. A soft smile hovered at the corners of her mouth, and through the half-closed eyelids of her she gave him a long, slow glance that was like the wave of an arm. The blood drummed at his temples and again the giddiness passed like a soft hand over the back of his brain while something clutched at his windpipe and sent a redness burning his cheeks.

"Well, I'll be off," said he lamely, and she sniffed through a lifted nose. Sniffed. She might as well have said the word and spat in his face.

He shifted from foot to foot. Then he made to shuffle past her.

"Well, I'll be saying good-bye, Murdo," said she, all friendliness again, "and I hope you'll be getting on well at your learning." And she held out a hand.

He took the hand and gave it a shake. It was plump and cool and moist, the kind of hand you don't know what to do with when you have it. You cannot go on holding it forever and yet you are afraid to let it go in case the thing will fall off the arm on to the road. You feel as if somebody had put a puddock into your hand.

Finally he let it go and strode off at a great rate round the bend.

"'Amadain, 'amadain, fool, fool," he was saying to himself, and wishing the road would open and swallow him and the blazing red shame that was on him. Fool and coward it had been before. But most men were fools and cowards at some point of them; *this* was a knife-cut at the most vulnerable part of him.

All very well to be striving with the flesh and despising it, but clearly enough a man must be a man, with all the parts and powers of a man, before he can affect to despise any part of him, even the lowest. Otherwise he is the greater fool, affecting to despise in himself what in fact he has not got. Dhia! was he not like other folk in any way at all? He could have had her, no doubt of that. The question was, would another man have taken her? It is to be supposed he would. But did he want her? Difficult question to answer. Probably not, except to prove certain things to himself and all the world, and that he wanted more than anything else at the moment. He could have held up his head after that, knowing what he did. It would have been the slash of a knife through this sticky jelly of the smugnesses and the known-but-unmentionables that had ringed him round for five or six years past and was pressing on him now. A clean slash and a letting in of clean air! So that was what he wanted it for? Then he didn't want her after all? Only as a knife. But would not a normal man, a man, have wanted her for its own sake? He could have had her without doubt. That little bit of acting was no accident. Deliberate enough the way it happened. But things were better as they were maybe. After all he did not know his way about with the creatures, and he would probably have made a bigger fool of himself than ever. He doubted not there was a definite procedure in the matter, a kind of ceremony to be gone through, a set formula of speech maybe, which everyone would know but him who had never been intimate with anyone but himself, and wanting the knowledge of which the thing would degenerate into a farce.

Suddenly he stopped dead in his tracks, gazed for a moment at a big grey rock at the side of the road, opened his mouth wide, and let a tremendous guffaw out of him. He gave a great push with his hands right down to the bottom of his trousers' pockets, tilted his head to heaven, and *roared.* "Eureka!" shouted he, and fairly yelled till the tears rolled down his cheeks. Eureka! He must look the newspapers for advertisements—"School of Procedure and Preliminary Operations. Theory and Practice. British and Continental Methods. Special attention to Formula. Special classes for Gaelic-speaking students. Text-books and appliances provided. Occasional lectures by distinguished Rakes." And there was student Murdo Anderson standing in the middle of the floor receiving instruction. "Murdo! Take up position 3! Cross the left foot over the right and place the right forefinger along the nose!" or, "Position 53! With the left hand make the sign of the cross, with the right hand unfasten buttons one to four!"

But in a moment he was serious again and striding up the road as before. After all there was one other person now who knew about him. That had never happened before. Various things had taken place and various scenes had been enacted, but always inside his own skull. He had always managed to put up a barrier and keep these matters to himself, unsuspected by the outer world. And now Annie MacIver must meet him like this. At the least she knew he had not been able for her, and probably, with the complete knowledge of these matters girls seemed to have from the age of twelve, she would suspect all. The question was, would she spread the news. Women seemed to have a sort of secret society that recorded and disseminated common knowledge of this sort, a secret society with its own private signs and ceremony in the form of titters and nudges and giggles behind hands and Bibles. He would probably know by the way the girls looked at him in the town after this, the poor fish! The blush rose to his cheeks at the thought. If he had not been already in a tremble when he met her things might have been different. He might have passed her with a look of disdain as if he would say, " I know all about that, my dear, and I'm sorry, but it doesn't appeal to me." And then it would have been she who would have been humiliated. Her breasts thrown back in her face. A curse on it all! A fellow never got a chance. No sooner does he set out to walk away from what is at the back of his mind than the flesh meets him round the next corner, with faint blue veins running into the hollow between her breasts.

There must have been a break in the clouds

that covered the sun, for suddenly a shadow leapt on to the road before him, a grotesque bobbing thing with a tiny body and little arms hanging to it and with enormous legs of a spidery thinness that marked time with a lift of about nine feet on each step. The sun was warm and up here the breeze had fallen away to nothing. Murdo gave a turn right about towards the west.

It was a world in the forging that he saw. A red haze of fire-mist filled all space to where the whirling gases surged and billowed in a welter of liquid heat that here was gold or copper and there a bloody red. All was ten million years ago and himself had slid back along a corridor of time, a memory of the future. Below him the Guala Mhór threw a magic shadow across a beach of colourless real world, a shore of prophecy, where far out on the end of a Presbyterian branch sat the monkeys in a row, hiding their tails and buttocks, in a loud chatter of assurance that they had reached the top.

The cloud-break filled and the light in a great beam shot up to the centre of the heavens. Murdo prepared to turn his step towards home. Bah! The chattering apes, not strong enough in the head to try the giddy heights swaying unclimbed above them, and keeping back him that would with a grip on his tail!

A chip of stone lay in the dust at the side of the road. He took a sudden run and kicked the patriarchs, the prophets and the Apostle Paul head first into a tuft of heather. A little dry dust rose where they fell.

Then he turned and strode off downhill in a fine healthy blaze of wrath. Hold him by the tail would they, the gibbering apes? He would have up to the fresher air whether or no. If only he could meet Annie MacIver now he would greet her in her own mincing English. Oh, Annie! I seem to have forgotten the beastly Gaelic word for the female breast! I wonder if you could supply the necessary information. Cìoch? Oh, yes. Many thanks. I had forgotten until you reminded me!

A figure appeared round the rock and turned up the hill to meet him, a little old man with a stick in his right hand and something slung over his left shoulder. As he came nearer Murdo recognised Calum Beag from the Torr, with a stick in his right hand and his week's groceries bobbing in the pillow-slip slung over his left shoulder, and he clumping along in his heavy, tacketty boots at a good, steady, hill-man's pace.

"Tha oidhche bhriagha ann, there's a beautiful night in it," said he as he went stumping past.

"It's a devilish cold, wet, stormy night that's in it," said Murdo loudly as he swung down the hill.

The little bodach tóok a half-dozen of steps before it came on him there was something mighty funny in what Murdo Iain Ruaidh had said. He stopped, cocked the bonnet over his left eye, and scratched the back of his grizzled head, settled the bonnet on him again and clumped off up the slope without so much as giving a look behind.

Not far from John the Elder's door, Roderick Urquhart was shambling along, narrow at the shoulders of him and with a ponderous blinking through thick glasses.

" It's a fine eeffening, Murdo," says he in his high-pitched voice, with just the smallest flavour in the world of the patronising for this quiet black lad that could seldom get up to him in the Latin or the Mathematics.

" Give the glory to Almighty God," declaimed Murdo as he strutted past on the other side of the road. " He has made a better job of the evening than he did of you, Rory Urquhart! "

The long lad turned round and watched Murdo swing up through the door, with the head of him in the air and a spring in his step as if the feilleadh itself was flapping at the back of his knees. What had got into the fellow at all ?

Roderick Urquhart was surprised and annoyed, with the annoyance of a man that is not accustomed to get problems set him that he cannot get to the inside of by means of x plus y. He had no great liking for Murdo Anderson just for that very thing. You could not understand him. You never knew what he would do or say next. You got ahead of him in examinations and so were entitled to think yourself superior, but the black fellow had a way of saying nothing sometimes that made you feel like a withered pea. In spite of yourself you felt it was no great honour to be at the head of the class. He would like very much at the moment to know just what exactly was inside that fellow. Tchah! More than likely there was nothing at all and this was just his way of covering up his jealousy and getting even with you. That was what the teachers thought, anyhow. Anderson, your very manner is a veiled impertinence! would intone the formidable Mr. Matheson. However, they were both going to Glasgow; they would be in the same classes and he would give the fellow a showing up.

Meanwhile Murdo strode into the kitchen, and the Books were already on the table.

" And where was you to-night again, Murdo ? " started his mother before he was all through the door.

" I was back at the beginning of things again, mother, communing with my Maker."

" What nonsense is this ye're at now, you rascal ? " says John the Elder, with a blinking of pale eyes, and he more than ready to fly into one of his rages.

" I decided, father, that I would be better to be mending my ways, and therefore, like one of old, I went up into a mountain apart to pray."

His mother looked at him, more than half certain that this was another of his games, but Murdo was as solemn as his words and never a twitch of the lips to give excuse for an accusation. This was more than she was equal to and with a helpless look at the Elder she sank down in her chair. John the Elder gave a little cough and bit a moustache-end, blinking round with the pale eyes of him and clearly not knowing what to say. Finally, " Let us turn to our deefoshuns," said he, and sat down, forgetting for once to wave his arm like Mr. John MacIver.

5

For some weeks more the weather held. If you chanced to wake up in the night you might hear perhaps a faint pattering of raindrops, but in the morning they had left no sign. Now and then a passing cloud might shed a summer shower, but in a while the sun was out again and a thirsty earth had drunk it up.

Then heather bloomed on the bens and Alba put about her the ancient purple of her royal state.

It is a strange thing you can never see that robing without a start of surprise. A man may see it every year of as long a life as is given to man but always it will be putting awe upon him, as if it never was so beautiful before, so that however much of sorrow is behind him he must be wishing himself back at the start of things again. God of Heaven, how beautiful it is.

And this was a year of all years, because of the fine weather that was in it. By day and all day the east was purple-red, so red and so purple it was sometimes like an insult the eye was giving to the mind. At evenings a strip of human world was borne on the edge of a purple cloud, and the sky was a wash of colours as the sun went down with a deafening clash of cymbals in the west, while a faint fluting of reeds in the pale east trilled along the ragged edge of rosy bens.

It was an early cutting, and not much of it. The stalks in this part of the world at any time have a way of keeping to themselves, and, though they may sway in unison readily enough when it is a matter of doing their little dance in the wind, each one prefers as a rule to have a piece of grey stone between him and his fellows. But this year they were short as well, poor, short things, with pale, thin heads that had never filled, forever trembling away and shaking like the head of a doddering bodach on the top of his scraggy neck. It was difficult to know how to get them cut when they were like that, there was nothing to swing a scythe into, and you would see a man stop in his cutting now and again as if he would be asking himself whether it was worth his while to go on.

"It's a pair of scissors you'll be wanting there, worthy man," shouted Murdo one afternoon as he was passing Domhnull Bàn's croft, and the man himself at the cutting.

"Yes, indeed," says he, turning round. "It's

the slow business this. But it's healthy; it's the fine walking you have going from stalk to stalk!"

"A kind of stalking the Sasunnaich are not likely to take up with much enthusiasm, I'm thinking," says Murdo in the Beurla, since the pun could not be made in Gaelic.

"Well, I'm thinking some of them would be a better hand with the scissors than they are with the gun," says Domhnull with a grin. "And I'm sure Murdo Alec over yonder would be agreeing with me, and he without a bit of his left ear, poor lad."

But indeed the crop was poor enough and when it was cut some of the sheaves leaning against the dyke were more like bunches of withered flowers than anything else. If a cow were interrupted stretching her neck across a dyke she would give her head a toss and clatter off down the road with a thing like a bunch of dandelions hanging to her nose.

The day came at last, however, when the clouds began to gather along the two horizons. At first there was but a long wisp trailing from summit to summit in the east, like a filmy scarf blown by the wind and caught there, and low down in the west a narrow ridge of cloud, a sky-shadow of the isles that lay just over the horizon. Then began a moving and a growing, and the sun shining only to the centre of the heavens gave but a filtered or reflected light to earth.

There was something deliberate about all this, as of some great celestial spectacle approaching at which the earth was favoured to be present, and the clouds, the audience, were being marshalled to their places by flying winds, slowly and with dignity. There came a time when all were ranked in order, massed in close formation so that all the sky was covered, all but one little patch of blue overhead. Soon even that was filled by a late-comer that came up flying, and the spectacle was ready to begin.

There was first a breathless while of waiting, when the thick, hot air stood still and the world was pressed on by a hush of expectation. On a sudden the jagged lightning flickered across heaven and leapt in among the furry bellies of the clouds. Thunder yelled, then rumbled among the mountains like the wheels of a million chariots of war. In the pause that followed the rain began to fall, first in a preliminary splash and patter of big, soft drops, then suddenly in a hissing wall that steamed a foot high along the road.

Murdo turned to run indoors and met his mother rushing out.

" Clothes! " she gasped, running past him.

He was round the end of the house before her and saw the water streaming from the sleeves of John the Elder's shirts as if they had been hosepipes.

" No use! " he shouted. " Better get inside! " and the two of them scurried indoors with rain running from wisps of hair plastered on their faces.

For a long time they sat in the kitchen listening, looking at the pale, grey, liquid light streaming down the window-panes. The room was almost dark. When the lightning flashed his mother's ghostly white face leapt towards him out of the shadow and the plates and cups on the dresser flashed a momentary twinkle. The only sound was the steady hiss of rain, except during a slight abatement when with a prodigious clatter of tackets John the Elder rushed in from the byre, where he had been imprisoned, puffing and gasping and shaking himself and slapping a wet cap against his leg. . . .

After that the rain continued. All the days were grey days, and it was seldom indeed the sun showed a blear eye through wet sheets of trailing cloud. In the early morning and at evening the hills were eloquent with the shouting of many running waters, strangely distinct when it came, mysterious, out of the white silence of a mist.

During these weeks Murdo went about as usual. He brought peats from the stack and water from the well, he served the folks in the shop, and at evening, whenever he was able to get out at all, he walked away from himself on the moors or by the edge of the sea.

To the folks of his world he might be just Murdo Iain Ruaidh, a quiet dark lad with at times a queer way of putting what he had to say; to himself as usual it was as if his state of mind were pointed out by a moving clock-hand on a dial of charted mood.

One morning he came slowly to his waking

out of a pleasant dream. For a time he lay with his eyes shut, knowing he was awake, but still not more than half across from the dream world, and scarcely conscious of his body. Then he opened his eyes, and it was as if he was looking at a familiar scene for the first time. Everything was there exactly as he had seen it for years, every morning of his life, the rafters, the chair, the chest of drawers with two knobs wanting, the open window, the swaying branch end. But it seemed he had merely accepted these things before, not knowing they had a meaning. He was coming at that now. Undoubtedly they had a significance. Even his trousers lying across the chair had a significance and the sleeve of his striped shirt stretched down to the floor with a limply significant gesture.

I have it! I have it! he said to himself, sitting up suddenly in the cold air. This is the morning of my last day of *this* place. One morning more and then every day and all the sun rises on a new world for Murdo!

He pushed a leg into the cold, then swung himself out of bed and began bending his knees and stretching his arms.

A familiar clatter of dishes began down below, unfamiliar too, like the chair and the rafters, as if a man should know a friend for years and only at the parting notice certain of his features.

The day passed quickly and early in the evening Murdo drew the old green door behind him and took up the road towards the town.

It was a grey evening, cold and hard. The even sky like a great sheet of lead rested one end on the hills and the other on the sea-horizon. The bens themselves were the blue of hammered iron, and the sea silent and motionless like grey steel. His heels struck loud on the roadway as with hands in pockets he swung across the bridge and up the slight ascent to the town.

At the first houses he turned to the right up a narrow close and stopped at the end, opposite a wooden building with "John MacKenzie, Joiner," over the door.

The half-dozen or so of men inside looked up as Murdo entered and then went back to their talking. Iain Beag himself lifted his head from the bench before the window where he was bending over some work, said, "Thig a stigh, a Mhurchaidh," and turned again to his tap-tapping with a little hammer.

Murdo walked over and watched him a while. Then, "What's in it to-night?" says he.

Iain Beag made some indistinct reply, because he had a nail in his mouth, and continued to present to him the bald patch on the top of his fair head.

Murdo cleared a plane and chisels from the end of the bench and perched himself on it.

Iain Beag's workshop was a rendezvous at evenings. At the far end of it there was a door to the house and old Iain Mór used to come hirpling through and spend his time in the shop when his son would be working there. The big-boned, broad-shouldered old man sat in his wooden arm-chair and mumbled the stem of his pipe with toothless gums, now and again bending stiffly forward and spitting at the fire, although for the want of teeth the spittle oftener than not ran down his beard. He used to be a singer in his younger days, and a notable piper, too, but his voice was old and cracked now and the rheumatics had put an end on his piping for good a matter of seven years before. Only once had he put finger to reed since then and that was five years back when he had the argument with the black Skyeman about a tune. His mind was active enough yet, however, and any young fellow that had an eye to the piping or the singing found him a shrewd critic. A philosopher, too, he was in his way and wonderfully noticing. It would surprise you the little things he would observe about the world, from the motions of a star to the habits of the little creatures of the earth. He would spend his days there thinking them all over, and—a strange thing in a man in these parts—he would never let the opinion of authority come between him and the end of his reasoning, but would form his own judgment on the matter in the face of the most precise statements of Scripture. He had no learning and not more than half a dozen words of English, though he would read the Gaelic fluently enough when he could get his hand on anything printed in it.

Naturally enough, it was not anyone who would drop in of an evening, but only those that were more or less of old Iain's way of thinking, that had a liking for the old songs and sgeulachd and for conversation of the speculative kind, and that were not too careful of their reputation with the mass of the stricter folk. Naturally, too, as you might have expected, none of the Seceding persuasion at all were of the company, only Murdo himself, when he could manage it, except that now and again Rory MacIver's grinning face would appear round the door if he happened to be passing that way and the laughing was louder than usual—but then the most half-hearted of giggles would have enticed that lad into Hell itself.

In this way it came about, therefore, that while anyone at all would have been welcome who was willing to make himself agreeable, actually on most nights you could have stood outside the door and guessed who would be there, and found when you opened it that you had not been far out in your guessing.

The folk sat or stood about as they liked and talked just as the talking went, having no objection as a rule to leaving the end of a topic in the air if one arose that promised to be more interesting, or if it was necessary for someone to illustrate a point by singing a song. Sometimes, too, the argument would get hot enough in a friendly kind of way, and if it was about piping it would end by someone taking down the pipes and striding out to the patch of grass at the side of the shop with the whole company trooping at his heels, all except old Iain Mór himself who sat in his chair and bent an attentive ear. Every now and then someone would come in to tell the stage of the argument and demand his opinion, which he would then carry out to the men at the gable, who would pause in their arguing to listen and then be at it again. At times a whole evening would be passed in this way, the men arguing at the end of the house and only pausing now and again when someone took the pipes and stepped aside to play over a part of the tune to illustrate some technical matter, and he as like as not continuing the discussion for a bit with the bag hanging limp and the chanter held ready between his teeth.

Iain Beag would always be out when it was a question of piping. He was one of the best of pipers himself and would stand there leaning his weight on his artificial leg and tapping time with his one own foot while he went through all the changing parts of a pìobaireachd, and he plainly in his glory. At other times he usually worked away at the bench while the talk was going in the shop and only paused occasionally when anything unusual or intricate was under discussion, or out of courtesy if the songs were going. He was a broad, strong man on the near edge of forty, with a big fair face and a way of keeping his own counsel, so that you were seldom sure what his real opinion of a matter might be. He had left a leg in France.

This night as Murdo entered Duncan Lachlan Iain of the Squint was saying, " Well, that's the queer thing you're telling me. Myself would not have thought the wren would have a song at all, unless it would be just a cheep or two."

" Well, I'm saying to you it has," says Iain Mór.

" And what kind of song would it have ? " says Duncan, " A sweet song, would you say, a little, low, sweet song ? "

" Indeed it is a sweet song," says Iain Mór. " But it is not a low song at all, but loud it is as if it would be coming from a bird the size of a lark. I have mind the first time I heard it, and I a lad going up by the big wood that was yonder at Strongorm, and it put surprise on me the loud and hearty song that it was."

" Eudail mo chridhe, cho breagha 's a bha e, Jewel of my heart, so beautiful it was," he added to himself, and the soft way it came out at the end of a little sigh you could tell it had brought the long memories on him, that first hearing of a wren's song.

Murdo was looking at the fine old man with the far-coming look of one that remembers in his eyes and was wondering to himself what he would have been doing that time going up by the wood that used to be yonder at Strongorm, the sun striking athwart the trees no doubt, and he a young lad.

There was a little silence, a natural politeness in the people of these parts to an old man having his memories, and then,

" Seall sud a nis, Look at that now," says

Calum Bàn Mac Ruairidh 'Ic Ailein Mhóir, as was his habit.

Old Iain bent stiffly forward and stirred the red peats with the end of his stick, sending a little shower of soft, momentary, peat sparks up the chimney.

" An Dreathan Donn," says Kenny Mhurchaidh Bhig softly, on an intake of breath.

" The Wren," says Duncan Lachlan Iain of the Squint, translating; and then, louder, " Is it not the queer language the English ? There's a great gabble of long words in it to be sure and there's a great number of people that will be speaking it (though I never met any myself that had anything much to say that was worth the saying) but there's no music in it at all that I could ever hear and the queerest thing in it is that the words seem to have no meaning to them. Now in our own Gaelic a man can't tell his name itself without every man will know his whole history and his people's before him; and the name of every place will be a picture of what will be there, so that a man will almost know a place on its first seeing by its likeness to the name that will be on it. Say Achadh nam beith to a Gaelic man and he will be seeing in his mind a level place and the birch trees growing here and there, and they white and slender. Say Achadh nan siantan and he will be seeing a little plain between great mountains and the rain driving down on it. But will a man of you tell me what Achbay or Achnasheen will mean in the Beurla, or what kind of a place is in Lowestoft or Dover ? "

" True enough," murmured a few of them.

" They will have a meaning, though, for them that will know it," says Iain Beag, hirpling over to put a match in the hanging lamp.

" And are you telling me that the Sasunnaich will know that meaning ? " says dark Kenny Mhurchaidh Bhig between puffs, and he putting a match to his pipe with horny fingers.

It was Iain Beag's match put it in his head to light his pipe, Murdo was thinking. Aloud he said, " There's no man of them that will, for one name will come from one old language and another from another and it would take a man a lifetime to be learning them all."

" Seall sud a nis," says Calum Bàn Mac Ruairidh 'Ic Ailein Mhóir, as always.

" And not one of these old languages as old as the Gaelic itself, I'm thinking," says old Iain Mór, looking round at Murdo.

" That is true," says he.

" O indeed it's an old language that's in the Gaelic," says Kenny Mhurchaidh Bhig, stepping over to spit in the fire.

" And it's a beautiful language that's in it also," says Duncan Lachlan Iain of the Squint.

Old Coinneach Mac Dhonnchaidh 'Ic Alasdair Ruaidh, who seldom said a word, opened his mouth to speak but shut it again and turned round, as did they all, when Iain Mór commenced in a low voice to recite. They leant forward to catch the words and as it went on and the voice became louder one or two sat back with a satisfied air, having recognised the lines.

The old man warmed as he proceeded; a flush rose to his cheeks, the eyes glowed in his head; and in a deep and resonant voice he gave the great, mouth-filling words. The liquid lines rose and fell and flowed and ebbed till the mighty sea herself was in the room, heaving up and sinking, breaking at the tops of billows into fragments glittering in sun-sparkle, rushing up long beaches and chittering among the pebbles, dashing with huge anger against tall cliffs and snarling round the roots of black, wet rocks. The sea, the sea was in it, the restless sea, the tireless one, the calm sea that lulls and laps and hushes, the greedy, cruel sea howling and gaping for bodies of men. And the soul of man was in it, loving the smiling sea, glaring under fearless brows at the roaring, wrathful sea, going down, clutching, in green waters, biting the seaweed in his teeth—but never conquered!

When he had finished a hush was on the company. For the moment they were under the spell of that great monster the sea, and of the poet whose unconquered soul was in it too.

Then Iain Mór turned himself round with a brisk and supple gesture, a young man again, and proud. The grey hair fell back from a smooth brow, the nostrils twitched, and an ancient spirit that will be always lurking somewhere in the Albannach sat right behind his eyes.

"*There's* the Gaelic language for you," says

he, like a challenge. " That's a bit out of the poem Alasdair Mac Mhaighstir Alasdair made on the birlinn of Clan Ranald. And if there is the like of it in any language in the world let the man that knows it stand to his feet."

There was a murmur of admiration now from the men as they relaxed. Murdo had been swept away by the fierce power of the thing and it happened that without noticing it he slipped to his feet from the bench where he had been sitting.

" Eh! " says Iain Mór, swinging round at him, " You that knows the Latin and the Greek and maybe the Hebrew also, heard you ever the like of that ? "

" I did not hear," said Murdo, abashed before the old man's fury.

" Indeed, I was thinking that myself," says Iain Mór, quietly, turning again to the fire.

The glow ebbed from his eyes and he sat back in his chair plainly exhausted, an old, done man. With a hand that shook he put the short pipe up to his mouth.

Then they all started discussing the poem and the Gaelic bàrdachd in general.

" And yet the ministers will be telling us it is the work of the Devil," said someone, far enough out of himself yet to be forgetting his habitual caution on these matters, " Myself was hearing Mr. John MacIver saying it yesterday itself."

" Bah! " says Murdo, " that same man should be in a halter, and them leading him round the country—like any other bull." And then right after that he said to himself, Coward! You're sore because that girl shamed you the other day!

"True enough!" says Duncan Lachlan Iain of the Squint, "that poor woman of his will never be off the flat of her back. Is it not fourteen of a family she has had by him?"

"He was saying the other day it was woman's lot to be bearing children," says Kenny Mhurchaidh Bhig.

"Yes, a hell of a lot," says Iain Beag half aloud in the English, with his head down, and he at the tapping again.

Then they went back to the bàrdachd. Others were dropping in, and before long the songs began to go round. Murdo slipped off the bench and mumbled something about going home. Iain Beag at that very minute laid down his tools, hirpled across the room and through the door to the house, as if he had not heard him. Murdo waited for a bit but Iain did not come back, so with an "Oidhche mhath leibh uile!" to the company he went out.

He stood a moment to get his eyes accustomed to the dusk and then turned down the narrow close and made for the road.

Before he reached it he heard "A Mhurchaidh" called in a low voice behind him and turned round to find Iain Beag hurrying after him as fast as his artificial leg would let him.

"You'll be going to-morrow, I'm thinking," said he, hobbling up.

"I'll be going with the mail-car to-morrow morning," says Murdo.

"I was thinking that and just came out to be wishing you a good journey and good luck. You'll not be staying in Inverness at all?"

They talked for a little time about the route Murdo would be taking, when he would reach Glasgow, how he had arranged about his lodgings, and so on. Murdo was thinking Iain was talking a lot more than usual and seemed by his voice just a little excited. He was wondering if old Iain's poem could have affected him as much as that.

"Well, I'll be going now, or the Elder will be preparing a sermon for my benefit when I'll come in," says he at last with a little laugh, and making a movement to be going.

Iain made a movement too. He was wearing a light tweed waistcoat against dark clothes and Murdo could see that the fingers of his right hand were fumbling in the lower pocket. Instinctively he drew back a step and gave an upward tilt to his chin.

"Now, Murdo, my friend, don't you be taking offence," says Iain, reaching for his hand and putting a folded paper that crinkled into it. "You'll be going off to the city and forgetting us all; and you'll be wanting books, I'm sure, that you'll maybe not have the money for exactly handy at the time, so you won't be refusing a little gift from a friend that'll maybe let you get those books; and so you won't be forgetting us altogether."

" Taing! " said Murdo, in a small voice, pushing the money into his pocket and blushing in the near-dark.

" There's just a half-word more," says Iain Beag's voice. " You're going out on the start of your road, Murdo, and I know what that will be like to your kind of a lad, so I would just like you to be keeping in mind that there's a few of us here that can see further than the rest and know the old type of stuff that's in you, and we're expecting you to go a long bit farther than most that went out before you or any that will be going out with you. I'm not sure myself that you're not the one biggest man that came out of this part ever. And it's the fine piper you'll be yet, I'm thinking," he added.

At this there was a lump in Murdo's throat and the tears came to his eyes; he was almost angry with Iain for it. He had no words to say when the other man took his hand in a grip like a vice, and as he returned the grip the only thought in his head was that it was strange he had never noticed before that Iain was a half-inch shorter than himself.

Then he turned on his heel and strode round the corner on to the road.

He had never in his life felt as happy as he was at that moment. His chest was out and his head was up and his arms swung by his sides, and he taking great breaths of the cold night air. That anyone should express confidence in his abilities was for him a thing hitherto unknown.

The road stretched out before him to a prodigious distance, without a hint of turning. It was flooded with a warm, golden light. Beautiful houses lined it on either side, houses with marble pillars, and great, cool halls inside floored with marble also. Strains of delicious music played with skill and feeling floated out from windows wide open to the balmy air, strains of bright yellow music that floated out to mingle with the golden light that bathed the street. People moved about with dignity and gathered here and there in little knots, conversing in low voices and with dignified gestures. And he paced along with his chest out and his head up and his arms swinging by his sides, taking great breaths of intoxicating air.

He did not notice that there were no female figures to be seen; but if it had occurred to him he would not have thought it strange.

II

Murdo sat in his corner, facing the engine, looking out the window with a fixed and gloomy stare. Nothing was left now of his liveliness of the morning, and at the start of the journey he had been as cheerful, and as tuneful, as the lark of heaven. The mail-car jolting along had been a triumphal chariot bearing him from the realm of shadows to the kingdom of the sun. The jokes he was making had set the car-full of people laughing, so that a man from Camus-long, pointing with his thumb at Fionnladh the driver, and he with the tears on his cheek, had said, " Shut you your mouth now, dark lad, before this man will be drowning us all down yonder in the Dubh Lochan."

At the station he had paced impatiently up and down the platform waiting for the train that was coming leisurely from Kyle with a few people out of the Isle of Skye.

Till long after Inverness the sun had shone and the train had run puffing among great mountains, over bridges across rivers, athwart fertile straths, through woods of tall pine-trees, out over the mountain moors. He kept the window wide open to let in a hill air that was rich and pleasing to his nostrils, heady a little and somehow unfamiliar from the lack of a hint of sea in it. Every now and then a racing stream or steaming eas would shout in the window and be gone. He kept crossing from one side of the compartment to the other lest any particular of the landscape should escape his eye, and often he would be stooping and craning half of his body out of the window. All the time he was humming away at the back of his mouth in time to the throb of the train, paying no attention to the glances of anyone who happened to be in the same compartment with him. Over and over again he would exclaim to himself under his breath, Alba, Alba, my own country! That's it there for you, he was thinking, the land of the people of my blood, —my fathers of the thousands of years, over the face of the world my roots in the soil of Alba.

This exalted state of feeling could not last, however, and by Perth the reaction had set in.

Clouds had come up and a cold wind was blowing. Moreover, in his excitement he had forgotten to eat for a long time. When the train started off again he pulled up the collar of his coat and settled down in his corner to study the people who had come in.

There were five of them. Two middle-aged women and a man did not surprise him in any way; in fact except for a greater smartness in dress they were so like some of his own people that when any of them spoke, which was not above once or twice, he was almost surprised to hear the Beurla and not the Gaelic.

Two men who sat together were unfamiliar, however, although if he had been put to it he would have found it difficult to say exactly where the difference lay. They were both very dapper and wore hard black hats. They were smoother in outline somehow, they gave you the impression that their bones would be softer. They seemed to exude an air of self-confidence and the tolerance of superiority, and to be shrugging their shoulders just a little contemptuously behind a wall of the most utter indifference. Whatever it was he felt a curious little tickle of animosity run along his spine. They talked away incessantly, and the voices—Now where had he met all this before? There flashed into his mind a bit of moor road. A big car was drawn up. Men in checked tweeds and some in kilts were taking guns out of it and talking and giving orders. The same arrogance, the same indefinable air of superiority and low-lidded indifference, the same voices, the same tickle of animosity along the spine! Sir Henry Sassenger and party from Torr House! Ah, yes, the Englishman!

These two were talking away still. Whether it was the conversation, that seemed to ramble on without coming to a point, and not more than a fair half of it intelligible, or whether it was the peculiar mouthing and meowling manner of speech that caused it, he gave a little shrug of dislike and turned again to look out the window. . . .

This was quite unfamiliar. He had neither

seen nor imagined the like of *this* before. He had never really thought about industrialism, merely been dimly conscious of it on the south side of his head, and had usually given it a mild and qualified approval, regretting the lack about it of that solitude so dear and so necessary to a hillman, but thinking of it for all that as somehow beautiful in its own mechanical way, a thing of great polished shafts rising and falling and of huge wheels revolving, beautiful for its polish and accuracy and dexterity, and for the power and inevitability of it. It had not occurred to him to imagine the like of this. The day was gloomy, of course, the sky banked up with dark clouds that dropped a spatter of thick rain occasionally, but he doubted if this country could smile even on the finest of days.

For a long time now the train had been running through a black, sad country, a country of ugly, irregular little towns, of scarred and blackened fields along whose edges dark trees waved despairing arms. Now and again huge black pointed heaps like hills of coal reared themselves up in air; long lines of coal wagons stood about or ran here and there across the fields—a black, sad country, a country of spattering brown rain and dismal skies, of coal heaps, and long lines of coal wagons, of ugly huddling houses and empty tin-cans.

It was so hopeless a scene that once or twice he looked round to see if his fellow passengers were not also dismayed thereby and was almost surprised to find them so seemingly indifferent.

The two middle-aged women beside him sat with their hands in their laps and stared stolidly before them, sucking sweets; the man in front was hidden behind a large newspaper; the two Sasunnach were still chattering together in their peculiar meowling speech, surrounded by that strange atmosphere that caused a tickle of animosity to run down the spine.

Only twice was he raised to a sudden and momentary cheerfulness.

Once was when a board passed the window and startled him out of a half-dream. He had been sitting dozing into the beginning of his melancholy when suddenly a board passed the window, a black board with white letters on it:

BANNOCKBURN

In a moment he was on his feet and fumbling eagerly with the leather strap of the window. He stuck his head out, conscious of that same little shiver and tingle of excitement he had felt in the morning when the train had been puffing along through a sun-bathed country of streams and woods and great mountains, and he had been looking out at it and saying, Alba! Alba! to himself.

But this was the black, scarred land; blasted and torn it lay under grey skies. Here no serried ranks of Albannaich to withstand the bleached Saxon, him and his speech, here only the desolate fields bearing their crop of twisted steel and ugly houses of men.

His heart sank.

The cold wind was blowing his black hair over his eyes and big splatts of rain were plastering it down there. He drew the coat collar together under his chin.

When he sat down he expected to find the folks looking at him. He had jumped up suddenly to look out and they would surely know why he would be doing that. But they were all there as before and no one seemed even to have glanced his way.

He suddenly realised that custom would have made Bannockburn nothing to them, merely a station to be passed on a train journey; it would not have struck them why he had got up.

The Englishmen were warming to their mouthing behind an invisible wall of cold indifference.

He looked out again at the scarred, cheerless land, and, " I'm thinking we've lost that battle," says he to himself.

The second time he had been thinking to himself that this was a black coming and a bad omen, and then he looked anxiously at the pale patch low down in the sky ahead where he imagined the sun would be.

Even as he looked the clouds began to thin, to tease themselves out, and suddenly with a loud laugh the sun burst through and looked him right in the eyes, and warmed him. The omens are favourable, thought he, and was almost cheerful again.

But in a moment a black mass began to move across the sun. He watched it almost with fear.

Almost immediately the light was snuffed out and the world was grey and cold again.

Once only, later, the sun made an attempt to struggle through. It failed, and thereafter there was naught to see but a gloomy, black land, cold and wet through a steady smurr of rain. A black coming indeed and a poor omen for a lad rushing in a train to the beginning of a matter. . . .

Now for a long time he had been sitting huddled in his corner staring gloomily out the window in a melancholy that was partly fatigue and hunger, and partly the reflection of the grey world darkening to night outside. The train was slipping between rows of high houses of a dirty grey stone, high dirty houses with innumerable windows in them, dirty windows they seemed, some of them broken and some with clothes outside drooping dismally on a line, sodden and limp and forgotten about. Lights were going in inside many of the windows so that in the passing you might get a glimpse of part of the interior, a patch of ceiling with moving shadows thrown on it, or a corner of a bare room; or else a figure would move mysteriously across the light, going about on some unimaginable business. Occasionally they would glide past some huge, black, silent factory, or a long board covered with bills would break the monotony, and then it was the tall black buildings again, with occasional sodden clothes hanging, and lights going in inside the dirty windows.

He shivered.

The rows of houses were receding to give place to a network of rails, the train was slowing down, and he concluded they were near the station. He glanced up at the two cases on the rack above him, realising he was tired and hungry and cold, and wondering in a sort of panic how he was going to find his way to the house of Mrs. O'Callaghan in Hill Street, seeing himself trailing along with the heavy cases in his hands between endless rows of tall black houses to find at last that his lodgings were up a prodigious long stair behind one of the dirty windows they were passing.

He had just begun almost tearfully to wish himself heartily back at home and the Books on the table when the people began to get up and take things down from the rack. Then lights flashed in the window and he looked out to find they were slipping along a great lighted platform, with knots of people standing about looking earnestly at the carriages as they passed. The train stopped with a little jerk and the people began to get out, grasping their luggage. Almost mechanically he did the same.

Now he was standing on the platform between his two cases, looking helplessly around him. Everywhere people were shaking hands and talking together, smiling into each other's faces. That put a great void of loneliness inside him and he seemed to recede till he was occupying a position of complete isolation.

Without doubt Murdo was conspicuous enough at the moment had anyone cared to look particularly at him, he standing there with his two cases at his feet looking from side to side, a dark lad in rough tweeds and an unaccustomed felt hat that shouted its newness to the world. Clearly none of its species had ever sat on that black head before. A hairy highland stirk that had somehow found its way into a herd of sleek southern cattle, you might have thought.

He was just going to pick up the two cases when suddenly a figure approached him, seemed to rush at him suddenly out of the middle of a seething crowd, a smartly dressed figure with an overpowering air of haste and efficiency.

" Are you Mr. Anderson ? " it said.

" Yes," said Murdo, after a little pause at the unusual name.

" I'm John Colquhoun. Mrs. O'Callaghan asked me to come down and meet you," said the figure, shaking his hand with an unexpected friendly warmth. It was a smartly dressed young man with a fair face and that air of efficient haste that made you feel like a clumsy sheep-dog alongside a thoroughbred; but the blue eyes were friendly.

" Is this all your baggage ? " said John Colquhoun, taking charge of the situation, " Well, we'll be toddling along."

He seized one of the cases and hurried off into the crowd with Murdo at his heels lugging the other and feeling as if his hat was at a slant, his collar to one side, and his laces loose.

They came out of the station and Murdo was immediately rolled head over heels and tossed about by a tremendous wave of roaring and rattling noise that swept over him, a great dark wave with moving lights shot through it. He strode along by the side of John Colquhoun answering his questions about the journey in what he felt to be a lame and rustic manner, bumping his case against the legs of people passing and hurrying on blushing for his clumsiness, sure the other would be laughing at him. Great iron monsters of different colours rushed roaring past, moved by no visible force, blazing with light above and below and with people climbing up and down at the back, or sitting inside strangely aloof and indifferent. He was afraid John Colquhoun would ask if he had ever seen a tram-car before.

They crossed a street to a corner where a crowd of people was gathered. Several tram-cars rushed up, stopped for a moment as the crowd surged forward, then rushed off again round the corner.

Of a sudden John Colquhoun shouted in his ear, " This one will do. Make a dive for it! " and dashed forward.

Murdo was to walk up to it but was pushed and jostled by the crowd, and the thing had started off again before he was able to throw the case inside and clutch the brass rod with all his might.

For what seemed a very long time he sat swaying in the tram-car, bewildered by the flashing lights and feeling like a great shaggy bullock among all these trim and purposeful people. Right opposite him sat a young woman whose remote and indifferent beauty increased his confusion so that he kept tugging his collar round and never seeming to get it right. Her face was peculiarly white and her lips surprisingly red. Her nose was tilted disdainfully as if to disclaim all ownership of her legs, and they crossed so as to reveal a disturbing shapeliness. He glanced at John Colquhoun and was surprised to find him staring in front of him as indifferent as herself. He felt he could never aspire to this Olympian indifference.

At last John Colquhoun got up and Murdo staggered after him and off the car. They turned a corner, walked for a little up a sloping street and eventually turned in at a door. In the passage John Colquhoun cried out, " Here's Mr. Anderson, Mrs. O'Callaghan! "

A little clatter of dishes suddenly stopped in a room on the left and Mrs. O'Callaghan came out. She took his hand with a warm and friendly pressure, a little woman with dark hair turning rapidly to grey who beamed up at him through her spectacles with the kindest pair of grey eyes in the world, so that he smiled back and felt at once at home with her.

" I'm not long after getting your telegram," says she in a soft, musical voice, with a blas on it that struck him as oddly familiar, " so I asked Johnny here to come down and meet you in case it would be you hadn't been to Glasgow before."

She led the way into a room on the right, a cheerful room with a fire blazing and a white cloth on the table.

"You'll be tired, I'm thinking," says she, "and hungry. Sit down now and you'll get your tea in a minute."

Murdo hung his coat and hat behind the door and sat down in front of the fire. There was a great singing and buzzing going on in his head, his eyes were hot and tired, and his bones were sore with the rattling and jolting he had got the whole of that day. He suddenly realised he had let John Colquhoun go without thanking him for his trouble. Then he thought what a clumsy fool he must have looked floundering along banging his case against people's legs, and then clutching that brass rod like a drowning man with a straw, and his mouth open, as like as not. He felt miserable again, tired and miserable.

Mrs. O'Callaghan came in and set his tea on the table.

"Sit in, now," says she.

He got up to go to his place and stumbled over the leg of a chair.

"Tigh an Donais! Hell!" says he, exasperated beyond measure at this new clumsiness.

Mrs. O'Callaghan gave a silvery tinkle of laughter so that Murdo looked up at her in amazement.

"Have you the Gaelic?" says he.

"I have, indeed," says she, and went out the door laughing.

2

That first term went over his head in a smooth and graceful curve. Quickly, too, it went, as time will do when you are happy.

To be sure there were episodes, and there were moods, but they were a mere momentary slackening of pace and not enough to disturb the smoothness of day slipping into day.

There was first of all the room. It was a large room, but not too large. On your left, as you came in the door, was a big double bed, beyond that the fireplace, and beyond that a bookcase with glass doors. Facing you was the large double window looking to the street.

Opposite the foot of the bed hung a picture of the Virgin; very sad she was, with the eyelids drooping and the tear on her cheek. "δακρυα θερμα" was the phrase that would come into his mind when he looked at it. At the head of the bed hung a large crucifix and the figure on it was white like ivory, a drooping, pitiable figure with blood oozing from the hands and feet where the nails were. These gave the room a curious air for Murdo, a strange and unaccustomed atmosphere about it, strange yet pleasing, mellow and clean and agreeable to the nostrils of a lad like himself new from the hot stuffiness of old Judæa. For some reason he felt he was in contact here with the generations of minds of the past. It disposed him to study and to thought.

This room was Murdo's kingdom. He would sometimes walk about surveying it from different angles. It was comfortable, and cheerful, and he liked it. Mr. Maclellan from Dumfries had sent word that he was taken ill and would be unable to come to Glasgow to begin the term. As the weeks went by he did not appear and no other boarder came in his place so Murdo had the room to himself, which was better and better. There were so many little human noises that would get on his nerves and Mr. Maclellan was almost certain to have had a habit of making some of them. He would certainly have made little noises when he was eating, or tapped with his fingers or whispered to himself when he was studying. Murdo himself was like a cat for silence, or if he made a noise it was a downright thing, clear away from the background, with clean, straight edges, not a little, indeterminate, shapeless, recurrent thing.

If Mr. Maclellan had come, of course, he might have turned out to be a pianist, and that would have made up for a lot.

The piano stood against the wall, the end of it facing you to the right as you came in. Murdo had never got his hands on one before, and it was two days before he had ventured to open the lid and take off the strip of green felt that covered the keys. He struck one of them high up and almost started back at the beautiful clear note that came out. Since Mrs. O'Callaghan did not come through to protest, he drew up a chair and began to explore the keyboard.

Soon he was discovering which notes sounded together, bending down with his ear close to the keys, and one day he fairly jumped with delight, like a schoolboy, when he succeeded in striking a great chord of five notes all together.

He would often spend hours at the piano, playing chords and running up and down the keyboard, pleased enough if the sounds were beautiful, whether there would be a tune in it or not.

When he happened to strike a particularly fine set of notes together he would stop and listen till the last pale edge of it faded out in the corners of the room, and then strike it again for his pleasure, or vary it a little to weigh the nice difference of mind-mood that got expression in it; and when anything had occurred to disturb him or when he had been too long at the reading he would sit down at the piano and let a cool stream of clear notes wash back through the hot fibres of his brain.

Before the end of the term he was playing so well that Mrs. O'Callaghan said once she would not have believed he had not had lessons in it if she had not heard him herself that first week, and he picking at the notes with one finger.

Mrs. O'Callaghan herself was a large part of the pleasure of that term. She was a widow, and Murdo gathered she was comfortably off. At least she confessed to him one day that she was in no great need of taking in students at all.

"But it's something for myself to do," she said, "and it's nice to have young people about the house."

After a week or two Murdo was in no doubt as to the real reason for it or as to the relation in which the young men stood to her while they were under her roof. It was that the kindly creature would be making sons of them for the time, for she had no child of her own. She would watch his food and his spirits and be angry if he went out on a cold day without enough on him; and once when he had caught a cold and the fever was on him she scolded him roundly, and she putting a cool hand on his brow and running her fingers through his black hair. With it all she was the most cheerful soul alive. Murdo would often go ben on some trivial excuse for the pleasure of leading her on to talk in her curious Irish Gaelic that always seemed to be putting the accent on the wrong place. And she no doubt was as much amused at the curious sounds and ways of speech of this dark lad from the north-west of Alba, who was so like one of her own Eireannaich. Often they would laugh heartily together when they failed to understand each other. She came from Donegal.

Then there was Father O'Reilly. Mrs. O'Callaghan brought him ben one day, and she must have been telling him the kind of lad that he was, for the priest strode fiercely right into the room with a loud: "What! a heretic lurking here!" Then he gave a rich throaty chuckle at the sight of Murdo's consternation and shook him warmly by the hand.

He sat down at the other side of the fire and began to speak in a beautiful mellow voice. A stout man about fifty he was, not fat but of a firm and healthy plumpness.

"I hear you speak the Scots Gaelic, Mr. Anderson," says he, and then he began. Murdo thought he had never heard his own language spoken so correctly and so beautifully. A little different at the vowelling it was from the Gaelic of his own district, like what he had heard at times with men from other corners of Alba, but perfect Scots for all that and with none of the English words and English modes of expression that were so common at home. He felt almost ashamed for his own ignorance of his mother-tongue.

Even on that first meeting Murdo noticed how the expressions kept changing across the priest's face and how his eyes were sometimes sad and sometimes dancing with an almost elfish glee.

Father O'Reilly was never in the house after that without coming through to hold a conversation with him. He visited Mrs. O'Callaghan fairly frequently in order to converse with her in the Irish Gaelic. His mother came from Donegal and her father, strangely enough, had been a MacNeill from Barra, which perhaps in some measure explained his love for the Scots Gaelic.

Murdo was never done marvelling at Father

O'Reilly. He would sit there with his air of comfort and culture around him, as of one who has savoured the essence of life and found it good, talking so beautifully in his rich, mellow voice that Murdo would look at him in amazement and say to himself: It's a poet that's in him! Or, carried away by what he was saying, he would stand to his feet, or walk about the room, fine shades of expression moving across his face, and with a gesture here and there like a shaft of light on his subject, and Murdo would say to himself: It's an actor he should be! Oftener than not he would be at the stories, his face solemn maybe but his eyes laughing till you thought they would dance right out of his head for glee, and Murdo would be able to say nothing at all but would slide down in his chair with the tears trickling out the corners of his eyes, helpless.

One day the priest lifted a solemn finger before his nose and began fumbling in an inside pocket of his coat. With a face of portentous gravity he drew out a silver-mounted chanter, adjusted the reed and fitted it together. Then he began playing, while Murdo tapped time with his toes, inside his boot. When he had finished the little reel he played he handed the chanter over to Murdo, who played another, the priest tapping on his knee with plump fingers and clearly delighted. They were there at the piping, laments, reels and marches and snatches of piobaireachd, sitting forward in their chairs as eager as schoolboys and the feadan passing between them until in the middle of a tune the priest happened to look at the clock, and he was up on his feet, clapped his hat on his head and skipped out of the room with the feadan still in his hand almost before Murdo realised the music had stopped.

But there was another reason why Murdo would look forward to the coming of Father O'Reilly, for the priest began to come with a book in his pocket, a volume of the Scots or Irish poets or of the old prose literature of the language, and they would sit there for hours with their heads together and the book propped up on the table while the priest read and discoursed and Murdo put questions to him.

Many a lovely thing did they discover in these readings, many a little lyric so light and dainty you were almost afraid the frail delicacy of it would fade before your eyes, a simple-seeming thing, and yet when you came to examine it of a rare intricacy of architecture, a marvellous interweaving of rimes and syllables and play of chiming vowels.

A strange effect these readings had upon you. It was as if a window of the mind had been opened upon another world, a very young world, with the high spirits and the deep feeling of youth, clean and healthy and strenuous, and with great sea breezes snoring through it and bright sunshine slanting through tree branches, golden on the dew-wet meadows and the open places, and with dark mysterious shadows in the glens. It was young with a youth that is not in the English anywhere, even at its most youthful, and strange too and hopeful with the boundless hopes of youth. A curious and refreshing air that was, that will not take expressing in the English, and if you asked yourself what it was, it was that every man stood more firmly upon his two feet, head up, the eyes looking straight forward with a steadfast gaze, rather upwards than down and with no use, yet, for trash.

One evening they had been more than usually fortunate and that strange wild wind was blowing strong, bearing the perfumes of flowers and the faint tang of virgin seas. They came to one that began "Binn guth duine and tìr an òir." Murdo caught his breath and sat back in his chair.

"O Ree, what have we lost!" says he.

"Say rather what we shall recover!" said the priest, and looked him square between the eyes—a strange look, half scornful and half questioning, as if he sought earnestly to find an answering look of understanding in the other's face.

Murdo was puzzled and turned again to the book, not knowing what answer he was wanting. But the priest would go no farther that night and after a few trivial words he rose to go, with a strange, sombre look, almost sad.

It was in that room that Murdo was happiest all that term. It was long that the streets affected him in a curious and unpleasant way.

He was from the region of great hills and wide moors where he had been accustomed to walk about leisurely revolving his thoughts in a world entirely his own, except when one would pass him as leisurely as himself. In the part he came from people had a way of their own of going about things. You could tell by looking at a man whether he was abroad on an affair of importance or merely for pleasure or on some ordinary routine business of life in those parts. If it was the last—taking peat from the hill or seaweed from the shore or provisions from the town—a man would be taking his time to it and looking around him. On the other hand if you saw a man, and haste on him to get to a place, you knew at once he had a very good reason for it—that there was illness, maybe, before or behind him—and without asking questions you did what you could to speed him on his way, even if it was only to give him the middle of the road.

In the streets there was no time for leisure or for thought. The crowds that seemed to be forever rushing here and there prevented anything but a rapid and bewildering flicker of impressions that, because they could not at once be arranged and assimilated, produced a sort of giddiness. It had been weeks before Murdo began to realise that these hurrying, scurrying folks were probably rushing to nothing more pressing than their tea.

After a time, however, he fell into the ways of the city. He would rush along to a corner and wait there for a car, with haste on him to be out of that place and going somewhere else. He would walk smartly along the streets, dodging in and out among the crowd, hurrying with a great air of purpose to get to nowhere in particular. He would even upon occasion knock against people and glare at them as they used to do at him, then hurry on feeling as genuinely annoyed as if he had really been going somewhere and they had hindered him.

And all the time he was falling into the bustling city ways he was feeling pleased with himself in some way, as if he was progressing well, getting free of his rustic slowness and coming abreast of the times.

When he went to Glasgow first what most of all made him conscious of himself in the streets was the young women. They would mince along in their smart dresses cut so as to reveal their calves and suggest the rest of their bodies, swaying their hips and generally carrying themselves as if they well knew every man in the street desired them. If one of them looked at you it was usually with an arch glance, as if to say: "I know you would give absolutely *anything* to sleep with me, you poor animal, but I am ineffably above all that sort of thing. It merely amuses me." He had always understood such was the feeling of most women about the thing, and when a girl looked at him like that, as not infrequently happened, he at once concluded the glance was critical and hurried past, very conscious of himself, feeling he had been detected in an act of gross discourtesy if he had not desired her or in a kind of vulgar dogginess if perchance he had. By the end of the term, however, for long periods together he even failed to notice the young women at all and would walk through a whole street of them with a calmness and indifference that was new and surprising and that he found very pleasant when at times the extent of it had come home to him. This indifference was partly no doubt the result of familiarity; and partly he knew it was something else.

In the life of the University he took no part. Indeed it early began to affect him with a growing sense of disappointment. His interests were in the sciences and the philosophies and in the peoples of the earth and the movements and stirrings going on amongst them. He ventured to talk once or twice with men he happened to be together with on subjects like that and they did not respond with enthusiasm as he had expected but turned the subject aside shortly after or even looked at him in pity or amusement. At first he thought it was their much greater knowledge that was the cause of that but later to his disappointment he had to conclude it was not so. He had to do that because he never overheard two men talking on such subjects to each other, but they would always be talking on some trivial matter, arguing together about the football perhaps, or discussing the ways of the professors, with little wit and much laughter. Moreover, when he once or twice got a man to discuss the matters that were interesting him he found him arguing with the same prejudices and unreasoned opinions you could get from a man anywhere. It amazed him.

There was, as an instance, a man he saw in the quadrangle the first day, a tall young man with a little fair moustache and an air of complete indifference and self-possession. Murdo felt like an ant as he passed by. Here was the real thing, he thought to himself. The very air about this place has a hint of ancient learning. Intellectual giants have paced to and fro in these cloisters conversing together in low voices upon deep and fundamental things. And this young man knows all that. He feels it. Yet such is his own knowledge that he can hold up his head proudly among them all. His researches must have been extensive and profound, yet he carries his weight of wisdom easily, with a light step. And he studies still! He met that man often after that because it happened he was taking one class along with him. Crow was the disagreeable name that was on him. On one occasion he got into a conversation with Crow and the conversation developed into an argument. Crow finished up by saying, "The Greeks! Rubbish! The Greeks kept the world back a thousand years. Look at the ideas they had. Besides, what did the Greeks know about modern science? Take Aristotle. He believed in real weight. The prof. told us yesterday. The man was a fool!"

Then he added as he turned away, " You take my tip and don't waste your time on stuff like Greek. *Science* is what you want nowadays, my lad! " And from the way he said the word " Science " he saw that Crow was a man like MacLean who taught Physics at home, a man with no reverence for the past and no appreciation of the finer things of the present. He had always hated MacLean more than any of the other teachers at home because he had burst out laughing when he saw him piping one day at the side of Iain Beag's workshop, and because once before that he had clouted his ear when he heard him speaking Gaelic in a corridor of the school, clouted his ear and said something about a " barbarous language " and " civilisation." MacLean came from Skye, and his English was not very good.

He came away from that argument with Crow very angry and hurt that fellows as stupid as that should be in the University, and also feeling a fool himself when he remembered what he had been thinking the first time he met the man. It was not knowledge he had been carrying so lightly that time; it was ignorance. The fellow had never been touched by any of the feelings he had credited him with.

However, the studies prescribed in the ordinary routine of class work he found interesting enough. They filled a wider horizon than the dull pedantic stuff the dignified Mr. Matheson and his colleagues had droned forth in the school; and he performed them diligently. But his real delight as has been said was to discover some new book about the sciences or the philosophies or about the peoples of the earth and the movements and stirrings going on amongst them, something advanced and heretical maybe that did not come within the compass of the University curriculum and that you felt would be frowned on there.

These when he discovered them he eagerly seized and carried home with a sense of elation as of one about to taste forbidden fruit. He would close the door behind him and settle down with the book, delighted to think he could count on not being disturbed for the whole night and wondering what strange and undreamt-of avenues of thought might be opened to him by the mere turn of one of its pages.

When the thing was more than usually interesting he would often stretch himself face downwards on the bed as he often used to do among the heather at home when a desired idea wanted a careful tracking and a quick grasping. He would lie there staring at the fire with the book before him and the toes of his right foot digging into the bedclothes, and he not making head or tail of the thing for a long time. Then of a sudden it would flash upon him, something entirely new and unsuspected that threw wide a whole region never yet explored, and it was as if he walked abroad in the great immensities, basing his feet on the gold, chiming stars, taking deep breaths of the clean cold air that came from out the vastness of illimitable space around him to touch his forehead and to stir among his hair. That was the sort of feeling he had, and he thought there could be no pleasure on earth to equal it.

So with the delight of books and Mrs. O'Callaghan's tinkling laughter, with chords and his own music on occasion, and with Father O'Reilly and his mellow Gaelic, the term was near its end before Murdo was half accustomed to the quick, impatient tread of life in a big city.

On a day in the second last week Mrs. O'Callaghan came in and handed him a letter from his mother.

" Dear Murdo,—we got your letter on this tuesday past and was glad to see you will be getting on allright with the lerning the thing ourselves never got. its necessary to have the lerning nowadays for a man will not get on wanting it. well theres nothing new with ourselves at the time but last night Ruaray Alastars red cow was in the bog the back of Drumuane and your father was at her taking out. they had a bad job taking her out and the ground so wet with the rains weve been having and your father was not the better of it at all I am thinking. I don't know how she would be getting there at all. your right enough about staying in Glasgo for the Christmas hollydays it would not be worth your while to be coming home for all the time. I don't know what your father will do about the spring work the year wanting yourself and the shop not doing too well at all. Roderic Gun is after having a big cheap sale too but the Lord will keep want from his own people. excuse the gramer for I was never very good at the English as yourself knows my parents did not have it at all. hoping this finds you well as it leaves ourselves. your loving mother Janet Anderson."

Well, that's all right, says Murdo, looking up at four thick volumes that stood in the bookcase. He could now look forward to a few weeks' solid reading without even the inconvenience of going out to classes in the streaming rain that looked like lasting forever. He smiled to himself and wondered if his mother would still be as keen on the learning if she knew the regions it was leading him into.

But his parents' position was now more incomprehensible than ever. They were browsing round and round behind a fence of fixed ideas, unthinking as cattle, while he ranged abroad in vast uncharted regions of the mind only explored as yet by a few intrepid spirits.

On the last Monday of the term Murdo walked up to the University to a class he had that afternoon. In the quadrangle a group of students were pushing about and craning their necks at one of the little notice-boards. As

Murdo walked up one of them said to another, "I don't see my name anywhere!"

"There it is!" said the other, pointing to a line of type at the foot of the paper which read, "The remaining twenty-five students have under 30 per cent."

There was a laugh at this and Murdo realised that these must be the results of an examination he had sat some time ago. He began to read up the column and when he had reached the seventies and his name had not appeared he began to be afraid that he was one of the twenty-five who had scored under 30 per cent. At last he found it:

"Anderson, Murdo . . . . 80 per cent."

His name was second on the list.

With that the little bell began to ring and the students moved up the stone stairs chattering together.

During a lull in the lecture, when the professor had paused to make clear some subtle point, Murdo happened to turn his head a little to the right. From the middle of the seat above him a familiar face was turned towards him, a long white face with the mouth drooping at the corners, looking gloomily at him through thick spectacles, with reproach in the eyes, for all the world like a sick, short-sighted horse. He suddenly remembered a name he had seen on the notice-board.

"Urquhart, Roderick . . . . 62 per cent."

It was all he could do to keep from laughing out loud.

After the lecture he was walking home down Woodlands Road, feeling pleased with himself and smiling from time to time at the blank dismay of the equine Roderick Urquhart, when suddenly something very unpleasant shot across his mind, one of these half-thoughts that come and are gone before they have taken recognisable shape. He stopped in his tracks and tried to recapture it, frowning the while, but whatever it was it was gone beyond recall, and he walked on looking at the pavement, with a vague sense of foreboding at the back of his mind. So intent was he that he had to jump aside to avoid a milk-van that was coming out of a side street and almost upon him before he noticed it. Just as he took a leap on to the pavement opposite a voice said in his ear, " You are young, my son, to be tired of life! " and he looked up into the twinkling eyes of Father O'Reilly. He chatted a moment with the priest, and he in his best humour, and by the time he walked on again had forgotten the unpleasant thing altogether.

He closed the door behind him and turned into the room. Suddenly there it was again, the same unpleasant thing, a shadow looming above him, the air of the room thick with a vague menace.

His eye happened to fall on the table and in a flash he understood all, as if he had known it before.

For a long time he stood there without moving, his back to the door, his hands half out of his pockets, his eyes staring into the room. How would it affect him? The thing itself he was strangely insensible to, but in some vague way he felt it as a threat to himself and fear was on him that somehow this would put an end on it all. And the beginning had been so fine!

He walked over to the table and picked up the brown envelope.

Then he let it slip from his fingers unopened and turned to pull his cases from under the bed. —A blue lip and the breathlessness that came on him when he stooped to pick anything up—and Ruairidh Alasdair's red cow in the bog behind Druim Uaine.

3

Among those of the Free Presbyterian sect, the Seceders as they are called, there will be no service over the corp, whether in the house or at the grave itself, because there is a hint in that of prayers for the dead, and that tastes of popery; but always before the service in the house begins the corp will be removed and put outside the door. So that when Mr. John MacIver stood up in the dark room that day, and his Bible in his hand, he first gave the order to take the remains outside.

Several of the men came forward to do this and when they were in the doorway manœuvring to get the heavy coffin round and out on the front door the only thing that was running in Murdo's head was the terrible lack of dignity about a man's end, the grotesqueness of it even, when you regarded the seat of Ruairidh Alasdair's trousers hanging like a bag behind him. It was an anti-climax at the end of even so ridiculous and grotesque a life as John the Elder's. The first part of the life he could not imagine, he had never been able to imagine; in fact it had seldom occurred to him to try to imagine it. It seemed like a breach of natural law to imagine a childhood or youth for such a man. It was far more natural to assume that he had come into the world by some peculiar process of his own, unhuman, and had always existed as he remembered him as far back as he had any clear memory at all, with a walrus tusk of moustache hanging at each side of a blue underlip, blue and red veins showing on his nose, tufts of red hair in the nostrils and the ears, and he throwing out his arm and declaiming loudly in the manner of Mr. John MacIver or stroking the Bibles with a hairy, red-tufted hand. He had the impression now that the man had never done anything else but that, that he had spent his whole life throwing out his arm and declaiming in the manner of Mr. John MacIver or stroking the backs of the Bibles with a hairy, red-tufted hand. He remembered too the shortness of the breath and the suggestion of a squint in the pale, colourless eyes; but even his passions had a something mechanical and forced about them, as if he were a sort of automaton set moving by order of a detached and independent brain which watched the whole performance, critically, judging the effect. And how ridiculous indeed, how meaningless and without significance all his theatrical shoutings and throwings out of arms seemed now. The man was nailed up in a kist! And the kist was stuck in the door. And a half-dozen of men in blue clothes were manœuvring it about and whispering orders to each other, each of them with a look in his face as if there were a dull pain in his belly. And the legs of Ruairidh Alasdair's trousers were very narrow and wrinkled up like the bellows of a melodeon, and the seat hung down loosely like a wet paper bag. If a man could only see how ridiculous he looked walking through life with a thing like that flapping behind him! It passed through his mind that his red cow ought out of decency to have been at the funeral too. Who indeed had a better right ? And she could have been trusted to go through the business with the utmost decorum. Her face would have been quite in keeping with the long dismal faces of the men around her, and her wheezing and lowing in tune with their melancholy coughings and groanings.

It was not with any sense of amusement that all this occurred to him. The grotesque pictures passed in front of his mind as if without any will on his part, and he regarded them from a great distance as a remote and almost indifferent spectator. He could not feel that he had anything to do with this affair that was going on. He was not concerned. He was merely present. He was held there, an unwilling spectator of a performance he could follow in an objective way but which had no subjective significance for him. It would have been more natural if he had got up and walked away, more natural than sitting there among a roomful of silent people. But he was held back by a compulsion he resented. For a moment a little flame of anger blazed up in him. What was this compelling force after all ? It was ridiculous to say it was connected with the man in the coffin or with the woman sitting over there looking straight in front of her, with a tuft of black hair sticking up on the top of her head and a large red hand with swollen finger-joints resting on each knee. It seemed now as if all *that* was only familiar to him by long custom, that there was no more essential connection. Looking at your hands and your knees you simply could not believe that story of the blob of protoplasm that formed and grew because the corpse in the coffin and the woman over there came together some nineteen years ago. The idea was fantastic and unnatural. But what was it that held him here in his chair ? It was not that something held him but rather that something would have kept him from getting out. It was that he was enclosed by an invisible wall it was impossible to break through. It was the soft elastic wall that had always enclosed him in this place and that he was more conscious of now that he had been outside it for a time. After a period of breathing the free air he was more than ever conscious of its stuffiness. It was very close around him now, formed of the expression on the faces about him, arrogance of self-righteousness in their forced melancholy and all that was implied of smugness and complacency. He felt resentment towards the whole lot of them, as if there was a struggle going on between them, a struggle in the plane of will and mind, unsuspected to a casual onlooker, he trying to get away and they keeping him back. What made him angry was that the calm unconcern of them seemed to suggest that their victory was assured, not to be questioned. There was a bond of silent understanding between them, a conspiracy to keep him from soaring and to tie him firmly down to earth. They were sure they would manage it, and he had to admit he was himself more than half afraid they would. He could almost have believed at the moment that they had driven the red cow into the bog on purpose. It was a plot. However would a cow get over there in the middle of winter by herself? Damn them, they would manage it yet! They would have him one of themselves before they finished with him.

Ruairidh Alasdair came in last and shut the door behind him, quietly, like a conspirator. Then he walked over to a chair and sat down on the seat of his trousers, right under the framed piece of yellow cloth with "Thou God seest me " sewn on it in red wool. Mr. John MacIver cleared his plump throat and started to read the psalm they were to sing.

Murdo could not have repeated a word of the service when it was over. He was too occupied with himself and his own sensations. He ran over them again and again, arranged them, savoured them, gloated over them, weighed his chances of resistance to the surrounding influence, took a sort of inverted pleasure in feeling thwarted and miserable; and to all this Mr. John MacIver's melancholy droning formed but an agreeable and fitting background.

Outside it was a hard, cold, dark-grey day. The window was tightly closed and the curtains were drawn across it, so that the room was in a half light and Mr. John MacIver where he stood had to give a turn on himself and tilt his Bible towards the window when he wished to refer to a passage, repeating several times in his greasy voice the word he stuck at and fluttering the pages with his plump and tapering mole's fingers until he found the place he wanted. If you looked steadily straight before you for a time the dark clothes of the men sitting or standing round the room merged with the shadows hanging about the walls to form a solid black background, and out of the corners of both eyes you could see the faces, very white by contrast, leaping towards you.

The room began to get stuffy with so many people breathing their own breath. You recognised your own breath coming back to you. Then you began to recognise the breath of other people coming back with it. Occasionally there would be a little bit of cold air in it too, a little wisp of clean air that had drifted down from some out-of-the-way corner where so far it had escaped the sucking mouths and noses.

A draught of cold air touched him and put a little shiver on him. Would Mr. John MacIver never put an end on his gabble?

He began to study the man, planted in the middle of the company on his plump legs. It would be a time yet before he finished, for clearly he was enjoying himself over there. He wondered the one outbye in the kist had never seen through him. The man was as plain as a book. With the way he had of slinking along like a beaten dog and never giving you a straight look in the eye, but just a flickering sideways glance now and again from the little pig's eyes of him, it was clear he was feeling inferior to every man that passed him on the road. With the folks about the place, of course, this passed for humility. O, Mr. John MacIver is the humble man! They respected him for it. But he himself knew better. It was grovelling he was before every decent man he met. And why? You had only to think of his poor little thin drudge of a wife and the fourteen children he had given her, and of the way he would open a pig's eye on the young girls in the congregation, and of his tongue flickering along his lips that day and he looking at the white neck of Mary Campbell, and of two or three rumours that had gone through the place about him and faded out again. Also if anyone commenced to laugh Mr. John MacIver would purse his lips and give a little cough behind his hand and glance from side to side, clearly annoyed. With the older folks this was regarded as another proof of godliness. The worthy man was vexing his righteous soul with the foolish talking and jesting that went on among the young folks nowadays. But he himself knew otherwise. Without any sense of humour himself, the man never could hear anyone else laughing without feeling he was being made a butt. And that of course explained why he had become a missionary. Only with God and His Hell at his back could he face a decent man. Of himself he could never hope for a respected place amongst them; but on his feet he had them at his mercy. Of all animals he must most resemble a bull. Curious how people resembled animals. His father had been a stirk, an innocent red stirk looking over a fence, occasionally stamping about with his hoofs and deepening his dismal lowings in a pitiably transparent attempt to imitate the formidable ongoings of the sleek black bull in the next field for whom he had the most profound, round-eyed, bovine admiration. Not that he had any conception of how the bull was affected by the succulent buttocks of a cow—he was only a stirk—but the stampings and lowings of the formidable animal impressed his innocent heart. There was a black Macintosh in Mellonree that was exactly like a frog. He had a round head and a flat face like a plate of porridge. He had wide eyes, a little flat nose, a long upper lip. A thin mouth extended half-way round his face. The lower buttons of his waistcoat were straining over a round, bulging belly, and he had slender bandy legs. A frog! What else? The Frisealach Ruadh up the town, the Red Frazer, had a pointed nose, a sleekit manner, small sharp teeth that snapped upon occasion. He was so much the fox that if you had discovered he had a long brush hidden in the leg of his trousers it would not have put the least surprise on you. There were also fish, chiefly codfish, and various birds. Fantastic thing that so many of the lower animals should be moving about the world only partially metamorphosed into human beings and revealing themselves now and again by an act or a gesture. This one here was a bull. Not a stallion; there was something noble, something beautiful about a stallion; it was as if it should say: I trust you don't think that that is my main purpose in life. I rather regret that, but one must have a means of livelihood. My real purpose in life, however, is to maintain the maximum degree of physical fitness and beauty. Observe the gloss of my skin. Note how the muscles writhe and ripple under it. Decidedly not a stallion. Not a boar either, although the clammy whiteness of the skin might suggest that; he stood too well upon his plump legs. Had he not become a missionary he would have been a boar, but having become a missionary he was a bull, a sleek black bull that took his business seriously and had acquired the gift, unusual among bulls, of conjuring up the cow-smell in his nostrils at will.

He shivered again and began to move his frozen toes about inside the hard toe-caps of his boots. It was one of the bare wooden kitchen chairs he was sitting on and when he moved the cold came through his trousers as if it was off iron. He glanced across at his mother. She was sitting exactly as before with a large red hand on each knee, staring straight before her with no expression at all on her face. Not even the flaps of loose skin between chin and neck moved. In the dusk of the room the hair on her upper lip looked very dark. Ruairidh Alasdair had happened to sit down next to her. He was continually sniffing and drawing the back of his hand across his nose.

He looked round at the people nearest himself. On his left was little Calum Beag from the Torr with his cheeks covered with a thick grey stubble lengthening on his chin to something like a beard. His legs were planted wide apart and the toes of his hard boots pointed outwards and turned themselves up in air. He also sniffed loudly now and again, squeezing up his eyes and pursing his lips so that the stubb of beard jerked up and down. On his right was the man they called the Bradan, the Salmon, because of the great number and prodigious size of the fish of that kind he would always be catching, according to himself. He was a long, lanky fellow wearing a hard white collar several sizes too big for his thin neck. His chin was a little round red ball in a straight line between his nose and his big Adam's apple, in fact no chin at all. His shapeless mouth hung half open. His pale eyes bulged and stared glassily straight before him. His nose was very long and very red and a big drop trembled on the point of it. Involuntarily Murdo put up a hand and found his own nose was cold and wet. If Mr. John MacIver would not put a stop on his gabbling soon the whole still company would be frozen where they sat, and years after someone from the world outside would come into the room and find them all sitting silent in their places, a stalactite extending downwards from each nose.

He shivered again and looked over at Mr. John MacIver. The man of God was planted firmly on his plump legs. The shadows marked out the fleshy bags under his eyes so that each little eye looked as if embedded in a ball of fat. Suddenly he contracted his brows and looked attentively at the man again. Extraordinary! A darkening on the cheek that was turned towards him seemed to suggest a patch of colour. Carried away by what he was saying the fat fellow was actually at the moment believing in himself, convinced he was in contact with the

Almighty, whose agent he was. His greasy voice had become almost musical. Amazing! At any rate he was warm standing over there in the glow of his enthusiasm and his own steaming breath. . . .

At long last the service came to an end. The people stood up and began coughing, moving their arms, stamping their feet. The men moved towards the door, putting on their caps and preparing for the job of carrying John the Elder to his grave. It was now Murdo's duty to go round with the dram. His mother was not fit for anything. She was still sitting in her place staring before her. The men were standing about in the room and in the little lobby and about the door, shuffling their feet and looking about them as if they were just standing there, well, just standing there, with no thought of a dram in their heads, of course—oh no! But an occasional one was sucking in his lips or drawing the back of his hand across his mouth, an unconscious and maybe habitual movement. Murdo went round with the bottle in one hand and the glass in the other. His fingers were blue with the cold and glass and bottle shook and rattled together as he poured out the whisky in front of the man that was to get it. Each man received the dram mechanically, without looking up, just as if it had fallen into his hand. Then he took it off in silence, looking gloomily, as if it was a solemn duty to be performed, not altogether pleasant and needing determination. Only young Kenneth Mitchell, George Washington, as the younger folks called him, coughed and spluttered and glanced at Murdo with the tears running down his cheeks; and Iain Beag gave him a long, unsmiling look out of wide blue eyes.

Going from man to man among them with the bottle he was near to hating them at that moment, the long line of familiar faces, each drawn out to a forced and exaggerated sourness which the owner clearly thought was expressive of the deepest sympathy and the solemnity fitting in the house of death. They did not look at him, but their whole attitude, their silence, their air of being clumsily at home in the situation, seemed to say: We know each other perfectly, don't we? I'm so-and-so, and you're Murchadh Iain Ruaidh. The man that was your father is out there in a kist. We knew him perfectly too, knew him for forty years before you were born. We called him John the Elder. He's dead now, and we're just going to take him to his grave. That's why you're pouring out a dram to us, because you're his son—Murdo Anderson—Murchadh Iain Ruaidh. You went to Glasgow to get learning in the college, and you came back to bury your father. That's how things stand. We understand the whole situation perfectly. There's nothing to be done about it. . . .

When he got to the last man he was still so cold that he would willingly have taken the fill of his mouth of the stuff himself, only he had never taken it before and did not know what kind of effect it would have on a man not accustomed to it.

Now they all went outside. The road was like iron. The Guala Mhór looked terribly dark and hard. A dry, black wind blew up flecks of white foam on the face of a grey sea. A flake of snow flew past occasionally or melted suddenly on a coat sleeve. The moors were heavy brown, and blue hills rose behind with here and there a swollen eas stuttering down the rocky face.

The kist was placed upon three struts of wood. Six men came forward and took each an end, remaining in a stooping posture for a few seconds so as to straighten themselves together. After a pause to adjust the weight equally they set off up the road, while the others fell in behind, silently, two by two. The wind was blowing almost in their faces, but when they turned to the right at the far end of the bridge in order to avoid the town it was blowing somewhat to the side. Half a mile beyond the last house they struck the main north road again and the going was easier. Every hundred yards or so the next six men came forward to take the places of those that were at the bearing, and these latter stood up three at each side of the road till the procession had passed, when they fell in again at the end of the file.

Where the road swerves up to the right over the shoulder of Càrn Bàn Murdo happened to be standing to the side. He had been taking his turn at the bearing with the rest because he was the only relative of the dead and did not like the colder job of walking alone. He was warm now. Behind him where he was standing the Càrn Bàn shut out the wind. A brown, wooden piping came out of the wood that covered the carn as the wind blew among the tree stems. The long double line of men filed steadily past, and it came on him that here was the first dignified thing there had been about the funeral of John the Elder. It was almost impressive the way those silent men walked past him with a steady rhythm. In the calm eddy of air formed by the hill between them and the wind the tramping of the heavy boots came suddenly clear and loud. For a time they were all walking in step, with a regular tramp-tramp-tramp of feet, and every now and then the clear ringing of an iron heel struck against a stone; then someone at the head of the line got out of step and there was nothing but an irregular clattering and shuffling until they picked it up again.

So they came to the churchyard, and Murdo in the middle of the line again, walking behind a man with sloping shoulders and a thick, clumsy seam down the back of his grey-green jacket.

The body was immediately lowered into the ground. The men standing round took off their bonnets and for a moment stood in silence, bowing their heads. Murdo stood staring at the tops of the heads of the men standing opposite at the far side of the open grave. A few white flakes of snow drifted past between him and their dark clothes. Mechanically he put up a hand and took off his hat. The wind blew his long black hair about. Then the first clods fell on the lid of the kist, which gave out a hollow sound. The men raised their heads, put on their bonnets, and began to move slowly away. A few of them came up to him and shook him silently by the hand or said a word or two to him that he did not catch the meaning of. He gave no words in reply because he had none to say.

Presently he was alone. His hair was still blowing about and he was looking at the words on the stone at the head of the grave.

SACRED
to the memory of
MURDO ANDERSON, crofter at Druim a' Choirc
who died 21st October 1895
aged 74
and of Mary MacKinnon his spouse
who died 30th December 1899
aged 69
also of Murdo Roderick their son
drowned at Warramulla, South Australia,
2nd May 1898, aged 35 years.

"Gus am bris an là agus an teich na sgailean."

"Until the day break and the shadows flee away." That at least was very beautiful, and incidentally the only part of the writing that his grandparents would have understood, for neither of them had the English. Well, well, that was his grandparents. Murdo Anderson his grandfather and Mary MacKinnon the red wife he had married out of Skye. Now they had put down his father to rot beside them. Later it would be his mother. Then as like as not it would be himself—Murdo Anderson, crofter and merchant at Druim a' Choirc, died 19—, aged — years. That was how it was. Five of them rotting quietly down there in one hole and the fat weeds waving in the wind above them. And there would be nothing to show for it. One million and more of people would still be tearing breathlessly about in Glasgow shouting "Progress! Progress!" But the only difference was that here men sank into a grave with some sort of dignity while there they flew at the business in a great dust of haste and jumped in with both feet or tumbled in head first, legs and arms splayed ridiculously out, so that the end was as noisy and undignified as what had gone before it. That was all the "progress" there was to it—a small matter of being tootled and rattled to your grave in a motor hearse. Here at least a man was borne slowly to his resting-place, a long column of men marching rhythmically on a grey road over the shoulder of Càrn Bàn, while the black wind of winter piped a lament among the trees. A small matter indeed after and all. Now if his grandmother had lived another two days she would have seen the dawning of a new century. But what indeed did it matter? Why trouble to delay for that? The life would have no more meaning or significance for having 1900 on the gravestone. The whole thing was meaningless. A vegetable process.

A spade struck sharp against a stone behind him where the men were waiting to fill in the grave, and he realised that more than once he had heard a little subdued cough from that direction. Without looking round he put his hat on his head and walked away across the uneven ground among the graves. He climbed the crumbling wall at the far end, keeping away from the road. Snowflakes drifted quietly past his ear as he strode home across a brown moor under a sky the colour of lead.

4

John the Elder's wife remained the rest of that day without saying a word. They had found her still sitting in her place in the room after the men had gone away. They brought her ben to the kitchen and since then she had sat in her sitting place by the side of the fire without moving or changing her position in any way, one hand resting on the top of each knee and her eyes, wide open, staring into the heart of the red peats. Once, however, she took a little food they put into her hands, lifting it mechanically to her mouth without taking her eyes away from the fire.

When Murdo got home there were still three or four women in the house. They had been taking the chairs out of the room and putting them in their places and generally setting things right. Now they were just looking for little jobs to do in order not to leave the house so soon, and they must have been hard put to it to find anything, for Liza Murray had taken a duster in her skinny hand and was needlessly rubbing it back and fore along the arms of John the Elder's chair in the intervals of chattering in a low voice with Jane MacKenzie, the two of them wagging their heads and sniffing now and again or heaving a sigh.

"Oh, he wass the good man indeed," says the latter.

"Yess, indeed he wass the good man, the godly man," says Liza Murray, giving a quick glance of her eyes in Murdo's direction to see if he was listening.

"Oh, indeed, it would be difficult to get his like in the place, I'm thinking."

"Indeed and it would that. A godly man he wass, and it wass the godly folk he came of—godly folk—oh aye, godly folk," says Liza Murray, heaving a sigh and glancing over at Murdo to see if he would still be hearing.

"You're right there. Oh, hiss folk wass godly; all hiss folk wass godly. Ah but it wass godly folk that would be in it in the old days. There's not the like of them nowadays—oh no—what with the way they will be breaking the Sabbath itself . . ." and Jane MacKenzie wagged her head and sniffed up her nose.

"Oh, it's terrible indeed the way folks will be going on nowadays, terrible indeed—they're telling me it won't be possible to walk in the streets of Glasgow to the church on the Sabbath day for the crowds of young people, and they going to the Moving Cinemas in their hunders. It iss an evil day."

"I'll believe that, oh, I'll believe that. I would be believing anything about the young people nowadays. It's the Lord's mercy there will be some godly folk left yet to be bringing up their children in the good ways, yes, indeed, or no flesh would be left living without perishing, as the minister was saying in Dingwall when I was visiting on my sister Annie, and he speaking so well in the Beurla"—and Jane MacKenzie spoke with finality, as if there was no limit to her knowledge of the English.

"And it's not the young people only," says Liza Murray. "They're telling me the schoolmaster at Mellonree was to be taking the children into the school on the day of the last sacraments."

"Are you telling me that now?" says Jane MacKenzie, and the ears of her spreading themselves out to catch a choice bit of news. "On the Sabbath day itself?"

"Oh no. It was the first day, the Thursday."

"Oh, not the Sabbath day," says Jane, plainly disappointed.

"But he didn't manage it, that man," says Liza Murray, who had forgotten where she was long ago, and had raised her voice. "The folks just kept the children at home. He just had to be shutting up the school, for only two children came that day,"—and she tossed her head as if she had gained a personal victory over the schoolmaster at Mellonree.

Jane MacKenzie was taking a breath to reply in the same tone when her eye happened to fall on the woman sitting by the fire. She remembered where she was and her voice suddenly fell to a whisper.

"Herself over there iss taking it fery baad," says she, nodding towards the far end of the hearth.

"Aye, she's taking it fery baad," says Liza Murray in a low voice, with a quick look at the woman and then at Murdo, and of a sudden rubbing hard at the back of the chair with her duster. "And well she might," she added, letting a heavy sigh out of her breast. "It's a godly man they're after taking up yonder this day."

And so on, clearly enjoying themselves, speaking in the shentleman's English for the benefit of the lad that had been out in the big world.

Murdo was sitting with his back to the big bed. The door to the little scullery place was closed and from behind it came the continuous hum of voices, with the rattle of a dish now and then when they remembered they were supposed to be working. They were enjoying themselves in there too. They were all enjoying themselves, Had it not been for the woman sitting by the fire, he thought with some bitterness, he would have told them something himself. He would have told them they were now in what Liza Murray had called the " Moving Cinemas." However, he said nothing, but sat with his legs stretched out and his hands in his trousers pockets, feeling humiliated and resentful, while the early dusk began to fill the corners of the room and the women continued their chatter, pretending to themselves that they were needed there.

The door to the little back place opened and figures loomed in it. It was by this time so dark that their features could not be recognised.

" Oh! I see you're sitting in the dark! " said the voice of his aunt Ealasaid from Mellonree. He recognised it by the quick, sharp, excited tones of it that always sounded as if she were in breathless haste to catch a train.

She turned to the big sideboard and took the lamp from where it sat and placed it on the table. The match she put to the wick caused the room to become quite dark, and against that blackness her face leapt suddenly out, very white. At that moment, blinking her eyes in the light as she replaced the globe, she was very like her sister. She had just opened her mouth to join in the gossiping again when suddenly her eyes enlarged to twice their size. Her mouth remained open with the word half out of it. With a gasp she clapped her hand over her left breast. Then she looked again, turned away and sank into a chair muttering something about " himself! " In the light of the lamp she had on a sudden caught sight of Murdo's eyes gazing at her out of his dark face, and the way the light was striking him he had strangely resembled his father.

Eventually, for very shame, the four women began to get into their things. They talked themselves to the door, running with expressions of sympathy, commiseration, pity, and from the way their melancholy voices came dwindling back from far up the road you could tell there must be snow upon the ground.

His aunt Ealasaid had come from Mellonree that morning and was to stay with her sister some days; and long before the evening was passed she had got already on his nerves. She was not capable of keeping herself from moving for a single minute. If it was not her thin legs that were forever carrying her aimlessly about the room it was her tongue that was going; and if she had nobody to speak to she would keep up a continuous patter of exclamations and phrase-ends to herself. This day in particular she seemed to be wearing a hair shirt that never gave her a moment's peace. She was a big woman, with big buttocks and big pendulous breasts. She was wearing a black blouse and a black skirt that rustled loudly as she trotted here and there setting up currents of air, muttering to herself in Gaelic. It was " A Chreutair! " or " Aree! " or " Is not that the sad thing! " every minute of the time. It took her a terrible time to lay the table. She never got anything on it right. No sooner was a thing set down than she would rush at it again and move it a quarter of an inch, blink—blinking all the time with her short-sighted eyes. She fussed round Murdo till he could almost have shouted at her. She would rush up to him and pick an imaginary hair off his shoulder, and Murdo would shuffle uncomfortably in his chair. This was going too far. A fellow couldn't think with this porpoise puffing about the place. She kept up a running stream of remarks to her sister, who never appeared to hear. It was " A Sheònaid this " and " Sheònaid that " all the time. Then she would blink at her and address to her remarks that were meant to be consoling. " Oh, a Sheònaid, it's the good man they're after taking away from you this day. It is indeed," and so on. And all this time there was no expression at all on her face that you could put a name on. A singularly stupid woman.

Meanwhile, his mother remained in her silence, sitting, sitting silent before the fire.

Gradually these two things began to oppress and weigh on him, the endless fuss and chatter of the one and the terrible stillness and silence of the other. After a few hours of it he was fidgeting constantly about on his chair, crossing and uncrossing his legs, taking his hands out of his pockets and putting them in again, unable to settle to the simplest train of thought.

Shortly after eight o'clock he got up and said something about going to bed. Ealasaid jumped up and said she was just after putting the pig* in his bed, she would now be going up

* In Scotland a hot-water bottle is universally known as a " pig."

to fold down the clothes. He stood on the floor looking at the door she had just closed, amazement on his face. Who ever heard of putting a pig in *his* bed? What did *he* want with a woman folding down the clothes for him? Preposterous!

He made for the door and was half out of it when he turned to give another look at the woman sitting before the fire. Something about her attitude struck him, the terrible desolation that sat upon her. He suddenly felt a warm wave of compassion for the poor creature whose life had also been torn in two before her eyes. He went over to her and put a hand on her shoulder, saying, " A Mhàthair! " It was all he had to say. A shiver seemed to pass over her. She stood up and looked at him for a moment with wide eyes. Then she threw herself on him, crying, " A Mhurchaidh, Mhurchaidh! " and burst into a convulsion of dry, hard sobbing with her head against his shoulder. Now he was terrified at what he had done. What must he do now? He put his arms round the trembling creature and patted her clumsily with his hand, trying to soothe her. But she only grew worse, shaking in his arms, the dry sobs tearing at her throat. He was helpless in a case like this, hot with discomfort, so that he was grateful when Ealasaid came fussing into the room and took the trembling woman out of his arms.

It was morning before he slept. For hours he could not get sleep for the woman downstairs and the terrible hard sobbing that would not give her rest. It was bitterly cold and when he moved out of one place the clothes of the bed chilled through him so that he drew a quick breath between chattering teeth. But it was his thoughts most of all that kept him awake and restless. For where were you to end if once you admitted there was so little difference in significance between a cow and the fulfilment of a young lad's dreams that it had to be decided by such a far-out chance as the cow falling into a bog at the back of Druim Uaine in the middle of winter? If the like of that was possible there could be no order or discrimination; and without order and discrimination how could there be purpose? And if no purpose then the cow and the dreams were alike without significance. A chasm yawned beneath him at the thought. He had often enough been miserable in that bed before, but he had always been conscious that there was a ray of sunshine and a clean wind blowing once he had turned a corner or two. Now there was but a long straight road before him, across a grey moor, the mist hanging so close around it that only the edges were his world to the last step, and a thick rain thrashing always down on the surface of that road. It was the end. He must reconcile himself to be a vegetable, nodding his head familiarly to the potato shaws in the next furrow.

In the first cold hours of morning he fell asleep, and the last thing floating before his eyes was a picture of a chinless Bradan nod-nodding his idiot's head, a quivering drop hanging precariously to the end of his tapering nose.

5

When Murdo opened an eye the winter morning had already been for some time in the room, but so thin was the light of it that tardy wisps of night were still holding their own in all the nooks and corners. There was a soundless hush, as if all Alba had for the moment ceased to breathe. You could tell by that alone that the earth was under snow, even if the black spray end at the window had not been holding itself stiff and motionless for fear of letting fall the inch-deep ridge of the feathery stuff that sat so lightly on it, gleaming white against a leaden sky.

Later in the day a wind rose, driving sleety rain in front of it, and before long the moors were sodden, like a bog, and the roads were ankle deep in slush. This was clearly the weather they were to have over into the new year, for day followed day and no abatement. Scarcely for an hour at a time was there any slackening in the harsh cold rain that lashed at door and window and found its way in through every warp and crack, bringing such a chill air with it that the folks were fain to turn themselves round occasionally where they stooped over the red peats, lest the side of them that was away from the fire should freeze.

That was not the kind of weather to brighten the mood of anyone who happened to be sorrowful and Murdo found that it accorded very well with his. Most of the time he spent in the shop by himself, crouching behind the counter with a book on his knees. Out of that he scarcely moved all day unless it was for a meal or to bring water from the well or attend to any of the little things that will always be causing a man that has a croft to put his nose outside. There he sat, hunched up, behind the counter, his coat round him, the collar over his ears, until sometimes he could scarcely straighten himself because of the way the cold had stiffened his joints. But although he had a book upon his knees it was seldom he read in it for long. That was too much like probing the wound, and little enough of that was needed either to let him know it was there or to discover the offending matter.

This stunned silence that was on his mother—so that she would hardly say a word or move from her place—was the very devil. It was impossible to discuss anything at all with her while she was in that condition. Not that he expected anything would come out of any discussion at all he might have with her—no amount of discussing would bring a man back to life or give a woman over fifty a grown-up son. He certainly expected nothing from the discussion. The situation was plain enough already. But the one pin-head of hope there was in the whole black business kept glittering just inside the corner of his eye, irritating and annoying him till at times he would have given something to be done with hope altogether. Sometimes when he looked steadily at this pin-head it began to enlarge until it filled the entire field of vision. It might happen that his father, against all the probabilities, had been a wealthy man. Undoubtedly it might so happen. Perhaps his brother, drowned at Warramulla, South Australia, had left a little hoard behind to which he had added from time to time. He had never heard anything to the contrary. Perhaps in that case his mother would already have decided that everything would just go on as before. Perhaps, perhaps, perhaps. . . . But it always ended by a coming down to the hard ground of reality again, and the hope that was in it dwindled once more to an irritating pin-head of uncertainty.

With his reason running round and round on that track the whole of every day, without change or halt; with the miserable weather remaining monotonously at the maximum degree of combined cold and wet; with the stale smell of a thousand dreary memories clinging to every one of all the deadly familiar objects about the house; with the strain of perpetual association with the two other inmates; above all with the continual staring into the face of the black future, without any illusions about it; with all that it is not surprising that he found himself gradually shrinking into what he had been before ever he lifted on him to go to Glasgow at all. He began to grow restless and irritable, unable and unwilling to fix his thoughts on anything (since it must always be the one thing), and before a week was out, as he had almost expected, he was reduced to turning the leaves of old newspapers and magazines, even old papers that his mother used to get, showing the latest fashions, and slim girls standing about in their corsets or pulling stockings on to their shapely legs.

Naturally he got more and more irritable and unhappy, and the place and the two women got more and more on his nerves. His mother still spent the day sitting in her silence before the fire, or if she moved about it was slowly, with her eyes looking straight before her, and if one spoke to her she would give but a word in reply, or give no word at all. Ealasaid was still fluttering and fussing needlessly here and there, crinkling and rustling her black clothes, blinking her short-sighted eyes, addressing a string of commonplace remarks and questions that would have been put out to get an answer to anyone that was present, and addressing exclamations to herself in odd corners of the house, where she went alone to shift the ornaments about and flick imaginary dust from anything that came within her reach. For such a woman there was possible a comfortable torpor of the mind; she met the world and all its changes with an uncomprehending blink.

Yet before the end he had reason to be grateful for the stupidity of Ealasaid. As it turned out it was that that solved his problem.

It happened that on what would have been the last Friday of the vacation if he had been going back to Glasgow he was by chance bending down to look at a calendar on the wall when Ealasaid rustled into the room.

"Oh! You're looking at the calendar," says she, breathless, "I see you're looking at the calendar."

She was on the point of turning away to move something out of one place and put it in another when suddenly she turned round again and looked at Murdo's bent back, and by the way she stood still, blinking more than ever and wrinkling her brows, it was clear to see she had been struck by an idea.

"And when will your college be opening again, Murdo?" says she.

"Beginning of next week," growled Murdo, wincing.

"O Dhia, Dhia!" exclaimed Ealasaid, waving her hands and glancing from side to side. "Am I not the stupid woman! Oh indeed itself! What was I doing at all, at all! He'll be going on Monday morning, says he, and I haven't looked to his clothes yet!" and she took out the door.

Murdo wheeled round and looked after her. In a moment he heard her crossing the floor above his head and rattling at the locks of his cases. He looked across at the back of his mother's head, and slowly he scratched the top of his left ear. Evidently it had never occurred to Ealasaid that he would not be going back. She took it as a matter of course that he would be going. Well, why not ? There was nothing here just now to keep a man's hands occupied, nor would there be for months. He was no use for attending on his mother in her present condition, merely in the way. He would be as well there as here, and if he were needed they could send for him. And perhaps Ealasaid knew that it was intended he should go from the beginning, and was supposing he would know himself! Perhaps, indeed! He would simply act as if he had expected to go back in the ordinary course of affairs, and if nothing was said, and nothing occurred to stop him, well. . . .

Meanwhile, Ealasaid came crinkling through the door, shirts hanging over her arms and a bundle of socks and collars grasped in either hand. For the rest of that evening she sat turning over a bundle of clothes, blinking as she held them up to her eyes, plying a busy needle. His mother sat at the other side of the fire and took no heed of what was going on.

It was still dark on the Monday morning when the mail-car stood outside on the road and Murdo came to say good-bye to his mother. She raised herself from the pillow and looked at him. For a moment he thought she was about to break once more into sobbing. Then he feared she was to ask where he was going.

But she merely said good-bye and mumbled something about remembering his prayers. That was all right then, he said to himself, it had after all been intended—but he had a lurking idea she had no clear notion where he was going when she looked at him there.

Ealasaid was at the door to let him out. He shook her hand and bade her good-bye. Then he turned back suddenly, put his arm round her shoulders, and kissed her.

"Beannachd leat, a laochain!" said she, somewhat taken by surprise, drawing the back of her hand across her mouth.

III

ABOUT the middle of the first term he had discovered a small lending library at the back of a bookseller's shop off Sauchiehall Street. The man that kept the shop was evidently a bookseller from choice and inclination rather than by accident or necessity for he was always to be seen standing behind the counter peering into a volume of some kind through a pair of gold-rimmed pince-nez which at such times sat awry on the tip of his nose and at others dangled from his neck at the end of a black cord. He had a devouring curiosity about everything that was new in human knowledge or opinion, and in anything that was not too technical for any but an expert was usually up-to-date in some corner or other of his shelves. Naturally he had gathered round him a small company of customers with similar tastes—there are more than a million people in Glasgow—and since that kind of book is usually dear he had begun to put a copy of any new book of the kind on a row of shelves in the back shop, and for the payment of a moderate sum any of the initiated was at liberty to take one of them away for a month.

Murdo had gained his respect and confidence

by buying, with part of the pound Iain Beag had given to him, a large number of second-hand copies of the Greek and Latin classics. Since then he had been a frequent visitor to the back shop and it was there he had found most of the books that were the most interesting and stimulating part of his studies since he came to Glasgow.

Since his return he had been depressed and irritable out of all measure, beyond anything, indeed, since he first left home. One evening he was unable to settle himself, and after wandering aimlessly round the room for a time decided to go out into the streets.

The lights of the lamps and the shop windows and the passing tram-cars shone bleared through the dropping rain and reflected themselves in the water that streamed down pavements and across the road. The few people there were abroad scurried past under dripping umbrellas, or with coat collars pulled up round their ears. He decided after a short time to go into the bookseller's shop, more to get out of the rain than from any desire to see what was going on in the heads of men with their minds ordered and disciplined and directed to an end.

Mr. MacPhee took his nose out of the book he was reading and looked at him over the gold rim of his eye-glasses.

"Good evening, Mr. Anderson," says he. "I see you've gotten back!"

"Good evening, Mr. MacPhee. Have you anything new since I left?"

"I can't remember if I have. Just go through and look for yourself, will you? I'm engaged with Mr. Bergson at the moment."

Murdo ran his eye carelessly along the backs of the volumes, not really intending to take his hands out of the pockets of his coat. However, at the end of a shelf was a new book, a comparatively small one, and when he opened it his eyes happened to fall on something that interested him extremely.

"Find anything?" said Mr. MacPhee without looking up.

"Yes, I wrote it down in the book."

"Righto! Good night, Mr. Anderson. . . ."

He had hardly got to the foot of the second page when he heard Mrs. O'Callaghan at the door with the cup of tea she would always bring ben at night. He closed the book and gave it a push under the bed, for she would often glance over his shoulder to see what he was reading. However, to-night he did not wish her to see what he was reading.

As soon as she had closed the door behind her he seized the book again, fluttered the pages and began to read.

For a time he went steadily forward, interested enough to be forgetting himself. Then suddenly he found himself reading a chapter which could not have been more apt if it had been a definite answer to the questions that were uppermost in his mind. Until the end of that chapter he was consciously keeping his emotions and logical deductions at the back of his head, as it were deferring them by an act of will, though now and then he would let an exclamation out of him,—'Dhia! 'Dhia! and, several times, 'Amadain! 'Amadain! 'Amadain!

When the end of the chapter came he threw the book on the bed and leapt to his feet. He stood stride-legs on the mat, thrust his hands down into his trousers pockets and surveyed the room.

In " Turus a'Chriosdaidh " there was a place, was there not, where Christian came to the cross, and immediately his bundle, the load he had been groaning under on every step of the way and only bore forward by dint of fortitude, fell off his back. Was not he the happy man at that moment? And no doubt all that hard journey the thoughts of Christian were fixed upon that burden on his back, so that he could think of nothing else, so that the burden itself seemed to get heavier step on step, so that it became bigger and bigger in imagination until at times it must have seemed to fill all space. Yet it was a very little thing that rid him of it at the end. And no doubt when the thing did tumble off, with all the feeling of lightness, of elation, that filled him he must have had a half-thought in his head that he had after and all been making himself just a little ridiculous; there had been no such tremendous big matter in it now that he was able to see it at its real size. So with himself, he had been torturing himself all these years with a shadow, a mere semblance of reality! And this knowledge had been in existence all the time, yet he had never thought of it! What an amadan! It is extraordinary how a man will trouble himself about a thing for years when a very simple idea, if it only occurred to him, would solve the problem in the twinkle of an eye. Calum Beag was an example. He had often heard the bodach grumble about his well. There was a terrible number of those little creatures that skate about on the top of the water in it, he said. It was not possible to take a pail of water out of it without there would be half a dozen or a dozen of them sliding here and there on the top of it. One day he happened to be there when Calum went to the well. " Look at the little beasts! " says Calum, flicking them out with his hand. He looked at the man in amazement. " Would it not be better to put them out on the ground instead of back in the well ? " said he. Calum looked at him, wrinkling up his face. " O dhuine, dhuine," says he, " I never thought of that." The bodach had been complaining for goodness knows how many years about the number of the beasts in his well and yet every time he went for a pail of water he carefully put them back where they came from. He had laughed at the old man at the time, and here he discovered himself to be in similar case.

He was just going to put out the light and get into the bed when his eye fell on the cup of tea. He took it in his hand, held it up on a level with his eye, said " Slàinte mhór ! " and drank the cold stuff in a couple of gulps. Then he somersaulted into the bed and landed with his two legs sticking up against the wall. For a long time after he had concluded this pantomime and wriggled himself, shivering, between the sheets, he lay on his back, his hands clasped behind his head, smiling up into the dark. Finally: "Buidheachas do Dhia," he said aloud, rolling over on his side.

It was about a week after this that Murdo found himself one evening on his feet addressing a company of students. (Greatly to his own surprise. But since the episode that was mentioned it had been with him: You are so-and-so. Well, I am Murdo Anderson. Such was his confidence.) He had gone to a meeting of that society which the Gaelic-speaking students have, for practising the English. Donald MacAskill, M.A., B.Sc., read a paper on " The Contribution of the Gael to the Making of Empire." The sough of the high winds of the Isle of Lewis was from his mouth; and for his complacency, for his hair that would have put shame on a carrot and for his insolent up-pointing nose, Murdo took great dislike. For three-quarters of an hour it was that a Lewis-man had explored a corner of Canada, a Skyeman had found a river in Australia, a Lochaber man had given his name to a hill in New Zealand, a Mullman had crushed a marauding tribe on the frontiers of India, a

Caithness man had become King of a South Sea Island and condemned his subjects to death in the Gaelic (huge laughter), a Cowalman had fought the Zulus in Africa, an Atholl man had irrigated a bit of Egypt, a Badenoch man had found a microbe in Nigeria. Donald MacAskill, M.A., B.Sc.(Glasgow), to his peroration: The '45 and the efictions were the Providence of God. But for them the Highlanders would neffer haff entered into their heritage, the map would not pee cuffered with Highland names. . . .

After him hippocephalous Roderick Urquhart bleating admiration for his prodeegious erudeetion. But his peroration. *That* showed him to be no mean philosopher, ass well ass haffing a deep releegious feeling. It wass indeed the Providence of God. *He* wass to go a little farther and say we had forgotten so far to put up a statue to one of the greatest benefactors of the Highland race—the Duke of Cumberland.

At this there was a sudden change in the atmosphere so that Urquhart, who had clearly intended to say more, changed his mind and sat down. He got his share of applause—although a little grudging in some quarters—but it was plain to see he felt himself he had gone too far. He had tried to say something striking and original that would reflect credit on himself, and he had overdone it.

Murdo was in a cold fury of indignation. He said he wished to disagree. They were orgies of rape and theft, of destruction and bloody murder. Any Highlander who gloried in them was a slave. Their " heritage " was a farce and a delusion. It was to clean the pots for the English. Their language was to die in two generations. They deserved it. They were assisting in their own annihilation. Their name would rightly stink in the nostrils of every honourable man until the end of time.

When he sat down the room went into noisy movement, with ominous patches of silence here and there. Clearly for most he had blasphemed. Mr. MacAskill was looking up at him over the top of the desk, making a great effort to maintain a sneering and contemptuous air—but clearly he had got a flea in his lug. Most of the others had had their breath taken away, and did not like it. But here and there a man was applauding loudly, and one big Lewisman in the seat below, with a soldierly set to his shoulders still, was slapping the only hand left to him, poor devil, on the bench in front and roaring out " Sin a bhalaich! Sin a laochain! " in a loud, deep voice.

There was, of course, a storm of criticism. But always he had an answer on the tip of his tongue. Rory Urquhart got up several times, white with passion, and each time he was flattened by a few well-chosen words his voice jumped up into a higher key with sheer bad temper and vexation. Eventually the last time he got up he was so angry he was altogether inarticulate. He opened and shut his mouth, but only a squeak or two came out. The folks began to laugh, suspecting a personal antipathy. Murdo was enjoying himself. They were unable to put forward any argument he could not demolish with a word. It was his day. For the moment he was invincible. And every time he made a hit the big Lewisman laughed out loud, slapped his hand on the bench and shouted " Sin a laochain! "

In that way the proceedings came more or less to a standstill, and when eventually Mr. MacPherson closed the meeting at the other end of the room with a prayer in which he thanked God for intelligence and the reasoning faculty everybody seemed relieved. They did not seem to be quite sure where they were, the sort of atmosphere there was as if someone were to tell a sex story in a room full of respectable maiden ladies with inflamed imaginations. On the way out he was given the middle of the floor to himself. At the door he passed the one-armed Lewisman coming in again for something. The big fellow opened his mouth wide when he saw him and let out a bellow of laughter.

When he got outside the night was clear and dry. He went for a turn through the Kelvingrove Park in order to cool his head and warm his feet and on the way home again he fell in with Donald MacAskill himself. He would have walked past, but the other spoke to him and fell into step alongside.

He began by telling Murdo he had made an

excellent speech, it was seldom they heard the like of it from a young chap who had tchust come up to the 'Varsity: It wass a splendid beginning indeed. . . .

Evidently the fellow was still sore and was trying to get back his self-respect by patronising him. For his part Murdo had no wish to humiliate the man, so he said nothing. He happened, however, when they were nearing Charing Cross, to drop an expression in Gaelic.

"Ah well, Ah well, yes, Gaylic," says MacAskill, pretending he had not understood. "Well, you see I wass brought up in Stornoway and we always spoke English in the house, so that I don't know Gaylic. A fine language no doubt, but I neffer learned it myself."

To this Murdo made no reply but he watched for an opportunity and a little further on kicked him right on the point of the ankle-bone, hard, with the toe of his boot, as it were by accident. MacAskill seized his foot in his two hands, hopping on the other leg, and a stream of Gaelic curses flowed out of his mouth. Murdo thought he had never heard the like, for comprehensiveness and the smooth way they came out.

"What language is that that's at you, Leòdhasaich ? " says he, and left him there, hopping.

2

The next day was Saturday. Murdo was reading all the morning and the afternoon, and in the evening, since it was clear and dry, decided to go out among the lights and the moving crowds. Now that he could do so without feeling he was at all conspicuous (or caring indeed whether he was or not), it was a great pleasure to him to walk alone through the streets, turning to left or to right as the fancy took him, examining the faces of the passers-by, speculating as to their characters and occupations, peering into a window here and there, on the look-out always for anything that was new or curious or amusing.

It was particularly interesting to walk abroad on a Saturday evening because on that night of the week the streets were thrang with people, and every man engaged in enjoying himself in the way he liked best. Some would be getting drunk in public-houses and going through strange antics on the pavement when they came out. Some would be waiting in long lines in front of the cinemas. Others would be courting a girl. And others would simply be strolling along looking around them, not very sure apparently what they wanted to be at.

On this evening he climbed to the top of a passing tram-car without looking to see where it was going, and when the conductor came along bought a ticket to the end of the route.

For a time they ran through streets that were familiar. Light streamed from shop windows on the moving crowds of people going up or down, passing each other, gathering into knots here and there, but always in restless motion, like a nest of ants. Gradually the crowds thinned out and the lights began to grow few and dim. Sitting there on the upper floor of the swaying tram-car he fell into a half-doze, and when he eventually came to himself it was to notice they were running through a street where there were no shops at all, in some part of the city he had never been in before; a poor quarter as far as he could judge. He looked round at the other people sitting in the car and discovered that a change had taken place while he was so busily engaged looking out the window. Where before there had been many well-dressed people there were now only a few men with handkerchiefs knotted round their necks, a woman in a Campbell shawl, and three young men in blue overcoats talking loudly together in the front seat. The rate seemed now to be quicker, the stops farther between, the lights fewer, the houses poorer. Murdo decided it was time for him to get out.

The street seemed strangely dark and silent after the lighted tram had hummed round a corner out of sight. An occasional lamp darkened the shadows in a gaping close mouth or on the walls of the tall black houses, but the general impression was of a street in half-light, a dismal street. Dim light filtered out through grimy curtains hanging in a window here and there, so thin and uncertain a flicker at times that it must have come from a single guttering candle. It seemed to Murdo that these must be the houses he had seen the backs of that first evening and he sitting gloomily in his corner while the train slipped smoothly along between the rows; if he went down one of these closes to the backs of them he would no doubt dimly discern above his head the dark shapes of garments writhing and contorting themselves or waving dismally to and fro between him and the pale reflection of the city lights in the sky.

Decidedly he did not like the street, neither the look of it nor the smell of it, nor yet the sounds he began to hear coming out here and there. Least of all did he like those gaping close mouths. They were mirk black and mysterious. As you passed, a strong stale smell came out of them and struck cold on the side of your face, a smell of cold human sweat, of breeding rats, of wet earth and rotting wood, of filth and disease and a hundred thousand greasy suppers; all these imperfectly mixed together in streaks and patches. Sounds came out of their darkness too, low voices whispering together, a cough, a short laugh, a girl's giggling. Once a voice shouted as he passed " Hey! " Then, louder, " Hey, you b—— o' Hell! " He turned round to see a drunken man swaying in the middle of the pavement, glowering after him.

Farther on a group was standing round a close mouth. Suddenly a girl ran forward into the street. He noticed the stockings hanging loose on the skinny legs of her. A young fellow darted after her and seized her round the waist. "Let go o' me, ye —— bastard!" shouted she in a loud hoarse voice, and the rest of them as he hurried past burst into shrieks of laughter right in his ear. Then a woman's voice shouted in sudden anger behind a window above his head, and a child broke into a thin wailing. Blessed God! said he to himself, are there children in it, too?

Later near a corner of the street a young woman was lurching along, the hat on the side of her head. She stopped in front of him, swaying slightly.

"Hello, Bob!" says she.

He stepped aside and quickened his step.

"Mother's darlin' boy!" says she behind him, bursting into a hoarse cackle of derision.

From the corner of the street he caught sight of a lighted thoroughfare below him, with shop windows, and tram-cars moving up and down. He made for that, and it was with a sense of relief that he found himself among the lights and the crowds again.

He was not long walking in it, however, before he realised he was still in that poor quarter of the city. The men mostly had coloured handkerchiefs knotted at their throats and caps slouched over their eyes. The older women wore shawls of various tartans and many of them were two parts drunk or more. Some of the younger women, however, had their faces white with powder, and the way their clothes were cut they looked, at a quick glance, almost smart. And there was a type of young man that lounged along, wide at the trouser legs, narrow at the waist, a blue overcoat flying open and a bowler hat set jauntily on the side or the back of the head, frequently with a white scarf hanging in front and coloured ribbons fluttering from the lapel, loud and harsh in the voice, with a defiant swing to the shoulders and a hard impudent stare from the eyes. Nearly all these people were under-sized, and every fourth one among them seemed to have some deformity. The shop windows were frequently dirty and the stuff in them, whether it would be clothing or sweets or fruit, was usually piled and huddled together in a way to make a delicate stomach turn. The street was dirty, the houses and shops were dirty, the people were for the most part dirty. It was a disagreeable quarter altogether. However, it was part of the city. People lived here, like this. It was necessary to see it and to know about it. There was a kind of exhilaration in exploring in this way, all the more so as you were not very sure there was no danger of something happening to yourself.

A man lurched out of a public-house he happened to be passing. A loud noise of shouting voices came out behind him, and before the door slammed to he caught a glimpse of a crowd of men seething about indistinctly in a cloud of tobacco smoke. He wished he could go in to see what they were doing in there, but it would be too dangerous in a place like this, for a man who had never taken the stuff before. A little farther on was an Italian restaurant. The noise coming out of it was like what came out of the bar, only here the loudest voices were those of girls. Murdo turned on his heel after he had passed it, settled the coat on his shoulders, put his hat on the side of his head and swung into the place as if he knew it well.

There was such a cloud of tobacco smoke in here that it was scarcely possible to see the other end of the room. He picked his way between the little tables, looking from side to side as if he was well acquainted and might at any minute see somebody he knew. By good luck there was a little table at the top of the room that had apparently not been noticed in the cloud of smoke, and he set himself down there. He pushed aside some cups and saucers and a dirty tumbler with a straw sticking in it and turned to survey the room.

It was a large room, although the clouds of smoke that surged about prevented an exact idea of its size. Between him and the door were a multitude of little tables, each of which seemed to be surrounded by a group of young men and women. These were lounging in a number of careless attitudes. Some young men, with their feet on the bar under the table, were tilting back their chairs at a dangerous angle, their hands in their trousers pockets, coat tails trailing on the floor, hats on the back of their heads, a cigarette drooping from the corner of the mouth. One at a table near him had fallen asleep with his head on his arms, and his bowler hat had tilted forward and now sat brim up on a plate.

There were girls at most of the tables, girls with painted faces who blew jets of tobacco smoke towards the roof, glancing under dark eyelashes at the men sitting opposite, girls who bent forward listening intently to what a talkative man was saying and going off every now and then, at set periods, into a loud harsh cackle of laughter.

But indeed the whole room was a pandemonium, everywhere people were arguing, shouting, whistling, cursing, shrieking with laughter, slapping their hands on the tables. Most of them seemed to have been drinking a little. Among the various dins he began to notice a continuous trampling noise above his head, from which he concluded there must be a balcony up there.

He had ordered a cup of coffee and now sat in front of it looking around him. For a time he seemed to have been completely unobserved; nobody paid any attention to him and he found himself interested and amused by what was going on. Then he noticed a girl with Jewish-looking features looking steadily in his direction from a near-by table, with an insinuating leer to him every time his glance happened to travel that way. He looked down at the plate in front of him, and in spite of his new-found self-confidence felt the blush rising to his cheeks.

Lest he should catch her eye again he did not look up for some time but kept his head down, nibbling the end of a biscuit and reading the few words on the wrapper that came off it—Kerr & Co.'s " Windsor " Plain Chocolate Biscuit, Kerr & Co.'s " Windsor " Plain Chocolate Biscuit—over and over.

Suddenly it struck him that his part of the room had fallen strangely silent. He glanced down sideways and noticed on the floor beside his table a pair of black shoes with the toes of them pointing his way. The man that's in these must be looking at me, says he to himself, and glanced up quickly under the brim of his hat.

A young fellow of about his own age and size was standing beside the table glowering down at him with a sneer on his clean-shaven face, his hands in the pockets of his blue trousers, his hat tilted far back on his head. The people at the nearest tables had stopped their chatter and were looking round expectantly. One young fellow smiled pityingly at him as his glance flitted round, as if *he* knew what was going to happen to him.

Murdo felt hot and bewildered by the fellow's unwinking stare and began to wish most heartily that he had never come into the place. He was just debating the chances of slipping out when the other spoke.

" —— the Pope! " said he, spitting the words out between his teeth.

Murdo felt more bewildered than ever. Clearly the fellow wanted to pick a quarrel with him, but why should he wish to pick a quarrel with *him*, and on such a pretext?

He looked down at his plate again and put his hands in his pockets, hoping the other would go away.

"Hey, you, Mickey! —— the Pope!"

Now Murdo did not care in the least what happened to the Pope. But he had a real affection for Mrs. O'Callaghan and Father O'Reilly and he objected to their religion being insulted in this way. Moreover, he objected to being spoken to in that tone of voice. A little flame of anger began to burn steadily in the middle of his breast.

By this time there was a hush of death in the room. Everybody was watching what was going on. The trampling of feet above his head had stopped altogether and he knew they must be peering down over the railing.

"Ah'll tell ye what ye are," said the ruffian beside him. "Ye're a dir-ty bastard!" and he struck him across the mouth with the back of his hand.

Murdo rose slowly to his feet. The flush of anger on his dark face gave him an almost Spanish look. A little trickle of blood was running out at the corner of his mouth.

The fellow took a step backward and drew a bottle out of his pocket, holding it by the neck. Out of the corner of his eye Murdo saw people half-rising from their seats. The ruffian ran suddenly forward, lifting the bottle above his head. Murdo waited till it was just about to come down upon him. Then like lightning his right fist shot up and struck the other under the jaw. Every muscle in his body had been braced up, and the whole strength of it went into the blow.

What happened then happened very quickly, but it seemed to Murdo as if it all took place with slow deliberation.

First the fellow with the bottle seemed to leap backwards into the air and to come down on his back across the table behind him. Two girls who had been sitting there sprang up screaming, and a tumbler splintered to pieces on the floor. The table balanced precariously for a time on two legs; then it began slowly to tilt over. At a certain point the man's feet seemed to shoot up into the air and the whole thing came to the floor with a crash. He lay still where he fell, among broken dishes, with the table on top of him.

Murdo had just time to feel surprise at the effect of his blow and the great strength that must have been lying unsuspected in his body when a man rushed forward from the right. Before he reached him a table came hurtling from the balcony, spattering cups and tumblers, struck him behind the shoulder and knocked him to the ground. Some fellows rushed towards the steps of the balcony and a fight began there.

Less than a minute had passed since the blow was struck, but the room was suddenly full of shouts and curses, of flying missiles and waving arms, of the scuffling and trampling of feet, the sound of blows, the breaking of glass, the shrieks of women. Murdo seemed for the moment to have been forgotten. He stood there looking on in amazement. He seemed to have nothing further to do with this extraordinary conflict he had set a-going. It was exactly as if he had merely been asked to kick off at a football match.

Then a young fellow pulled at his sleeve and hissed in his ear, "*You*'ll be'er get oot while ye can, mate. Come owre here—quick!"

Just before following him through a door under the stairs Murdo gave a glance back at the room. Through the smoke and the dust he could dimly see a number of blue helmets coming in at the front door. The next minute he had stumbled out into the cold of the open air.

"Quick! Owre the wa'," said a deep voice beside him. "We'll need a' wir time."

Murdo could see the dim shape of a wall before him. He scrambled over it, crossed a courtyard, stumbled through a dark close, and was out in the street. The figures in front, three of them, turned to the left and started off at a run. He ran after them.

After about ten minutes, when he was quite out of breath, they stopped in a doorway.

"Ye'll be'er come in here for a while," said the man who had first approached him. "They'll be watchin' for ye. Some o' them got oot afore us."

The steps of the stone stair they climbed were worn almost flat, the walls were wet to the touch and gave off a chill air. For what seemed a long time they climbed upwards, Murdo at the tail, feeling his way and stumbling occasionally. Once a voice came down out of the dark above his head. " Watch yersel' here; there's nae railin' ! "

" That'll be that thievin' bastard MacGurk again," said another.

At last came the sound of a door opening and a thin shaft of light appeared on a landing ahead.

" Come richt in," said the third man to Murdo. " Dicht yer feet on the Persian carpet. We dinna gang in for mats i' this distric'."

Murdo went into the room. A nauseating smell of grease and sweat struck him flat in the face so that he was on the point of putting up his fingers to his nose. Instinctively he looked towards the window on the left and saw that a piece of sacking was pinned across it. An iron bed stood behind the door. A few rags and some articles of a woman's clothing were scattered on top of it. There seemed to be no other furniture in the room at all. There was a little fire in the grate and a girl of about fourteen was crouching over it, her elbows on her knees, a mat of fair hair falling over her eyes. She was evidently trying to read a magazine by the light of the candle sticking in the neck of a bottle on the mantelpiece above her head.

"Whaur's yer mither?" the first man was saying to this girl as Murdo came in.

"Oot," says she, looking up and scratching her head.

"Whaur's Meg?"

"Oot," says she, turning again to the paper on her knees and taking no further interest.

The young fellow shrugged his shoulders.

"We'll gang in here," he said, making for a door on the right.

When they got into the room he lit another candle. Then he turned round and surveyed Murdo slowly from his hat to his boots. He himself was a well-built young man of about twenty-five, with a pleasing fair face. The thin-lipped mouth gave him a look of determination. He wore a blue overcoat and a bowler hat. Murdo was surprised that anyone could look so clean and neat coming out of a place like this.

"Ah'm Jim Pa'erson," says he, when he had finished looking Murdo over.

"I'm Bob MacDonald," says Murdo.

"Well, ye're a bloody good man at onyrate," says Paterson. "Shake!"

Perceiving his rôle Murdo gave a prodigious grip on the hand the other held out to him.

"This is Chay Harris," says Paterson, pointing to a wiry long-nosed little fellow in a brown suit—the man with the deep voice, Murdo guessed, as he shook hands with him in silence.

"An' this is Mulligan," says Paterson, pointing a thumb over his shoulder at a merry-eyed youth in a worn grey suit. "He thinks he's funny."

"Ah'm an Irishman like yersel'," says Mulligan, shaking hands with Murdo.

"Aye. Ancestors cam' owre aboot the time o' the Flood," says Paterson.

"Man, yon wis a heluva dunt ye gied MacVey," says Mulligan, looking at Murdo with undisguised admiration. "Christ, yon wis a sappy ane."

"Aye," said Harris, solemnly running his hand along his jaw.

Murdo shrugged his shoulders, as if to say, "Man, yon wis naething. Ye should jist see me when ah'm on ma game."

It was the first time he had been conceded superiority over the rest on their own ground of their common manhood. He was enjoying the sensation. He was deliberately putting to the back of his mind the knowledge that the whole thing had been more an accident than anything else, and encouraging the impression that it was the result of skill and much experience. However, he was clearly conscious of two reasons for doing this. Firstly, because it is not every day a man will find himself a hero, and it is a pleasant sensation. And secondly, because to admit anything else would have been a pitiful anti-climax, and unartistic; everybody would have been disappointed.

"Aye," says Mulligan again, looking at the floor. "Yon wis a heluva dunt."

Suddenly he looked up quickly as if struck by

an idea. "Ye're nae by ony chance Jack Dempsey in disguise?—visitin' Glesca incognito to get a tip or twa?"

"Oh, shurrup, Mulligan!" says Paterson. "Ye're aye yappin'. Gang doon tae the wine-cellar, Mulligan, and see if ye can find a bo'le o' champagne."

"Verra good, yer Lordship," says Mulligan, lifting a finger to the snout of his cap.

He stooped down and felt with his hand round the inside of the chimney. A few pieces of cement rattled out across the floor. When he straightened himself he was holding a whisky bottle by the neck—Murdo thought the gesture was familiar; another man had been holding a bottle just that way not so very long ago.

"Pit back thae bits o' cement," says Paterson, "or the auld bastard 'll be findin' tha' place next."

Murdo was now in a terrible difficulty. He was about to be offered a drink of whisky. Either he refused it, which would spoil everything (whoever heard of a bold, fearless, self-confident, hard-hitting, death-dealing, invincible hero refusing a drop of the uisge beatha?) or he took it, with heaven knew what strange, unlooked-for effect on himself. Either way he was almost bound to lose his hero's crown and expose himself for an impostor—the fellow who happened to hit a man on a vulnerable spot and took advantage of the accident to pose as a champion. He began to feel very uncomfortable indeed. Heroism plainly had its drawbacks. However, there was only the one thing to be done. Having hit his man like a hero he must now take off his dram like a man.

Paterson was pouring the whisky into a cup without a handle. As Murdo took it from his hand he suddenly remembered young Kenneth Mitchell at his father's funeral, how he had coughed and spluttered and the tears had run out of his eyes. At all costs he must avoid that.

He lifted up the cup and said, " Good Health ! " Then he poured the stuff down in a gulp, turning the cup round in his hand before putting his mouth to it to avoid the mark of an under lip that was plainly to be seen on the rim.

As soon as it was over his throat he opened his mouth wide and said, " Ha ! " Then he took a step or two up and down the room, striking himself hard on the chest. In this way he kept the tears from his eyes and led the others to believe he was merely expressing the keen enjoyment of a man that likes his dram fine when anything of the kind happens to be going.

" Noo we'll be'er gang an' see hoo the land lies," says Paterson, when they had had their drink and Mulligan was putting the bottle back in its place.

" You'll be safer tae bide here, Mac. It looked like a nesty business yon. Hooever, ah'm gled ye slipped it across MacVey. He's been askin' for it for a lang time, the b——. It'll be a lesson tae them. The bastards winna let us alane. The priest himsel's nae safe tae gang aboot."

"Sit doon, Mac," he added, following the others out at the door.

Murdo turned round and saw that he had been standing all that time in front of a bed. A blanket was spread across it and at the back, under the blanket, was a heap of something he did not care to examine.

He sat down on the edge of the bed, a hand on each knee, whistling softly to himself. All his limbs were full of a delicious pulsing heat. Never in his life had he felt so comfortable, so absolutely at peace with the whole round world. Problems? The solution to all the problems was to sit still and make no attempt at all to solve them. The problems were the pieces of a crazy puzzle. Each piece in itself as you took it up was a puzzling thing, with incomprehensible crabbed outlines. But put them all back in their places and the whole was a round rosy earth birling merrily at the end of a ray of sunlight. There could be no problem about that. It was the most delightfully simple thing. He asked nothing more of life than to sit there—But was it life? Would you call it *alive* in the ordinary sense of mortal man? It seemed to him, he sitting there, that the connection had been cut that bound his consciousness to his body, and all it implied of dimensions and space and time, and that while as he sat there his consciousness was still inside his head it was now capable of free and independent motion, and he, the essential conscious self, could if he wished float out forward or backward into spaceless timelessness and be at once contemporary with, say, the Fingalians, feasting on a sloping hillside among trees, and the man that will be living a thousand years after Murchadh Iain Ruaidh, the mortal creature, has headed a procession over the shoulder of Càrn Bàn.

At any rate he asked nothing better than just to sit there on the edge of the bed, his feet on a piece of worn waxcloth, looking round the bare little room, and it without any furniture at all, at the strips of paper hanging down from the damp walls, at the greasy workman's clothes hanging behind the door. The trousers were on top of the other garments and the way they hung the seat of them was turned towards him. It was that that was funny? Could it be—? Yes; undoubtedly there was a broad smile on the seat of yon trousers! Murdo chuckled.

Instantly there was a movement in the bed behind him. He twisted round quickly and found himself staring down into the wide-open eyes of a youngster of about ten years. Even as he looked there was a renewed heaving in the bundle at the back of the bed and another head popped suddenly out, a very similar head, but younger. These two little fellows continued to stare at him in silence over the end of the blanket, their eyes round with excitement and astonishment and perhaps a little fear, their brown hair sticking up on end. For his part Murdo stared down at them as if he had seen a pair of ghosts. Then the thing struck him as funny. He winked knowingly and began to laugh. If anything they became more solemn than before. "Ee!" says the older, "Ah heard a' thing. Wis there a fecht?"

"Aye," says Murdo.

"Wis you in it?"

"Aye," says Murdo.

"Did you swipe onybody?"

"Aye," says Murdo.

"Ee! Whaur did ye hit 'im?"

Murdo pretended to hit himself under the chin and jerked his head suddenly back.

"Jesus! A sock on the jaa!" says the boy, his eyes growing rounder with admiration. "Wha wis't?"

"MacVey," says Murdo.

The older boy looked solemnly at the younger and winked. The younger boy looked solemnly back at the older, and winked. Then the first spat fiercely.

"The B——!" says he.

He wriggled himself further out of the blanket.

"Man, ye maun be a richt fechter! Hoo did it happen?"

Murdo stood up on the floor and began to tell the tale. With awful solemnity he related how it came about, and for the benefit of the boys, whose eyes now threatened to jump out of their heads with excitement and admiration, he put in many sickening blows and many pools of blood. He acted it. He was himself, the innocent drinker of a cup of coffee, the hero arising in his wrath; he was MacVey, MacVey swinging a bottle aloft, MacVey on a table with his feet in the air, MacVey prostrate under that table with a clot of ice cream sitting on his lug; he was a man rushing from the right; he was a table hurtling from the balcony . . .

Just in the middle of his hurtling there was a sudden noise in the other room, and his audience disappeared with the speed of light. He was left standing in the middle of a gesture, with a word half out of his mouth. Between the beginning and the end of a word he was addressing two adoring boys, their hair standing on end with delicious terror—and he was addressing a motionless heap under the blanket, at the back of the bed. It was as if no boys had been.

He shut his mouth and gave an ear to what was going on in the other room. Evidently a woman had come in for he heard the first few words of what was clearly going to be a shrill scolding.

"Ssht!" said the voice of the girl who had been reading by the fire, and he could tell by the loud whispering that followed that she was telling her mother about him. After that the woman spoke no more, but occasionally she gave a short, dry cough.

In a little time another person entered the room, with much noise. He recognised the stumblings and mutterings of a drunken man—the father, he supposed. What he was saying he was saying to himself, and Murdo caught nothing of it except once when he raised his voice. "Whaur's tha' bi'ch Meg? Nae in yet?"

From the loud creak that came suddenly from the bed he imagined the man had thrown himself down upon it. Murdo clapped his hand to the seat of his trousers and grimaced as if in pain. There was something very funny about a drunk man falling into bed.

Then Paterson came in, alone. There was a dent in the side of his hat and his right shoulder was covered with dust. He looked worried and angry.

"There wis anither row," says he, "an' Mulligan's nabbed. Christ! the bastards 'll suffer for this yet. We're nae feenished wi' them, by Jesus we're no'!"

"And whaur's Harris?" says Murdo, as calmly as possible, trying to hide the fact that he wanted to burst out laughing every minute and dance about the room. Inside himself he was wishing he had been there. *He* would not have allowed Mulligan to be nabbed; by Jesus he would not!

"Chay?" says Paterson, "Oh, he gaed doon tae see if the road wis clear. But ah think ye'll be a' richt noo. He'll be back the noo onywye."

He took a step up and down the room, frowning at the floor.

"Here he is!" said he, lifting his head as someone entered the other room.

"H'm! jist Meg," he added, turning again to his pacing up and down.

" Here, Mac," says he suddenly, " Ye'll be nane the waur o' anither drap afore ye gang."

While he was putting back the pieces of cement that had fallen as he put the bottle back in its place, there came a shrill whistle under the window.

" That's Chay," says he.

He took the candle, now burned away to a stump, and led the way to the door.

In the next room there was a mattress lying, and two people were sleeping on it. A girl of about nineteen rolled over on her back and looked up at them, blinking in the light of the candle. They had to step over her feet to get past. From the bed on the left there was coming a sound, like a woman's low moaning. Murdo was to look there but Paterson came in front of him, leading him to the door.

An hour afterwards Murdo was standing at the corner of a street, alone.

That second dram had been a big one too and since they got outside his sensations had been strange entirely. Whatever the reason was his body seemed to wish to go against all the laws of gravity. He had had to be very stern with it. He had had to put his feet down on the pavement very firmly indeed to keep his body from flying up into the air with him. He had managed very well as long as those two delightful fellows had been there—who were they again ?—because he had had an arm round each of them; but they had suddenly disappeared a long time ago.

Now he was alone, nobody in sight. He was standing at the corner of a street, on the edge of the pavement. Opposite him was a church. Every minute he gave a low and stately bow, sweeping the hat up to his chest.

A policeman was standing in a doorway at the other side of the road watching the performance. After a time he came across to him.

"I'm thinking you'll better be going home now, Jim. You're not like yourself to-night at all."

Murdo caught the familiar blas.

"Oh, man," says he in the Gaelic, "Is it not the sad thing I'm a polite man? I can't be moving out of here for the steeple up yonder, and it always bowing to me."

The policeman began to roar with laughter.

"Where are you from, dark lad?" says he.

Murdo told him the name of the place.

"I was thinking that same myself, Rosaich," says he. "Your like never came out of the Island whatever."

He walked away down the street, that Skyeman, laughing in his throat.

3

The evening of the next Tuesday was dry and almost warm, and Murdo decided it was time for him to be taking another stroll.

Since the episode of the Italian café he had

been very pleased with himself. He had wakened the next morning chuckling, and the sight of his trousers draped carefully over the picture of the Virgin had brought everything to his mind and set him off laughing again. Just at that minute Mrs. O'Callaghan had come in with his breakfast and he had pulled the bedclothes up to his head and pretended to be still in his sleep, but he watched her with an eye through a fold in the blanket. First she stopped in surprise, with the tray in her hands. Then she set the tray on the table and came back to look at the thing again, putting up an undecided hand to the leg of her spectacles. Finally she took the trousers down and folded them up, shaking her head half in amusement and half in disapproval. When she spoke to him he pretended to come confusedly out of a deep sleep, and he did not mention the matter afterwards since she did not; but he was rather pleased than otherwise to think she would guess he had been drinking and would know he was not altogether the porer over dusty volumes but was also, unknown to her so far, the man of the world as well. He had tried to eat as much of his breakfast as he could and had not yielded to the craving for innumerable cups of tea.

He found himself very well pleased, in spite of the thickness of his head and the sharp pain that shot through it if he looked quickly in any direction. He had in one evening taken two long steps forward. He had gone down into the places where men fight and breed and altogether live at the level of their animal parts, and he had come up out of it not only not humiliated, as lacking in some coarser energies nevertheless necessary to the man, rounded off and complete, but even in a cloud of glory as above the rest at that common level itself. That was altogether satisfactory and settled one question, filled up one gap, for good. And he had also made his bow, and quite a graceful bow, to the rosy god, and had discovered avenues of the senses that must be further explored without more delay. A thing was none the worse of being looked at from another angle, and that was what happened—you slid into another position, impossible to the merely sober man, from which you saw not perhaps a different truth but at least another side, perhaps the backside, of the same truth; and that was what was wanted, the whole truth, the naked truth, not truth with its backside hidden in the breeches of sobriety. But, seriously, it was necessary to explore those avenues of sense, something of value might come out of it; and whether it did or not, it was necessary to explore them. There was only one thing more now that required to be done to complete his experience at that level—but that was a big thing, you would need to take a breath before tackling that.

Throughout the day he had kept chuckling from time to time as some forgotten episode came slowly back to mind.

On this Tuesday evening he turned down

towards Charing Cross, crossed the road there and strolled down the right-hand side of Sauchiehall Street. At a certain corner a number of people going in different directions had happened to meet and get in each other's way and to avoid them he turned slightly into a street on the right. Then a tram-car met him so that he was forced to turn still farther in that direction, and by that time it was not worth his while to go back into Sauchiehall Street; he continued to saunter along the street he was in, Hope Street it was.

He came to the offices of a newspaper and stooped down to peer at some photographs that were in the window. When he had looked at them he was about to pass on, when he suddenly saw something that caught his attention.

In one part of the window he could see the reflection of a lamp at the other side of the street, and the light of it was falling on a group of men who seemed familiar. He recognised Donald MacAskill, and with him Angus MacLeod, one of the ex-Service men that were in the University at that time, and Tommy Ross, the terrible little shinty player, a man namely for the bottle, with a voice in his throat like an iron gate rasping on its hinges. There was a fourth man there too, a long thin fellow he did not know.

As he watched he noticed that MacAskill had looked across and recognised him. He touched MacLeod with his elbow and said something, and they all turned and looked across the street. Then MacAskill said something else in what looked like a whisper and they laughed and looked across at him again. The long lad seemed to ask MacAskill a question and stooped down to hear the little red fellow's reply. Then he straightened himself and gave a nod of comprehension or agreement.

A tram-car passed at Murdo's back and obliterated them for a moment, and when he caught sight of them again they had crossed the street and were close behind him.

On your guard now, Murdo, my love! said he to himself, and quickly looked at another part of the window.

" So it's to be the journalism, is it ? " said MacAskill's voice in his ear. "Well, you're the man for it right enough."

Murdo wheeled round with surprise itself on his face.

"Hello, Anderson!" said MacAskill in a loud voice, and laughed, slapping him on the shoulder with an exaggerated gesture of friendliness.

The rest of them burst into a loud laugh too; even the big long fellow opened his mouth and let out a deep " Ha! Ha! "

You overdid that badly, my lads, thought Murdo to himself. You'll have to be a lot cleverer than that if you're going to catch *me*. Aloud he said, " Hello, MacAskill! I didn't know you. You've changed a lot since I saw you last!" Then he added, "Of course, you were speaking in the Gaelic that time."

For a second MacAskill drew his scanty red eyebrows together in a frown. Then he forced out another loud laugh and the others joined in again, and the sudden way they stopped together it was exactly as if they had let out a bark. Murdo kept back a smile at the obviousness of the thing.

" You know those chaps, of course, Anderson," said MacAskill, pointing to MacLeod and Tommy Ross and they grinning. Then, " I want you to meet my friend Mr. Duncan MacPherson."

Turning to the long lad he said, " This is Mr. Anderson, one of our most promising young Highlanders."

Damn your patronising impudence, thought Murdo, and took the hand the tall fellow held out with exaggerated spontaneity, like a part rehearsed, as if he had never heard of Anderson, not even at the other side of the street a minute ago.

" How do! " said Murdo to him and then added, for MacAskill's benefit, " 'Bheil Gàidhlig agaibh ? "

" Tha," said MacPherson. " 'Sgiathanach a th'annam."

After they had exchanged a few trivialities MacAskill said in what was meant to be an offhand manner, " Mr. MacPherson iss tchust in town for a couple of nights and we were haffing a little celepraytion. Would you care to tchoin us ? "

" With pleasure! " says Murdo.

(He wondered if they had thought he would not drink and the request would embarrass him.)

They set off down the street, MacAskill and MacLeod in front, Murdo behind between Tommy Ross and the long MacPherson.

" Are you the man I was hearing about that made the eloquent speech at the Seltic ? " says the latter, in the Beurla.

" Oh, nothing, nothing to speak about," said Murdo in a tone of indifference. " A thing was mentioned I happen to feel rather deeply about. That was all."

" Still, I hear you made quite an impression," says MacPherson patronisingly. " Eloquence is a thing you want to cultivate. It will be a great help to you in getting on, you know."

MacPherson reminded Murdo very much of the Bradan. He had a big black head set on a thin neck, and nothing very much in the way of a chin.

They turned into Argyll Street and the two in front stopped before a public-house.

" This place will do," said MacAskill, and they followed each other in the door.

Murdo walked up to the bar with the rest as if it was a thing he was in the habit of doing every day of his life.

" Five large whiskies," said MacPherson, " Eh, what whisky do you prefer, Mr. Anderson ? "

Murdo happened at the moment to be looking at a bottle on a shelf.

" Glen Fruin," said he without a moment's hesitation (in the mirror behind the bottle he had distinctly seen Tommy Ross wink to MacAskill).

" We may ass well haff something to wash it down," said MacAskill as the man was putting the glasses on the counter. " Five pints of beer! "

When they were lifting up the glasses Murdo caught Tommy Ross grinning at him in a strange, knowing way, and it came to him in a flash that they were going to make him drunk in order to have the pleasure of making fun of him—MacAskill's idea of course; he would still be sore. Very well, he thought, let them try. He had at least this advantage over them that they had clearly been drinking already.

" Slàinte mhór! " said he; and took off his dram at a gulp.

When they were getting to the bottom of the beer, the taste of which was strange and disagreeable to him, he thought to himself, Now the thing to do is to gain time.

"Here, boys," says he, "I know a better place than this. What about going along there ? "

" Righto! " said they, and turned from the counter.

When they had walked along the street for a bit Murdo saw a bar that looked more attractive than the others.

" Here we are," says he, and pushed open the door.

He strode right up to the bar and nodded to the lad behind it.

"Five large whiskies, Jim!" says he familiarly.

In the mirror he saw the men behind him glance at each other. Clearly they thought they had mistaken their man and their little game could not be played.

Very good, thought Murdo. He would be able to get away now after this one—and not any too soon either, for his head was beginning to go round, and he did not know how soon he might be lying on the floor. Fortunate I got this this morning, he thought, laying a dirty pound note on the counter.

But when that dram was down MacPherson, who seemed to have money, wanted another. He was clearly a bit drunk by now. Murdo thought he would be able to carry another one home with him, and moreover he did not wish to risk spoiling the impression he had made, so he remained.

The consequence was they were in that bar until it was time to shut the doors. Before long they had forgotten what their little game was, forgotten they had ever had one. Before the end they were all drunk. MacPherson had put his arm round Murdo's neck and the two of them were saying endearing words to each other in the Gaelic and swearing an undying friendship. MacLeod was leaning his shoulder against the bar and meditating with bowed head on the little gutter running along the bottom of it, dropping a spittle from his mouth from time to time. Little Tommy Ross was standing sturdily on his two feet and the short hair stuck up fiercely on his head like spikes, but fixed on his face was a wide and terrible grin and his eyes stared straight before him; he dared not move so much as a muscle of his face or he would have lost his balance. MacAskill was spending a very long time behind a little door at the far end of the room.

Eventually a bell began to ring loudly and a voice shouted "Time, gentlemen, please!" over and over again. They were ushered out into the open air.

They were all drunk. They knew they were drunk. And nobody cared a rap. They went through the streets describing strange curves and angles, tacking and veering in the breeze, shouting and clutching at each other. At one place MacAskill turned deadly sick. He went to the edge of the pavement and began to spue on to the road. Somehow there shot through Murdo's mind a half memory of how the evening had begun, a little pin-thrust of antagonism to the man. He went over and stood beside MacAskill, and he bending over the gutter. Then he seized the fellow's wrist in his two hands and began to work the arm violently up and down like a pump-handle, pumping the drink out of him on to the street, Murdo laughing like a devil, the hat sitting right on the back of his head.

A little farther on he thought he saw a man

he knew, a man from Achbay, and he turned round to go after him.

What happened after that he could never remember, there was a gap there he was never able to put anything into, except a shop he had sat in, eating something. He must have sat there for a very long time for the next thing he remembered was walking up Renfield Street, and there were no people in his part of it but himself. He remembered almost everything that happened after that very clearly, very very clearly. He was still very drunk, but he was at that dangerous stage of drunkenness when a man thinks he has become sober, that he knows exactly what he is doing, that he will not do anything that will not be approved by his sober mind.

At one part of the street two young women stepped out of a doorway. He stopped before them, took his hand out of his coat pocket and made them a low bow, sweeping his hat wide at the end of his arm. When he straightened himself one of them had miraculously vanished.

" Fair maid," said he to the one that was still there, " it is unseemly that a damsel should walk abroad in this wicked city, alone and unprotected. May I escort you to your dwelling ? "

" Aye," says she, parting her very red lips in a captivating smile. (Murdo very boldly resolved that he would kiss those lips before the play was played).

They set off walking through the streets

together. Murdo swaggered along by her side, spouting in high-flown English, declaiming poetry, addressing her as Helen, Deirdre, joking, making puns in Gaelic and in English. She walked stolidly along beside him, not understanding half of what he said but giving a short laugh now and then, trying to keep him quiet.

"My dear, you walk too fast," said he at one place. "Tha phallus orm."

At that joke, he stood still and roared with laughter. "What a pity you cannot understand that," said he, and burst out laughing again. "It's the misfortune of your sex, my dear, that however *hot* you are you can never say 'Tha *phallus* orm.'" *

Then he stood still again in order to laugh, "Ho! ho! ho! Damned clever!"

"Haud yer tongue," says she. "Here's a bobby."

Murdo saw no reason why he should not laugh in front of a bobby. In fact he thought he would speak to the gentleman, introduce the girl he was taking home. That gentleman, however, looked at him in a way he decidedly did not like, and said in a very impressive manner, "You'll better tak' care o' yersel', ma lad, or ye'll land the nicht whaur ye dinna bide."

Murdo walked on shrugging his shoulders, muttering to himself, "Incomprehensible!" "Unsociability!"

* Pun on the Gaelic *fallus*, i.e. perspiration.

Eventually the girl turned in at a doorway.

"Ah!" said Murdo, peering into the blackness, "I had better escort you upstairs!"

"Aye, ye'll be'er," says she.

After a long time of stumbling up a stair that was mirk black, without so much as a pin-head of light anywhere, the girl pushed open a door.

"Hae ye a match?" said her voice before him.

"I believe I have," says Murdo.

He took three steps into the room and struck a match. A white candle seemed to leap out of the darkness under his hand, startling him with its sudden tubular shape. While he was putting the light to the wick of it the girl closed and locked the door and when Murdo dropped the stump of the match and turned round she was taking off her coat.

"Ah! Allow me!" said he, and took off her coat for her. Then he unfastened her dress. He went on to take off all her garments, one by one, until she stood before him, shivering, naked but for her shoes and stockings, a plump girl, and young.

He turned her round to the light and stood back to look at her, saying, "Ah! Very nice! Very pretty indeed!"

She submitted to all this in silence, merely looking at him in some surprise.

He came over to her and turned her round a little, posing her in the candlelight, running his hands over her body, her breasts, her belly, her thighs.

"Very nice! Very pretty indeed!" said he,

stepping back and looking her over again with an appraising eye.

And then a drunken lust clutched him suddenly at the throat.

4

They had taken him and put him on his back on an iron bed among rags and some articles of a woman's clothing. Lying there he had not the power to move his hand or his foot because of some hideous influence they had put upon him. They were all around him, everywhere. Their faces, terribly pale, came suddenly into the candle-light, leered at him with mouths like bleeding wounds, and faded slowly back into the darkness again. He was oppressed with a terrible sense of guilt, though he could not imagine what it was that he had done; but it must have been a horrid thing or why should they torture him so? They went round and round the bed, leering down on him, waving long slender lances with glittering points. Then the leader came forward and stood above him, naked. He recognised those plump and pendant breasts with the blue veins under the white skin; and then his brain reeled as the horror of the thing came on him—crime and punishment. He had committed the unforgivable sin against the sex; he had not desired; they had offered and he had not taken. As a punishment he was to die a lingering and horrid death, extended there at their mercy pierced all over by those slender lances that only after a long age would reach a vital part and put an end on his misery. Even as the thought came to him the thing began. This Annie MacIver with the painted face took a long lance and began to extend it slowly, very slowly, towards him, staring with blood-shot eyes at the part she was to pierce. The hair stood up on end all over his head. He tried to move and could not. He tried to scream but the tongue stuck to the roof of his mouth. Then the sharp thing touched him. There was a little pain like a pin-thrust on the inside of his right leg, about four inches above the knee. With a great effort he sat up in the cold dark, wide awake, scratching his leg.

A moment he sat like that. Then he began to blush all over with shame. He could feel the sweat coming out, prickling, all over his body, and he turned deadly sick. Lying on his back he extended his right hand and moved his fingers about, feeling the darkness. By good fortune they fell upon his clothes where he had thrown them on the floor beside the bed.

He began very slowly to crawl from under the blanket.

Once, when the heavy breathing beside him suddenly stopped, he lay still for a long time with the breath in his breast and one leg out in the cold.

He struggled into his clothes, the brain reeling inside his head, retching every moment with disgust and loathing.

The lock of the door creaked loudly and set his heart thumping, so that he almost fell several times as he fled down the black pit of the stairs, pressing against the cold, sweating walls, remembering gaps in the railing of another stair.

When he darted out into the pale light of the street lamps a chill wind was blowing in short gusts, lifting up pieces of greasy paper and fluttering them against walls or thrusting them into the mouths of doorways. Without thinking where he was going he started off running along the empty street, fumbling with his clothes as he ran.

Long after he was out of breath and panting, the sweat pouring from him, the tongue sticking to the top of his mouth, he continued to run on, driven by shame and a nameless fear of he knew not what, looking neither to right nor to left of him except once when he glanced up at the illuminated dial of a clock in a steeple and saw that the time was half-past four.

When at last he got into his room he threw himself down in a big chair. The heart was knocking furiously against his ribs. A cold choking tightened his throat as he gulped air through a dry mouth. His hands hung limply down to the floor, as heavy as lead. He could feel the little strength he had left moving down his legs and running out at his boots. He was trembling with exhaustion, with the red shame, with something like terror. The dregs of the drink were still in him so that he felt sick and giddy and savoured the taste of filth in his mouth. He felt as if he were coated with an obscene slime within and without. After a time he could bear this feeling no longer. He forced himself up on to his feet. He washed his body from head to foot, gasping as the icy water touched his skin. Then he crawled into the bed; and if the outside of his body was now clean the inside was still full of reeking filth.

For two days this feeling of contamination clung to him. In an effort to get rid of it he took long walks in the open air, carrying his hat. He kept the windows wide open, shivering in the cold air that blew in, choking in the smoke that blew out into the room. He washed his hands continually. Yet he knew all the time that the contamination was inside him and that by none of these methods would it be washed away. Everywhere he went the red shame sat on him, and when he thought of the thing a hot flush came out all over his limbs. He was driven by a vague and nameless fear that kept his foot going by day and at night sat on his heavy eyelids and kept sleep from him.

Gradually, however, he began to find himself forgetting about it for long periods together. He began to eat hearty meals and to fall into his sleep at nights almost before his head was on the pillow. The last dregs of the drink were out of him and in spite of himself he found that he was in a gay and cheerful humour. After and all there are limits to the amount of worry a healthy young man can indulge in, and he had never in his life been more healthy than he was now. The hot young blood went leaping through his veins and he found himself doing strenuous exercises for the mere pleasure of feeling the muscles ripple under his skin.

One evening, after putting some reels on the piano in so jaunty a manner that Mrs. O'Callaghan had dropped from her a small matter of thirty years and had begun to dance, he sat down to consider the matter.

He decided first of all that the greater part of his sensations had been due not to anything that had actually happened but to the depression that will always follow on the heels of a bad bout of the bottle. He had been looking at the affair through the fumes of stale alcohol. In view of that it was just a little ridiculous the way he had been going about recently, dripping with wet shame. There had certainly been the filth of the place, the smell, the vermin even, but you cannot have everything made to your requirements. In order to settle certain questions he had wanted a woman; well, he had had her; the questions were settled, there was nothing more to be said about it—no regrets, please! He really felt much the better for it, another gap filled up; he could now go forward to other things with an even mind, having settled forever any doubts as to one side of himself. And it had been very enjoyable, too, while it lasted. She had certainly known how to see to that, yon one. Fortunately he had nothing much in the way of a private moral code to regret the breaking of. (He put his hands into his trousers pockets)—ah, as to that, he could easily walk for a month, all things considered it was worth it.

As for the other thing, the vague uneasiness, almost fear, that had been haunting him, he felt he could have laughed out loud now when he thought of it. It was as clear now as the ragged back of Isle Tanera on a day of frost! He had not had any private code of morals to break. No, he had nothing but his curiosity to satisfy. But the others, they had a code—and he had broken it. They had a code, a stout matronly person with a dirty mind, and he had raped her—and perhaps he had been upset not so much at the act itself as at the feeling that she had liked it; she had enjoyed being raped, this respectable person. His people and all their people before them, not to mention all the people around them, had erected a great edifice of beliefs and attitudes, of taboos and silences—he had himself been brought up within it—and he had, at one blow, thrown it down. Any young man might be forgiven a little momentary terror at such an act, even if it was only at the terrible cloud of dust he had raised. There were things, right enough in themselves, that a young man could not do, himself and unaided, without a momentary tremor. One of these was to strike an old man in the face, and that was what he had done. He had given a certain reverend old patriarch, one John Knox, a bloody dunt on the nose. And although the old cod-fish had needed it badly, inverted libertine that he was, it was but natural that a sensitive young man should be a little upset at seeing the blood trickling down among the white hairs of his beard—he would have to wash that before he went to bed with the child that was his wife, and she scarcely a woman yet, the villain!

But, seriously, he thought he could see this affair now from the right angle, and he thought he had every reason to be pleased with himself. It had been a strong dose of medicine, perhaps, and a little terrifying in its effect, but it was another long step in the right direction. He was glad he had taken it. He looked for much less trouble in future from certain directions—"Ho, mo Mhàiri laghach 's tu mo Mhàiri. . . ."

5

"Dear me! dear me! I was thinking you wouldn't be coming to-day at all," said Mrs. O'Callaghan, bringing his tray into the room. "I hope your dinner won't be cold."

He made a loud rattling in his throat by way of excuse, taking off his coat, a huge hairy coat, so thick that the edge of it filled his hand and the hairs on it, tickling his palm, sent unpleasant little shocks up to his brain. He made a wide detour round the corner of the table, which was liable to rush forward and butt into his thigh, and looked at the face that leaped up before him into the glass. The face was pale, as pale as a dark face like that could be, a black paleness, almost a blueness. The lips were about to turn down at the corners. Then the mouth would open and say " Maaa! " plaintively, like a sheep. Terrified lest that should happen he forced himself to look up at the eyes which glowed steadily from the far end of two corridors leading half-way to the back of his head. Suddenly he jerked forward the head that was loosely joined to his neck and peered attentively into those eyes, looking from one to the other, trying to detect in them a gleam, a momentary tell-tale glitter. They looked calmly and steadily back at him, with a serene, almost indifferent, expression which terrified him more than if he had seen madness sitting there. It terrified him so much, that calm look in the eyes of a man almost mad, that a number of little wheels began to go round and round at a great rate, purring, in the middle of his belly. The door flew open and Mrs. O'Callaghan was into the room, carrying the second part of his dinner.

" Oh, you haven't begun yet! " said she.

" Oh! " he roared, so that the house shook, and dived head first at his chair. Strangely enough Mrs. O'Callaghan did not seem to observe his strange behaviour or to be surprised at it if she did. She put down a plate beside him and vanished.

He ate bending forward with his head over his plate so that the food would fly up into his mouth and not over his shoulder towards the ceiling. Each time he put a morsel past his iron teeth the Adam's apple fell back into his throat and the food sat in a lump on top of it until it fell forward again. The keyboard of the piano annoyed him greatly by sticking out halfway across the room so that he could hardly move his elbow up and down. If the corner of his eye happened to fall upon a chair it annoyed him by leaping forward into the middle of the floor with a cheerful bounce and a loud Here I am! and then jumping back again into its place by the wall. A man was going down the steep incline of the street selling something. Suddenly his head came flying in the window, mouth wide open, and shouted two words right in his face so that he jerked back his head. After a minute the same thing happened again through the other side of the window. He could stand this no longer. The wheels were going round and round in his belly again, setting up a great heat there. He jerked himself up on to his feet and began to walk about the room, avoiding the furniture when it jumped at him, his feet splaying out and flying forward in jerks at the end of his loose legs. He wanted a note-book but he dared not stand still long enough to select it from the pile on the bookcase. He had gone five times round the room before he was able to seize it in both hands, expecting to find it heavy and finding instead, to his surprise, that it was so light it threatened to fly up above his head, with his hands clinging on to it.

As he jerked himself loosely along the street

he noticed a number of buildings standing solidly where they had not been before. Grotesque figures constantly bobbed in front of him out of the crowd, leering at him with idiot faces. He was suffocatingly aware of the fact that in the city of Glasgow there were at least a million of people deformed, malformed, idiot-faced, loose at the mouth, with pendant ears. Cars jeered and hooted at him as they rushed past. Tram-cars clanged a loud metallic derision. The noise was terrible. . . .

The black buildings leant steeply forward into the quadrangle where a huge crowd of people was seething about. Some were leaning their backs against the walls to keep them up. Others were rushing here and there, giving huge bounds into the air, like deer. All were shouting, chattering, laughing, grimacing into each other's faces like monkeys, their arms whirling about like flails or thrashing the air like the sails of windmills. Out of the corner of his eye he distinctly saw a man's arm fly off his shoulder, fly off, up, past the spire, over the roofs of the buildings. A red cloak going past leapt suddenly out of the crowd and slapped the side of his face.

Going up the steep stone stairs they were all around him, pressing on him. They whispered in his ear, they breathed on his neck, laughed loudly up the leg of his trousers. If one of them touched him he shrank back in terror. Contamination! He wanted to run, to leap up the stairs, three to a stride. He began to choke and suffocate. He opened his mouth. A man above his head turned round and coughed hot stinking breath into it.

The professor came hopping on to the floor, wide at the knees, his back bent, a huge volume clasped across his stomach as if there was a pain there. He looked sulky.

"Aw! Pea-soup again!" shouted a voice from the top of the class, and the room went into a black roaring.

He pulled his pen down out of the air, pressed the point firmly to the paper and began laboriously to take notes of the lecture. But by the time he had written the first sentence, tracing out the letters with much labour, the man beside him was fluttering a page for the third time. His arm was sore with keeping the pen from flying off the page. He let it go and it fell on to the desk. The big clock tapped him twice on the temple. He felt himself slipping. . . . You will remember that I had occasion to mention this point last day and that I illustrated it by an lobhar air am bheil a'phlàigh reubar 'aodach agus glaodhaidh e, Neoghlan, neoghlan. Ré nan uile laithean a bhitheas a'phlàigh air bithidh e salach tha e neoghlan, which sometimes takes a different form gabhaidh e còmhnuidh 'na aonar somewhat surprising an taobh a muigh de'n champ bithidh 'ionad-tàimh* consider the other manifestations of the same is duine lobhrach e BUT, and here tha e neoghlan, gairmidh an sagart e

* Leviticus XIII. 45, 46, etc.

neoghlan gu h-iomlan which illustrates my tha a' phlàigh 'na cheann the oftener this occurs the imichibh, tha sibh neoghlan, tha sibh neoghlan comes into operation tha sibh neoghlan, tha sibh neoghlan -ing to another side of the is duine lobhrach e, tha e neoghlan find that imichibh, imichibh, tha sibh neoghlan. . . .

A ray of pale sunlight struck suddenly athwart the room. Immediately it was set upon, pounced down upon, swarmed over, eaten into, by a million million loathsome germs. In a moment it wilted and faded out. Blessed God! Even the little ray of sunlight? They were everywhere. They filled the air. The whole earth was full of them, millions upon millions of them, loathsome things that crawled and flew and swam and burrowed, with hooks and claws and hateful sucking mouths, exuding their vile excrement. Even the pure gold of the sun's rays—when you examined it—red rotten! The whole earth was rotting, full of pus. Perhaps man himself was but a white maggot, product of the earth's disease—a sperm kicking uselessly in the sticky fluid of the air, itself a foul exhalation of a sick, a masturbating earth! Merciful Christ! Only to discover at the last that the earth had dirty habits!

The wheels began to go round, vibrating, in his belly. Then a loud purring began at the back of his brain. The men behind him had stopped writing and were aiming pens and pencils at a spot on the back of his head, just above the neck. It began to get hot, that spot.

He jerked his head aside, expecting to see them fly past his ear. But they had been attached to the hand by pieces of elastic and by now were being aimed at him again. Sweat broke out on him. There was a prickling over the skin of his head and face. He had made the mistake of sitting between two enormous men. They heaved up on either side so that no air could get near him. He was too far from the window. All the air was breathed up before it reached his side of the room at all. It was second-hand, hot, diseased air that was going into his lungs. He began to suffocate. His heart was beating so loud that he could not hear the professor's voice. He must, he must, get up, get out, run, put his head somewhere, take it off, put ice on it, squirt cold water among his brains. He shrieked "Excuse me!" with all the breath left in his body. The two men between him and the passage shot to their feet as if pulled up from behind by a hand in their collars. He saw the door at the foot of a thousand steps and fled towards it, loud shrieks echoing in his head, thrown back from the concave dome of his white skull. . . .

How many days? How many days since he had been an outcast calling Neòghlan! as he moved between men? He began to count, by the beat of his quick steps along the empty pavement. Before he could stop he had counted fifty. Fifty! Incredible! Fifty days without sleep, fifty days of ceaseless walking,

walking through the streets by day, walking round the room at night, even when he was putting off his clothes, unable to stop for a moment, driven on by terror. Fifty days! Fifty days! He began to count his steps again. Ninety-three, ninety-four. There was the house, 203, in clean white figures on black tiles. Could he push open that gate and climb those stairs? His step wavered, then hastened on again. At the fifth passing he rushed at the gate, flew up the steps and threw himself at the bell. Then he tapped with his toe and hopped from foot to foot, his strength running away from him down the inside of his legs, his heart bobbing in his throat. The big man that looked out at him, a big, red, round man, full of blood! If you were to cut him he would run out like a sink.

"What do you mean, sir? What the devil do you mean, sir? Have you had YOUR lunch? Come back at three o'clock."

When he was at the foot of the steps the door slammed behind him. He leapt nine feet straight up in the air and came down on stiff legs, jarring his brain. Now he walked almost double, shrinking into himself, the sweat running on him. It began to rain, heavily. He went into a doorway, but the fear that gripped his heart whenever he stopped moving drove him out again. He ran from doorway to doorway along the street. Then the rain went off. A car came along, running after him, humming loudly in his ears. He darted up a side street. The car followed, made up on him, was on him. He pressed himself against the wall, scratching it with his nails. The car roared past behind him, blaring a loud Ha-Haaa! of derision.

The big clock in the steeple said three o'clock. But was it three? Was it not quarter past twelve? It must be hours since he had fled out at that gate.

When he got to the street he had to take the coat lapels in his two hands and pull himself along. Would his knees hold him up till he got that length? Only ten yards more now. He pulled himself up the steps and leant against the wall, fear gripping him at the throat, gulping air. When he got into the dark gullet of a lobby he would have turned and run, but he had not the strength. Then the man slammed the door behind him and he was caught, trapped, his retreat cut off. What could he say? What mistake could he pretend to have made in order to get out again without speaking about it, about it, about IT, to another person? His brains began to swell up inside his head. Another minute and his skull would fly in two.

A hand was gripping him firmly by the shoulder.

"Well, my boy, been careless again, have you?"

The voice of God out of the cloud! The voice of God, all-knowing, all-powerful, all-forgiving! The lightning flash of hope before his eyes blinded him. The tightening spring of terror that had kept him on his going feet, unsleeping, for four days and nights, was suddenly relaxed within him. He breathed, and all the strength ebbed from his limbs. All his body ached, creaked, with fatigue. An overpowering desire for sleep came suddenly upon him. He wanted to burst into tears, to weep for hours. His knees began to bend beneath the dead weight of his body. With a little cry, a moan out of a dry mouth, he collapsed into a chair. . . .

As he passed under it the clock at the end of the street was striking four—four deep, musical, bell-like notes that fell agreeably on the ear. Three hours before, on the same spot, one loud note had struck him a fierce blow on the temple. But what a difference! Then he had been full of a demon energy, wound up like a clock, unable to stop for a moment in the quick walk that was almost a run, he an outcast from the world of men and almost mad, wud, with naked terror, the door of humanity slammed behind his back. Now he could hardly walk forward at all for the fatigue that was in all his limbs and the ravenous hunger that was in his belly, but he wanted to run, to leap, to break into song. He was so wondrously happy, and oh, so repentant, so sorry, so good! He would never, never, do it again—like a little boy that had just, only just, escaped a thrashing and greets with the wild relief of his letting-off.

Mrs. O'Callaghan was waiting for him anxiously when he came in. Why had he not come in for his dinner?

"Oh, I was at the house of the professor and he kept me till now," said Murdo, and smiled at the falseness of a true word.

Mrs. O'Callaghan smiled back at him through her glasses and the wrinkle went out of her brow.

"Well, it's glad I am indeed to see you laughing. It's five days now since I didn't see that."

EADAR-UIDHE

Murdo was upstairs in his room and busy at the packing. It was an afternoon at the end of the second week of April and he was preparing to go back to Glasgow for the short term that would complete his first session there. A white mist was coming up out of the sea and from time to time wisps of it drifted in at the open window. His mother and Ealasaid were at the gossiping down below and their voices came up to him through the floor. He was on his knees, whistling as he put things in their places in the case before him, watching the muscles bulge and ripple under the skin of his bare arms. The muscles were big with a month of work in the open air, in cool windy weather.

The last two months of that memorable second term had been a period of unceasing work on the tasks prescribed in the regular course of his curriculum. That was the curious way in which the matter had affected him. As long as it was hanging over his head he had worked feverishly, going over a thing again and again long after he knew it almost by heart, and never allowing his attention to be attracted elsewhere. The fact was that he had been frightened into a return into that structure which he thought he had demolished a short time before. Now the Gaelic writers, the books that were in Mr. MacPhee's back shop, the excursions he had begun to make into various parts of the city (not to mention his own mind), all led him outside that venerable building. It was through these he had stumbled so badly, therefore, he was terrified of them. He had sinned; he was being punished; he must not be tempted outside again. He had tried to overthrow that edifice in which he had been reared, and all that had happened was that a slate had tumbled off the roof and struck him a sore dunt on the head. So he kept himself from thinking and applied himself only to those studies—and they harmless entirely—which he had been sent there to attend to. They were safe.

He had felt that he was really marking time mentally, and so wasting time, but he could not help it, he was afraid. However, he had his reward. He had taken his place at the head of all his classes, and a few days after the end of the term he had walked out of a certain house —No. 203 of a certain street—a clean man again. He had felt that it had been worth it, a hundred times worth it, for the sensations of that moment. He did not regret it a bit. He had gone into a quiet lane and thrown his hat up in the air.

During the month that followed he had laughed a great deal, and in particular it was long since he had begun to laugh at his ridiculous repentance. It was an accident, yon thing, and had no significance. A little more knowledge and it need not have happened. He was going back to Glasgow and he promised himself a surfeit of all he had denied himself. Mr. MacPhee's back shop would see him often, he had some leeway to make up there and orthodoxy would suffer some shrewd clouts in a number of places. Father O'Reilly would be greatly pleased. He promised himself some surprising mental acrobatics, some very cunning and delicate little blasphemies. But as for the bottle and—that other—no! They had served their purpose. Let them stick there. No more slips!

He gave a last pull on the strap of the case he had been packing; and it seemed to him as if the finality of that pull corresponded to something in his mind, as if he were putting " finis " to another chapter. His mother's voice was coming up loudly from below, in the middle of a long speech about—against—something. He thought that he had been fortunate in being on the croft or on the moor most of that month, away from the woman's voice. She was almost her old self again, not so fleet perhaps, not so vigorous at the head-tossing, but with all her old gift of disjointed and never-ending speech. As long as the eye would be open the tongue would be clapping. However, it had not troubled him, neither that nor any of the other things. The place was harmless. He had found when he came back that the conflict was over forever, that he had conquered at the last. Because of some new influence inside him the spell would not work. The air that blew about the place now was a fresh, invigorating air. Let them stop him now on the road, let them call him familiarly by his name as if to say: Yes, yes, my lad, I know you. I knew your grandfather. Let them ask how he was getting on, as if to say: Take as many prizes as what you have of brains will let you, so that we may have some satisfaction in having reared you here among us. But watch you don't go too far, of course. No adventuring where we cannot follow! Remember your mind belongs to us! Let them; he laughed and passed on. Murchadh Iain Ruaidh? Yes, still—but with the emphasis no longer on Iain Ruaidh! . . .

He went for two days to Mellonree, to the house of his mother's-brother. In the middle of the Sunday night he woke up suddenly out of his sleep. He was immediately wide awake, staring into the darkness. He wrinkled his brows, trying to think what it was that had made him open his eyes. It could not have been a noise, because Alasdair Dubh was still sleeping heavily at his side, snoring loudly out of an open mouth. He put his hands under his head and tried to recall the thing to mind. Something had certainly occurred to wake him, something very disagreeable. It was not far away, whatever it was, lurking in his mind somewhere, just eluding him and no more.

That annoyed him, because he was sure that at the moment of waking he had known what it was. He tried for about an hour to recapture the thing, but it only got farther away from him, until at last he was not sure if anything had happened at all. He turned on his side and tried to get sleep. However, he kept coming suddenly wide awake every now and again, and when eventually he did fall into a deep slumber he seemed to have been in it but a few minutes before Alasdair Dubh was pushing a finger into his ribs and telling him he would better be getting up now if he was to catch MacKinnon Bros.' van in the passing. He jumped out of the bed in a cheerful humour and was putting on his collar when he remembered about his waking in the night, and the face before him in the glass changed suddenly.

He was under anxiety all the morning after that and impatient while the van made its customary stops in Camuslong and Achbay. He gave but half an ear to the gossip of Archie Robertson, who was driving, and craned his neck for the first sight of the house.

As they came in view of it a blue car was just driving away from the door.

" Hullo! Anybody sick at your place ? " said Archie.

Murdo clenched his teeth together and jerked his head aside as if someone had aimed a blow at him from behind.

" Not that I know of," he growled, anger on him at the careless tone the man had used.

He was out of the car before it had stopped

and running for the door of the house. In the middle of the floor the nurse was standing, looking at the bed. In the bed lay a woman. Only the face could be seen and that so twisted and distorted that he could not for the life of him have told, where he stood, whether it was Seònaid or Ealasaid that was in it.

" Is it my mother ? " he asked of the nurse.

" It is," she answered, in her sharp, professional manner.

" Will she get better of this ? "

" She might."

This nurse was a stout woman a little on the far side of thirty, not bad-looking, but forbidding. She came from Dingwall, and she added to the hard manner she had by nature, and no doubt also from her trade, the contempt that the people of that part feel, or pretend they feel, for the people of the West. She had no Gaelic, of course, or pretended she had not, and would snort through her nose if anybody spoke it before her—but once she had smacked the face of Dan Neill a'Chàirn at a dance they had in Camuslong because he said behind her back to the man beside him: It's myself that would be comfortable and this one in the bed beside me—a queer thing that for a woman to do that had no Gaelic and could not be supposed to understand.

When she said these two words to Murdo she turned and looked him coldly in the eyes, as if she feared he was to make a scene.

He turned on his heel and walked out of the room. He went slowly up the stairs and began to take out of his cases the things he had put there the Friday afternoon before, and to put them away in the drawers. He did all this carefully, with deliberation, as if it interested him. Then, although it was not necessary to do so, he went up to MacIver's and told him he would not be wanting that seat in the mail-car on the morrow. For the rest of the day he was very busy on the croft, and when the rain drove him indoors he rearranged nearly all the stuff there was in the shop, taking it down from the shelves and putting it back again.

Ealasaid was going round the place like a wild bird in a cage, fluttering wildly about for a time, making little cries in her throat, then sitting in a corner trembling, pressing a handkerchief to her swollen eyes. They had had to put her out of the room at the beginning of the affair and she was still quite useless, unable to do the simplest thing.

Murdo did not notice that he had nothing to eat in the middle of the day, but when evening came on he began to realise there was something wrong with his inside. He was at that time busy shifting the stuff on the shelves. After a while he realised it was hungry he was.

As soon as he went into the kitchen he saw the state of affairs and that it would be useless to expect Ealasaid to do anything. He prepared a meal himself for the two of them, going quietly about it, with deliberation, in no way different from himself except that the mouth was shut like a trap and a strange, hard look flickered at times behind the eyes.

IV

THERE is one thing peculiar that people have often noticed about the high parts and lonely places of Alba, especially about the little glens and the countless bays and inlets that open on the western sea and about the islands that are lying out yonder on its breast; that is, the way time has of passing there.

It is not that a man's life will be a whit the shorter there or that there is any difference in the actual speed of time's passing, it is simply that life in those parts goes to a different tempo. It is an amazing thing, and one not readily to be understood by any that have not had the fortune to live there, how day will slip into day out yonder, and month into month, and year into year, until a man will wake up one morning and find, to his surprise as it were, that he is in his ripe old age, and he more than likely thinking himself till then little more than a stripling. And that is true.

What it is about those islands and those hidden places that causes this it would be hard to tell; but to a man that has lived there it needs no telling. It is a something in the places themselves and in the air about them.

They are there, the islands, floating on the

western ocean, moil and pother of busy waves about their rock-bound coasts, the sea swimming far in upon white beaches, salt breezes blowing always over their moors and their machair lands. When it is weather they tremble in the grip of the black tempests, and the pulse of the islesman throbs exultant, glaring out into the storm. When the long days of summer are over them they quiver far ben in a warm cloud of rising light, the swooning ecstasy of a maiden in the first embrace of love. Tang of sea tangle, salt on the lip, the heavens throbbing with the ocean's pulse, the seabird's cry—*that* is the islands, their like is not in the world anywhere.

They are there, the little bays and inlets, the nooks and coves and sheltered places, strung along the shore of the great-land of Alba, set on the western moorland's border, like green beads at a brown garment's edge. The great bens sit behind them, the wide moors circle their greenness, they slope down to the sea loch's shore. Between the two ends of a day there will be more lights there—sitting or flitting, on moor or ben or the loch's face, lights or coloured shadows—more of them than a man-of-the-brush himself could put a name on. There is not an hour of any day there without its miracle; things unnatural, incredible, happen there—red bens rearing out of a black land; out of a sky like ink a yellow finger feeling, silently, along the side of a black mountain, finding strange things in it, a rock that flashes, a tree standing alone. Verily and indeed an enchanted land.

That is the country; the spirit of the north is in it, blown spume and wild sailings and the sword-keen mind; and the spirit of the south is in it too, colourful, sensuous, hot with passion. That is the west of Alba. The Good God made it. He meant it for rearing men.

However, that is the country as it will be to a man with eyes to see; it is not telling us how it happens that time seems swifter in its passing there. That is a thing that maybe will not take explaining, it is part of the bewitchment the place lies under, a difficult thing to put a finger or a name on but real enough to them that know those parts. It is not that a man will necessarily be happy there; it is not that, it is that time will go past in his running whether a man will be happy or not. That is the strange thing. A man's sorrow may come to him with his waking in the morning, but whether there be much or little to fill his day the night comes swiftly and his rest of sleep. And so the days pass, and the years.

So it was with the young man Murdo Anderson.

It was a morning more than two years after that day his mother took to her bed that he came down to his breakfast in a bad temper. He had slept past his time and woke in consequence in an irritable mood. He sat down at the table and ran his hand across the black rasp of hair on his chin and his collarless neck. That made him worse; it always irritated him to have anything on his skin, dark and as smooth as silk, and here now was the second morning he had not had the time to shave.

Ealasaid put out his porridge before him. He raxed across for the jug of cream and then took up his spoon.

" Ealasaid, Ealasaid, Ealasaid! Am I to be lying here in the dark all the day ? Will you put back these curtains now and let me be seeing out ? "

(Seònaid had forgotten her English since she had taken to her bed.)

Ealasaid hurried across and pulled back the yellow curtains the woman in the bed must always have round her at night because of the draughts she said were always coming in on her.

" M'eudail, m'eudail, I was thinking you would be still in your sleep."

Murdo went on eating his breakfast. That querulous voice was beginning to get on his nerves.

" Will you be cutting in the high field to-day, Murdo ? " said Ealasaid, for something to say, pouring out his tea.

" I will," says Murdo.

From the bed, peevishly—" You're not cutting that field right, Murdo. Your poor father would always be beginning at the other end."

" Ach, what does it matter what end you will begin at ? Anyway, it's too hard on the back the other way."

" Oh, well, whether it is or not that's how your father would be doing and he was on the place forty years before you were born. But that's the kind of you. The old ways are not good enough for you. That's what's wrong with the young folks to-day. It must always be something new, something new. Your father didn't know how to cut a field of corn, poor man. *You* will have a new way of doing it. The house itself isn't good enough for you. You must be putting in a new window here and a new window there. There'll be a big draught from that window I'm thinking. You'll always be having it open, too. Oh, indeed, there's nothing right; windows or corn, you must always be changing something."

" Well, it's you that has the fine memory, mother. There was never corn in that field so long as I mind."

"Well, whatever, there was at one time, and when there was that's how he would be cutting it."

Murdo got up at last and went through to the shop, irritated beyond measure at the constant complaining of the old woman lying in the bed.

He was just inside it when he stood still and stopped chewing the morsel of food he had in his mouth.

The shop had been in disorder for a week because he was enlarging the window of it. The stones were now all in their places and he had sent for Iain Beag to attend to the wood and the glass. He was outside there now, his head and shoulders appearing at the other side of the big hole in the wall. The moment Murdo caught sight of him he was just in the act of looking with great earnestness at his chisel's edge. He looked at it gravely for a time. Then he touched it gingerly with a finger. He wiped it carefully on the sleeve of his shirt. Then to his looking intently at the edge of it again. Murdo was wondering what would be wrong with the edge of that chisel. He was on the point of speaking when it suddenly struck him there was something strange in yon, that he should be looking with such terrible keenness at such a tool. He looked closely at the man and could have sworn that he saw a momentary upward flicker of the fair lashes of the eye nearer him. His cheeks flushed suddenly—it was as he had thought, there was nothing wrong with that chisel edge, nothing at all. He turned quickly and went out.

For a time he pottered about round the byre. Then he seized his scythe and strode off to cut the fine crop of oats in the field his father had not worked since the bad illness he had a few years after Murdo was born.

It was about ten o'clock of a fine autumn morning. A little wind was blowing steadily out of the south, and the corn was dry. He threw his jacket over the top of the dyke, rolled up his sleeves, and began swinging the scythe in among the yellow stalks. For a long time he kept at it, frowning and laying the corn down in long swathes, as if he had a personal dislike to it. Then suddenly he stopped and leant upon the scythe.

It seemed to him there was no use playing this game, this farce, with himself any longer. It was becoming more than a little ridiculous, and tiresome. Indeed, the farce had been carried far enough. For more than two years he had been carrying on an elaborate piece of self-deception; it was high time to face the situation as it was.

He swung the scythe once or twice into the corn. Then he stopped again and began to look the situation in the face, for the first time in two years and a half.

When his mother took to her bed yon time it was to him like a hammer-stroke on the head, so sudden and unexpected it was. He had employed himself on the croft or in the shop all day, in a sort of dream, and working like a fiend for fear he should come out of it. In the days that followed he had continued to work feverishly, not daring to stop lest he should begin to think. There had been some mention at the time of recovery, and he had clung to that. And he had succeeded remarkably in deceiving himself. Then as a result of yon letter from Mrs. O'Callaghan he had for a time been brought face to face with the naked truth. He had read the letter crouching over the fire. She had not tried to get anyone for his room. It was not worth her while for the last term, and anyhow the rest would do herself good. She was glad to hear his mother was to get better and the room would be waiting for him when he came back the next October. She enclosed a Gaelic poem she had found in a drawer. She had not known it was his and had shown it to Father O'Reilly. The priest was delighted with it and wanted to know if he had any more, if so would he let him see them. She was sending also an old Irish poem Father O'Reilly had written out with his own hand, thinking he would like it. The house was very empty now and she was missing the tunes he used to play on the piano. However, he would be back next session and no doubt some new tunes with him.

He had crushed up the letter in his fist and tossed it into the fire. Then he put flame to the corner of his own poem and watched it burn. He was going to do the same with the other but opened it in order to read it first. It was beautifully written out in Father O'Reilly's small round hand.

"Gile na gile do chonnarc ar slighe i n-uaigneas
Criostal an chriostail a guirm-ruisc rinn-uaine
Binneas an bhinnis a friotal nar chrion-ghruamdha
Deirge is finne do fionnadh n-a grios-ghruadhnaibh.

. . . . .

"Fios fiosach dham d'innis is ise go fior-uaigneach

Fios filleadh dhon duine dhon ionad ba
righ-dhualgas
Fios milleadh na druinge chuir eisen ar
rinn-ruagairt
'S fios eile na cuirfead im laoidhthibh le
fior-uamhan.

. . . . .

" Rithim le mire im rithibh go croidhe-
luaimneach
Tre imeallaibh curraigh, tre mhongaibh, tre
shlim-ruaidhtigh
Don tinne-bhrogh tigim ni thuigim cia an
tslighe fuaras,
Go hionad na n-ionad do cumadh le draoi-
dheacht dhruadha.

. . . . .

" D'inniseas di-se san bhfriotal do bhfior
uaim-se
Nar chuibhe dhi snaidhmeadh le slibire
slim-bhuaidheartha
'S an duine ba ghile ar shliocht chinidh scuit
tri huaire
Ag feitheamh ar ise bheith aige mar chaoin-
nuachar.

. . . . .

" Mo threighid! mo thubaist! mo thurrainn
mo bhron! mo dhith!
An soillseach muirneach miochair-gheal beol-
tais caoin
Ag adharcach fuireann-dubh mio-caiseach
coirneach buidhe
'S gan leigheas n-a goire go bhfillid na
leoghain tar tuinn."

When he came to the end he got suddenly to his feet and went and stood in the shop. For a long time he stood there, looking out at the falling rain and swallowing down a dryness in his throat. Then he took the paper out of his pocket and read the poem again.

"Gile na gile. . . ."

He leant his head against the wall and allowed the tears to follow one another down his cheeks.

They were bitter days that followed. The "gile na gile" had shown up the actual blackness of a future he had been trying to think was only grey—black indeed, with the woman in the bed little more than a living corp, unable to speak or move. Although his case was no better now he shuddered yet when he thought of those days when the black desolation came on him, and the great emptiness.

Then his mother began to get better and he set feverishly to work to build up again the flimsy structure that had collapsed above him. When she began with her constant complaining speech he was running at all hours to serve her and sitting up through the night at his books. When they began to prop her up in the bed—it was September—he was thinking of beginning to his packing so as to be ready to go if she was about again in October. When she seemed to stop there and get no better he told himself he had been a little too hasty; it would take a person a good year to get the better of a turn like yon—patience for one year more.

That was two years ago and she was now as she had been then—and would never be other until the end came—two years hence or twenty, people lived long in these parts, well or ill. One thing was certain, she would never be out of that bed again. She had never got back the use of the whole of one side and was able to do scarcely anything for herself. But her tongue could wag. All day and every day it ran on, the high complaining voice coming strangely out of the half light behind the yellow curtains. It was Ealasaid this or Murdo that, all day—she was not comfortable in the bed, the light was in her eyes, it was too dark in there, there was a draught from somewhere. The people going bye on the road would always hear that voice running like a burn in spate.

For those two years he had continued to play this game of deceiving himself. He had gone on as he had done at the beginning of the matter, never allowing himself to look beyond the day that was in it. And such is the way time has of passing in those parts that in spite of however vehement his desire might be he had scarcely been conscious until this minute of the passing of two whole years.

It had not been easy all the time, of course, to keep deceiving himself. There had been times when the air itself of a man that was speaking to him had come near to making him lose the guard he had on his mind. Yes, yes, you're Murchadh Iain Ruaidh. You were in Glasgow to get learning. But of course that's all over now. Nothing came of that. You're back here again, here again, with us, among us, quite one of ourselves. How is your potato-planting getting on? Some of them even seemed to have an air of triumph about them; there are envious people everywhere. It was certainly high time he put an end on this farce and faced the fact.

He gave a short, hard laugh in his throat and began to cut the corn, admiring the supple strength of each long curving stroke.

In the afternoon Murdo the Flea came up to give a hand and later on Kenneth Mitchell, the lad they called George Washington, came up also—he had not got away to the hotels this year with the rest of the young men because of a poisoned foot that kept him on his back for a good while after the beginning of the season.

Murdo set the pace, with the easy, rhythmic, tireless energy that was in him that day. The Flea worked his jaws furiously and squirted tobacco juice among the stubble, sweat running on him. Big blobs stood out on George Washington's white brow and his damp hair curled up in little ringlets all over his head. Murdo looked at him once or twice out of the corner of his eye, noting the pale face and the drooping movements of him, and smiled a little smile to himself.

Before long the stooks were sitting up amongst the stubble where in the morning a fine crop of oats had been waving. Not for nothing had that croft been called Druim a'Choirc, the

Ridge of the Oats, thought Murdo as he put his jacket round his shoulders and turned his steps towards the house.

Seònaid, behind him, was in her most peevish mood, continually asking stupid questions about this or that. Murdo answered her shortly, mumbling through the food that was in his mouth, and as soon as he had finished eating he got up and went outside.

It was a grey, windy evening. Flecks of white foam ran up swiftly on the face of the sea. The bens were blue and hard, lying under a skyful of moving cloud. Swirls of dust rose up and sailed along the road. Sand gritted in the teeth.

For more than two years, when he went abroad at all, reluctantly, Murdo had walked firmly and with purpose, as if he had something to do, and something else waiting on the doing of it. To-night he strode along with his hands in the pockets of his trousers, loose at the knees, shoulders and elbows swinging forward carelessly, his jacket flying open and flapping about him, and he whistled loudly, "*Gabhaidh sinn an rathad mór.*"

He went through the street and up the north road. At one point he lifted his head and saw a group of figures coming towards him, and behind them Lovat's van rattling down the road in front of a great cloud of swirling dust, so he turned sharply to the left along the track that led round Strongorm to the four crofts of Cladach.

For about a mile he went along that track,

stumbling among the ruts and loose stones that covered its surface and at times taking to the edge of the moor that bordered it where at every step his boots sent little clouds of dust out of the bone-dry heather tufts.

When he came to the Allt Dubh he stopped and leant over the little bridge that was there. The brown water ran out below him, going swiftly to the sea. For a time he watched it, bending over with his elbows on the stone parapet of the bridge. At the bottom of the water a little fish was lying, half under a ledge, quivering, with his nose upstream. His back was so like the surroundings that after a time he began to appear and disappear until it was not certain whether he was there at all. Murdo pulled out a fragment of loose plaster and dropped it into the water right above him. There was a little splash, and a few bubbles were carried swiftly down-stream. If the fish had been there the dart he made had been too quick for the eye.

At his back the woods kept up a continual sighing and creaking and rustling as the wind went through them. Sometimes a gust instead of coming up at the back of the wood took the Stron sideways, lifting a long swirl of dust that ran along the road, curved over his shoulder and came down on the surface of the running burn in a momentary soft opaqueness. As he bent over the parapet the water was continuously running up towards the top of his head. It began to stroke his brain, upwards, with a soft, soothing hand, gliding out from under the bridge with a smooth surface and a low gluc-gluc at the edges; and the trees behind him sighed and rustled in his ears. Gradually he fell into a kind of dreamy stupor, thought-less.

At length a red leaf drifted slowly past his eye and he raised his head and saw her coming round the bend of the road, to his right. She had come back about six months before from her place with the Rev. Mr. Morrison in Inverness and some vague story had come after her. He had seen her several times, of course, but had not spoken to her. To-night she had clearly been visiting her mother's people, the Chisholms of Cladach.

As she came towards him round the corner of that lonely road he was suddenly reminded of a previous occasion about three years before and out of the corner of an eye began to watch her as she came along, stouter now than she was, her full breasts bobbing before her as she walked. As she came up he felt an idle curiosity to see again those blue veins running under the white skin.

" Oh, Murdo, we had a letter the other day from Rory. He's getting on fine in Canada and was asking for you. It's more than two years now since he went out. . . ."

She began at her usual chatter, standing close beside him. He let her run on, merely grunting in his throat occasionally, leaning over the parapet and thinking about something else. Then her knee touched him, with too snuggling a movement if it was meant to appear accidental, and he stood, erect.

He glanced down at her, and, Why not? thought he.

They went up into the wood of Strongorm where wisps of the blue dusk were beginning to flit between the tree stems, clinging half hidden below the leafage. Branches waved and swayed and tossed above them. Leaves red and brown and yellow came fluttering in showers on them.

The second time, she scratched and bit like a cat.

2

Murdo pulled the old green door to behind him.

Standing outside, in the dark, just outside the ray of light from the window, he fastened the coat collar under his chin, and then set off walking up the road, bending forward, pushing against the cold north wind that drove the rain like melting ice against him. He clutched the snout of his bonnet and strode forward, slanting into the wind, staggering in the darkness, splashing in the pools and rain-filled ruts.

She had called to him last night from the dark outside; when he opened the door of the shop the beam of light had shot out and found her feet; he could see no more of her for a moment, looking suddenly into the dark, and she, invisible, saying in a loud whisper she had something to tell him. He knew at once what it was, of course. It was inevitable, the way they had been going on until the cold rains set in a few weeks ago. The idea had occurred to him several times and he had shrugged it aside, not caring very much either way. The cold, hard, careless frame of mind had stayed with him ever since that day a few months before when he had begun to review the situation, accepted the inevitable—the first evening, as it happened, they went into the wind-shaken wood of Strongorm. Let it happen; it mattered little to him, now. In any case he had no choice in the matter now, seeing he would be in the place the rest of his life. He was Murchadh Iain Ruaidh already, Murchadh Iain Ruaidh that had gone to Glasgow to get learning and had come back before he got much of it—that was enough, without any other thing to be between them, without mention put on it but heavy in the air, when they spoke to him on the road, looking straight at him with the calm security of complete understanding, and asked how he was getting on at the peats.

When he turned off the road and began stumbling in the darkness up the path that led to the house, with the wind and the rain now on his right side, he began to wonder how Mr. John MacIver would receive him. Apparently that conversation of two days ago was all through the town already and no doubt it would have come also to the ears of that lump of greasy sanctity.

He had been talking with a group of men in

Hector Matheson's shop and had got into an argument with old Angus MacDonald, about religion. Angus was an elder in the Free Kirk and Murdo had always disliked him because he had that arrogant smugness and overbearing self-confidence that is always to be seen in those that have the private ear of the One-that-is-Highest and know His entire mind.

Angus had been speaking about the evil-doers, pulling at his broad beard, speaking in a loud and righteous voice, smelling very badly of whisky. He was describing how he had seen Calum Mac Dhonnchaidh Odhair and Shonny Eachainn, two lads belonging to the United Free Kirk, kicking a rubber ball to each other on the afternoon of the Sabbath Day. This was what young people were coming to to-day. It was tempting the long-suffering mercy of God. It was bringing disgrace on a place that had always been namely for holiness and God-fearing ways. But they would give account of that yet. God would judge them on the Gathering Day, and He sitting on the Great White Throne, and all the righteous standing round giving Him a help at the judging.

Murdo usually said nothing when such a conversation was going on. However, it happened that he had eaten something at his tea that was lying heavy on his stomach and the arrogance of the grizzled old fellow annoyed him more than usual. Also, the ideas the folks had about things like that were so familiar to him that usually he hardly thought about them at all, the words simply went past his ear; but on this occasion, perhaps because he was annoyed and gave more heed, he suddenly saw a vivid picture of the thing as they conceived it, and it was so ludicrous that he would have laughed if it had not also appeared stupid and childish beyond words:—The Day of Judgment, and the God of the little Presbyterian sects sitting on His Great White Throne. He is a smallish, elderly man, about sixty years of age, thick-set and of a portly body. A short, square, iron-grey beard sticks out on His chin and His long upper lip is shaven, under a hooked and very Hebrew nose. Under the iron-grey stubble His cheeks are plump and red; and the plump cheeks are always puffed out, the iron-grey beard is always bristling, the bushy eyebrows are always drawn together, the eyes are always smouldering with a perpetual irritability and bad temper that is liable at any moment to burst out and demand for its satisfaction strange things such as that so many pregnant women have their bellies ripped open, or that so many chubby infants be dashed against the stones, or that so many Philistines have their foreskins chopped off. His religion is Presbyterianism; altogether He is a very disagreeable old fellow. He rests His elbows on the arms of His Great White Throne, crosses His chubby legs and folds His hands upon His fat little belly, glowers around under His bushy brows and prepares to judge the quaking throng before Him. These are all the sinners. There is a great number of them, in fact the great majority of all that have ever lived since the world began, since Adhamh Lack-rib was driven out of the Garden, since the tower-builders were smitten so that they forgot their Gaelic and began jabbering together in a bar-bar of outlandish tongues, Teutonic, Slavonic, Semitic. All the murderers are there and the adulterers, all the whores and whoremongers, the thieves, liars, vagabonds, Sabbath-breakers, scoffers, Catholics, Episcopalians, Moslems, Buddhists, Unitarians, agnostics, atheists, disobedient to parents, lovers of pleasures rather than lovers of God—all these and many more, including an enormous army of little children that had snichered behind the minister's back or shown an unclean interest in their physical parts. All these are now about to be judged individually and by name. And lest God, the Omniscient, should make a mistake, He is to have the assistance of the Elect, the Righteous, in His judging. They are standing there now, round about, behind, and on the steps of the Great White Throne, chief among them being the patriarchs, the prophets, the apostles, the ministers and elders of the Presbyterian Kirks, with such of their congregations as by godliness, by Sabbath-observance, by abstention from dancing and the singing of vain songs, by down-looking humility and interminable groanings and rumblings, have merited a forward standing among the Godly and a place of honour near Himself. On His left hand are those that were members of the Established and the United Free Kirks, never quite free from the taint of laxness and worldliness; but on His right His particular friends, His holy, His unreasoning, His groaning, moaning, chest-rattling, His sour-faced, His bovine, His dear, His constipated Seceders and Little Frees, the holiest of them all, those that never hesitated to condemn the indulgences of anyone else whatever, that never deviated from an iron adherence to the *letter* of the law, the dear old belly-ripping, baby-killing, foreskin-chopping Jewish law, and who even knew when to disregard the grosser indiscretions of one Jesus Christ, an incorrigible latitudinarian, who even went so far as to say once (but of course he couldn't have meant it) that the Sabbath was made for man, not man for the Sabbath. Old Angus MacDonald would be there, looking especially for young lads that kicked a rubber ball to each other on the Sabbath day; Mr. John MacIver would be there, glancing here and there for pretty girls that had committed fornication with men, other men; John the Elder would be there, the worthy innocent man, looking for nobody in particular but dutifully working himself up into one of his purple and cross-eyed rages about everything in general, and, with a learner's eye on Mr. John MacIver, jerking his stiff arms and waving his hairy hands about, advising God.

Usually, as has been said, when they were talking about the theocratic system of the universe they believed in, Murdo remained silent; indeed, from courtesy he did not even allow himself to smile. But this time the childishness of the thing for some reason made him angry.

"Are you telling me," said he to Angus, referring to something he had just said, looking innocently at the old man as if nothing was farther from his mind than to be sneering at holy things, "Are you telling me now that God has a body in every way like ourselves?"

"Indeed, I'm telling you that."

"In every way?"

"In every way, a Mhurchaidh. We are made 'in the image of God'."

"Well, now—a thing that's often troubled me," says Murdo, with some hesitation and a look of perplexity, "how is it now with Him, would you say—will He be going round the corner to the byre, like you or me, or will He be using one of these new-fashioned affairs with water that comes down when you pull the plug?"

"Oh, it's you that's ignorant, a Mhurchaidh. There will be no need for God to be going round to the byre at all. . . ."

So to many questions about God: Did he lie with women? What? Did He then lack the organs? . . .

Old Angus was too proud of his knowledge to let it appear that he could not answer any question whatsoever. Indeed such was the old man's pride in his knowledge and his position in the Kirk that Murdo might have gone on teasing him for long enough without its occurring to Angus that there was anything behind his questions but a shameless ignorance. There is no telling what laughable things he might have been led to say.

Unfortunately some of the young men behind Murdo could restrain themselves no longer and at this moment began to titter, and the Bradan, standing under the hanging lamp, suddenly dropped a giggle as if it had been a spittle out of the corner of his sagging mouth.

Old Angus, about to speak, was instantly suspicious. He glanced first at the young lads, who quailed before him and became silent, looking uncomfortably here and there, and then at Murdo, who, caught suddenly off his guard by the titter behind him, had himself been on the point of laughing and was now trying to recover himself by screwing up his face into too complete a look of innocence.

For a breathless second the old man glanced here and there among them. Of a sudden his cheeks and brow went scarlet and his broad beard bristled with rage, so that you could almost hear it bristle. He burst into a torrent of speech, waving his arms about, belching whisky breath into Murdo's face. Then his passion took him at the throat and he commenced to choke and stutter. It looked as if he might have a fit. Finally, raising an accusing hand aloft, he shouted out, " Behold ye despisers and wonder and perish! " and rushed out into the night.

And so it had gone abroad that Murchadh Iain Ruaidh had been blaspheming God in the shop of Eachann Alasdair. Much had been added to the tale as it went from mouth to mouth, and some of the older people had been going about with bated breath waiting for the wrath of God to fall upon that place.

So as he came up to the house, and a rain sheet falling white through the watery beam from the window, he was wondering how Mr. John MacIver would receive him. He must have heard of that childish outburst and it would complicate the position for him.

When Murdo opened the door Mr. John MacIver looked up suddenly from where he sat with the table before him. He had been at his meat. A trickle of grease at the end of his mouth showed in the lamplight. The fat throat, collarless, rose white out of the neck of his shirt, and the round belly bulged unsuspectedly big through the unbuttoned waistcoat. He stopped chewing, put his two fists on the table before him, a knife in one and a fork in the other, and stared at the man in the door, steadily, warily, with a look in his little eyes that might have been anger, might have been fear, certainly was amazement. Anti-Christ comes visiting, said Murdo to himself. Having looked for a while Mr. John MacIver began again to move his jaws, but without taking his eyes off Murdo. Clearly he had no intention of saying anything, not so much as, You're there! He watched in silence as Murdo took a step into the room and closed the door behind him, watched him carefully, unwinking, an animal look, moving his jaws slowly up and down. When Murdo turned round he found five or six more pairs of eyes upon him. Several children watched him from different parts of the room; a little one raised himself in the bed and looked at him; two older ones looked up at him from the floor; Annie herself looked at him over the top of a paper book she had been reading; the wife herself, the little bedraggled wisp of a thing, got up from her knees where she was working by the fire and looked at him as she straightened her back. This lasted several seconds. Then Annie with a little cry in her throat threw down the paper book and ran past him out of the door. Her mother with the back of her hand put up a lock of hair that was trailing over her eye, and drew forward the chair. She gave a quick glance at the man by the table and, " Dean suidhe, a Mhurchaidh," she said, with a little timid smile.

Murdo took a look at the missionary, then, " Thank you," said he, " I prefer to stand."

He stood where he was in the middle of the floor. He was wet and uncomfortable. Water was trickling down his neck, water was dripping from his coat on to the floor. He was beginning to get angry. Mr. John MacIver continued to stare at him from the table, where he was now gobbling up the last of his meat. Then with great noise he slobbered tea out of a big cup, holding back the spoon with his thumb.

"What are you wanting?" says he, just like that.

"I'm wanting to marry Anna!" says Murdo, plain out.

The man's head suddenly bobbed down between his shoulders as if one had aimed a blow at him, and into his eyes came the same look that was there before, the look that was anger, and maybe fear. He stared at him a while in silence until the anger became uppermost in his little eyes, and Murdo became angry too.

"What!" says the missionary, "The unclean blaspheming devil that's in you!"

"Oooh!" says the wife in a little voice and tears in it. "It's the good lad. . . ."

"Be quiet!" snapped the man, without looking at her, and at once she became silent.

"What!" says he again, "You're wanting to marry Annag? Indeed and indeed you'll not do that ever! I'll be looking another road for a man to my daughter!"

"As you desire," said Murdo, and strode from the room.

As he shut the door he could hear him stamping and shouting, and the woman broke into her shrill wailing.

He was too angry to think while he stumbled down the path, but by the time he got on to the road he was calmer. Of course it was natural the man should be angry, he thought to himself. Of all sins unbelief was worst to him, and of all men he must hate most the man that scoffed, or even doubted. Because he had no hold over that man. With *his* mind he must be feeling inferior to all men unless he had the terrors of religion to overawe them, and that he could not do to the man for whom there were no terrors there, because he did not believe them there. Any other sin he might forgive. Even fornication and adultery he might forgive, because they did not challenge his authority. Indeed, he might even feel friendly to the man that had committed that sin, because he would enjoy feeling superior to him and would be able to speak as haughtily as he liked without fear of check. But blasphemy was another thing. Weakling that he was, he could never forgive a man that would not bow to his authority without question. Apparently his hatred of that man was so great that he would endure the other thing rather than not indulge it.

He came up to his own door almost running before the wind. But as he opened it he thought another thing—maybe they had not told him about the other matter! Maybe he did not know! He paused a moment to consider that thought. Then he shrugged his shoulders and shut the door. After all it was not his affair, that. He had done all that was required of him. But if Mr. John MacIver really did know, he was a better man than he had thought he was.

But the next morning Mr. John MacIver came down in a storm of wind and rain and met him at the door of the shop.

"It's me that's the hasty man," says he. "You'll have to be forgiving me, a Mhurchaidh. I'm thinking a different way about it this morning, and herself yonder so set on having you."

All the time the little pig's eyes of him were darting from side to side. To look Murdo in the face was one thing he would not do.

They've told him, thought Murdo, and loathed the pig.

3

The day Murdo brought home his wife, Ealasaid stumped out of the house, her nose in the air. She took his marriage as a reflection on her ability to run the place. He had found someone to do it better. She was not wanted, apparently. One would have thought she would know best how to attend on her own sister. But apparently not. However, she still had her pride. She could go. Murdo stood at the door in his best clothes and watched her heaving herself up into the mail-car, he shrugging his shoulders. She went back to Mellonree where there was more need for her.

This was in February and preparations for the spring work began that year without delay. Shortly he was out again on the land from which a few months before he had taken a harvest.

Quiet hills, high-headed, sat on one side, and on the other stretched the sea. Between them lay the little fields, grey dykes tracing their oblong shapes on the face of the brown moorland. And among them day by day moved the dark figure, stooping, treading the slow length of them, up and down, turned earthwards. Cloud-shadows and sunlight patterned the plain ; grey rain, a slanting sheet, shrouded it; nightly the blue dusk crawled across it; mornings dawned; the watching hills sat on one side and on the other lay the sea; and day by day, under the sky, moved the dark figure, treading up and down, turned earthwards. That was he. The work of his hands was like the green points pushing out from the brown earth, or like the sap rising in the stems of trees. Like them was his earth-labour, quiet and sure, not hesitating, a natural thing, and good. For them the morning came and the evening, and for him.

So he toiled, not with much joy and not with sorrow. But when his foot turned home at evening there was food for his hunger, a quiet word for the woman that in her body bore his young, for her and for the other that had carried him, and then the sleep of the labouring man, which is sweet.

Five months passed in this way and then one day his mother died. It was just at the time when the earth was green and the sun was taking the longest road in its journey from hill to sea. There was no fuss about it at the end. One evening she was at the scolding as was her custom; the next morning she was lying, grey-faced, behind the yellow curtains, and her scolding days were over. She had been cold for hours when they found her, so that at the yonder end she went out on her road unspeeded and alone.

And scarcely had she been carried to her grave when Annie took to her bed. That is how it is with us, one dies and before you have the time to turn round another is born in the self-same bed—life and death, and please yourself how you get from the one end to the other. It is no great matter.

V

It was a few days after the birth of the child that Murdo came into the house one afternoon and seeing that the woman's mother was with her, went straight upstairs to his room. He stood a while at the window looking out at the little fields, at the green of waving corn and the darker green of the potatoes. Then his eye travelled slowly over the blue expanse of sea, very calm and very blue and with a long wisp of smoke trailing across the far corner to the left, from the funnel of a ship going up and out to Leòdhas. Then he looked up into the deeps of a sky cloudless and blue. For a long time he remained staring into it, standing motionless by the window with his hands clasped behind him. He heard the little bedraggled creature in her hurried timid voice saying that she would be going. He heard her go out and close the door behind her. Just under the window she twice cleared her throat loudly, then the sound of her boots on the road came up to him clear through the buzz of a blue-fly inside the window. Then the baby lifted its wailing voice. The thin piping sound came up through the boards of the floor and swayed about the room, an unpleasant thing somehow, demanding, impossible to escape or ignore. He turned round and began pacing up and down the room. The pathetic little piping noise, extraordinarily thin and clear and bright, continued to waver up through the floor and trickle into his ears. He shrugged his shoulders in displeasure. This was a new noise in the house and took some getting accustomed to. The quavering infant wail was a new noise, as was also the rhythmic hissing sound the mother was making in order to quiet him. They made the objects in the room change and look unfamiliar, expanding, contracting, changing colour. None of the old noises remained that had given the room its colour and shape, not the heavy tramp of John the Elder's boots or his sonorous rumblings, not the scolding voice of Seònaid, as he used to hear it with an undertone of cheerful contentment or latterly complaining always. None of these noises that marked the place he was born in and bound to. They made a world he was not part of, nor bound to, as he had been to the other.

He stopped in his pacing where a board had been put across the corner of the room to make a shelf for some of his books. The noises below had died away. He stood before the books and ran his eye along the backs of them. Horace, Virgil, Cicero, Lucretius, the venerable Aeschylus, Sophocles, the sceptical Euripides. At the end of the line a thick red-bound *Odyssey*. He put out his hand and took it down. Dust flew up into his nose as he opened it and looked at the type, grown unfamiliar. He ran his finger along the edge of the shelf. It too was thick with dust; not for a very long time had a cloth come that way. He went to a drawer and tore a large piece off the back of an old shirt. Then he returned and lifted down the line of books. He first dusted the shelf; then one by one he wiped the books and put them back in place, setting them carefully edge to edge, running his fingers slowly with a lingering motion along the backs of them. When he had finished he went downstairs. A child was standing in the shop. He put down the cloth he still had in his hand and held out the box of boot polish she was wanting. Then he picked up the coppers she laid on the counter and slipped them into the pocket of his trousers. As she went out a car ran swirling past the door, going at a great rate. He walked to the door and stood there for a while looking at the cloud of dust retreating rapidly down the road to the south, and as he looked he rattled the coppers in his trousers pocket and felt the sun striking warm on his face. After a while he turned and sauntered slowly up the road to the town.

He was standing on the bridge when MacKinnon Bros.' van from Achgarve rattled up and stopped beside him. Archie Robertson stuck his head out, laughing.

"Hello, Murdo! I was hearing about the happy event. Congratulations!" says he, and stuck out his hand.

Murdo took the hand and stood still where he was, saying nothing.

" Hello! " says Archie, joking as always, " You're not looking very like the proud and happy father. Are the responsibilities weighing on you already ? Come up to Mexico and take a drink to celebrate the occasion. Jump in! "

Murdo looked at him a moment as if he scarcely understood what he was saying. Then he smiled faintly as if an idea had come to him. And if he went up to Mexico to take a drink maybe it was not for the same reason as Archie thought he was giving it to him.

The two men that were standing at the far end of the bar stopped in the middle of the conversation they were having and stared at him in his going from door to counter on the heel of Archie Robertson. The like had never happened before in the place, Murchadh Iain Ruaidh to go into Mexico's for a drink of whisky. Mexico himself lifted a pair of red eyebrows on him as he came over and after Archie had asked for the whisky, while he was pouring the stuff out of the bottle, tilting up his elbow, he kept turning the sandy head of him round to look over his shoulder. When he put the glasses down before them and swept the money off the counter with his hand he had yet another look at him—as if the lad had pointed ears or a boil on the end of his nose.

" Well, here's warm days and hot nights to the little sinner! " says Archie, in the way he had.

He always spoke in the Beurla, and in a hard crisp kind of it, always making little jokes like that and laughing in a hard manner, with the lips and teeth only, so that you felt it was more in the way of business and not from any human friendliness. The feeling you had was as if the bones of his jaws were cold iron, and the teeth would make a clashing noise if they came together.

The shadow jumped away along the polished counter as Murdo took up his glass.

" Taing," said he, lifting it up to the level of his eye and looking across the rim at a row of square-edged teeth. He took down the dram and rapped the bottom of the glass on the counter.

It was the first time he had taken a drink since a certain night in Glasgow and now the stuff ran through his veins and curled about his heart as it did the first time of all. He twirled the tongue round the cavity of his mouth and was aware of a swelling at its farther end like the start of a throaty chuckle. In the beam of yellow sunlight that struck across the room the dust danced up and down. Outside the sun was shining on the face of the world, on hills and glens, on mountain streams and rivers bending on the plains, on the streets of strange far towns, on winding roads, on a young lad taking leave of a girl at a little gate, by a winding road, in the sunshine.

After Archie Robertson left him he remained at the counter, drinking with himself. From the back room came a warm hum of talk and rising above it now and then the sound of laughing voices; and in the beam of sunlight that struck athwart the room the points of dust went dancing up and down.

Before long, however, he was putting his hand into his pocket and finding no money there, so he turned himself round and walked towards the door. But because no drop of whisky had gone over his throat for a matter of three years he had to stand for a while when he got outside, unsteadily, putting his mouth in order so that he would be smiling equally on both sides of his face.

That was the start of the many visits he began to make to Mexico's in the evenings. Before this for long periods together he was never near the town at all; after this he was forever on the road, going and coming between his croft and the town end.

For a time the men in the bar, and Mexico himself, continued to look up in silence when he came in, and his glass would usually be set before him before they took themselves to their talking again. But it was not long till they got accustomed to seeing Murchadh Iain Ruaidh standing in his place at the end of the bar. They accepted him at last as one of the company. When he came in they would nod to him and pass a remark about the weather, and now and again a man of them standing beside him or strolling over in a casual way would attempt to start a conversation. But if he did it was little encouragement he would get from Murdo. He would answer him with a half-word, unsmiling, or with no word at all, and plainly showed that he preferred his own company. Nor could he ever be persuaded to take a drink from any of them. The result was that after a number of them had retired, looking surprised and a little resentful, they began to give him his end of the counter to himself, and not even if one of them was drunk would he approach the corner where Murdo would always be standing. Indeed they got into the habit of leaving that part of the room alone whether Murdo would be in it himself or not, or if anybody was there when he came in he would immediately pick up his glass and go to another standing-place.

Murdo would stand there by the hour, silent, by himself at the end of the counter, looking straight before him at the bottles sitting on the shelves in rows. What was passing in his head, he standing gloomily there, nobody could tell; but occasionally the black eyes of him would suddenly light up and a smile would play round the ends of his mouth; and now and again he would cast a sullen glance over the company, a slow dark look, as it was of reproach and resentment.

One evening he went out in a boat with a few others, to fish. It was a thing he had liked to do as a boy; the air of the sea, the lift and fall of the boat, above all the strange and unfamiliar look the land had from the water, these used to calm him always; it was not to catch fish that he would go, it was to taste contentment.

This evening he went out to catch fish. They rowed out a little distance from the shore and then threw over their lines. But the fish were not taking well that evening and after trailing his line for some time without getting a nibble Murdo turned round from his seat in the bow to see what the others were doing.

The black curve of the gunwale drew a sharp line round the four of them in the boat, hemming them in from the waters without. All around was the grey expanse of the sea plain lifting up on end, and inside, in the black shell of the boat, were the four of them together, himself and three others. In this way there is less air for each man on the sea than on land.

Before him sat Murdo the Flea, a round black lump of a back with a raw red neck above it that thickened and thickened again as he lazily drew the oars. Beyond him old Coinneach Mac Dhonnchaidh 'Ic Alasdair Ruaidh was leaning over the edge, holding his line. The snout of his sailor's cap hid the top of his face and the beard hid his chin; only the end of his nose was visible and his mouth, and the tongue quivering about behind an occasional yellow tooth in his lower jaw. There was nothing in his mouth but slavers and nothing in his head but the fish he was maybe going to catch. He was in his place there; between himself and the outside there was no secret struggle but the peace of the first beginning or of a won battle; he was content. As he crouched there the outlines of his hunched body repeated the curves of the hills in a way no wise displeasing to look at as a thing in itself, and his lined face looking down into the water reflected the grey of the sea. In the stern sprawled the Bradan. Nothing was to be seen of his head or his narrow shoulders, only the seat of his trousers sticking up and his reedy legs twining together, but his mouth would be sagging intently open over the side where his red and bony hands would be tit-titting at the line. For him also there was no doubting. For answer the Bradan sprawled his ungainly form contentedly upon the earth and in the face of the riddle of the universe turned up a shameless arse.

A red serpent of anger began to twist and coil in the middle of his breast. Like a red-hot wire it writhed within him. Looking at them there, cooped up with him in the boat, he hated them, hated them. He suddenly hated them so that he trembled with the anger that was on him. He hated them so that his hands shook visibly, and the intensity of his anger frightened himself. The unbroken face of the sea around the boat lay on him with a feeling like suffocation. Never, he vowed, never again, of his own will, would he shut himself up in the same room with compliance or satisfaction. He feared lest they should notice his emotion and could hardly wait till it was time to turn the nose of the boat towards the shore.

In the end it was he that proposed that since the fish were not taking they should return to land, and all the way he rowed in a fury.

After that he withdrew himself even more from any dealings with the people of the place, and with such a surly grace that even the most long-suffering of them began of their own will to avoid him. And his visits to Mexico's continued. There was some slackening of them when the harvest was claiming his attention, to get any of it in dry at all between the cold showers that came slashing down at the back end of that year, but when the winter was once in he was hardly ever out of the place whenever it would be open, and scarcely the spring-work itself when the time came made any difference.

2

It was almost a year after his mother's death, in another June, that he was sitting one evening in the kitchen, by the side of the fire. Outside the window behind him a warm mist was distilling itself in a thin, quiet rain.

At his side was the table, with the dishes and remains of two meals sitting about on it. He ran his eye over them with an expression of disgust. Some of the dishes had been sitting there since he had his breakfast, never a dish-clout near them, pushed aside to make room for the next meal. At the place he had just risen from himself there was some appearance of order. Without thinking about it he would be always setting things right, putting the cup straight in the saucer, the knife at right angles to the table edge and so on—as fastidious as a cat. But where she had been sitting everything was here and over there. The saucer was half full of tea which had soaked into a piece of bread that was lying in it. The cup sat on the table, the spoon sticking out of it and the mark of a mouth on the rim, and all round that place the white oilcloth was marked with brown rings where at different times she had set down her cup between her noisy wauchts. There were other things on the oilcloth too, spilt food, the rinds of cheese, jam, unwashed spoons, pieces of biscuit the baby had chewed into a sticky pulp. He gave a grimace of disgust as his eye fell on the things she had just been using before she went out. She had stood at the table and plastered her face as she was always doing with whatever it was she had in these little smelly boxes, stood over the dishes making faces at herself in the little mirror she held in her hand, and when she had done she put the things down on the table among the dishes and spilt food. Then she had gone out to visit her mother, so she said, leaving him sitting there to watch the baby.

The baby was sitting opposite him now, in a high chair at the other side of the fire. His face was smeared with some brown matter, and he was contentedly slobbering something which he clutched in his two hands. The loud slupp-

slupping noise he was making caused Murdo to writhe with acute discomfort. He stuck his hands down into his pockets, sliding his hips forward in his chair and glaring across at the child. He, however, paid no attention, but went on with his loud and cheerful slobbering, squinting down at the sticky matter he was holding to his face.

Murdo had never been able to stand the child. He was now near a year old and very big and fat, so fat indeed that he had made practically no attempt as yet to walk or even to crawl. His occupation was to sit about and slobber food. He was always slupp-slupp-slupping at something, seizing it in his fat fingers with ferocity, glaring at it with lust and forcing it into his gaping mouth, emitting his beast-like noises, so that it was revolting even to look at him. The result of all this eating was that he was completely buried in fat, a mere mass of white creesh. When his mother attended to him, he lying belly downward on her knees, from pink buttocks to ankles he was fold upon fold of soft flabb. Worst of all was his gross and shameless resemblance to his grandfather. He was Mr. John MacIver over again, his look, his skin, the pig's eyes of him, his ways even. It was an obscenity. It was unnatural. It smelt of incest. It was also a perpetual insult to Murdo himself—in his own house, bearing his name, the incarnation of all that he despised as stupid and vulgar and beast-like. He had never been able to stand this beast-like in man. When the child was born he had been deathly sick for a whole day. He had gone away from the house and busied himself outside on purpose to be out of the road, and only returned when he expected it would all be over. But apparently the birth had been unduly prolonged. He was approaching the house when he heard it, and he ran immediately round to the byre and stood there, retching, leaning against the wall and trembling from head to foot. Later, the nurse had come out and beckoned him and he had gone inside. She was lying in the bed, sweating, a smile of heavenly content upon her face. It was the same moist look that will be in the eyes of a cow when she looks round at you after she has dropped her calf, and he had gone out and been sick again. He could not help it.

It was long since the woman had affected him with a kind of disgust. She was grown monstrously fat now, so that it was a sight to see her moving about the place, her stockings wrinkled and twisted on her legs, her hair in disorder, fat bulging above and below wherever a garment was tied. Only once since her child was born had he slept in the bed with her, and that was one night he had taken a little more than was customary with him. In the morning she had raised herself on an elbow and leant over him, passing her fingers through his hair and smiling down into his face. He overcame his dislike and submitted to it thinking that he had been too hard on the woman and that maybe after all she was fond of him in her own flabby way. But while he was waiting for his breakfast his eye happened to fall on one of the little paper books she was always reading, lying open on a chair where she had thrown it the night before.

> " Gladys leant over him on the grass, leaning on one dimpled elbow. And while she gazed down at him with the eyes of love she passed her slender white fingers through his hair. Her man! . . ."

So the creature had been play-acting after all! It was the heroine of a sixpenny novel she was all the time! He had cursed and thrown the thing on the fire; and that strangely enough had been the cause of the only real quarrel they might be said to have had together. The burning of her love-story was the only thing since she came to his house that had ever made her angry. Nothing he had been able to say had ever succeeded in piercing through the thick wall of fat that overlay her pitiable little brain. She simply gave her head a little toss and went on as before, secure in her rôle of heroine of a sixpenny love-story, and no doubt in her stupid head she even managed to feel contempt for him, the mere man who could not be expected to understand the sacred mysteries of the female heart. It was in her rôle of sixpenny heroine that she would always be speaking in that silly mincing English. The Gaelic was not good enough for her—although she would always be more at home in it, and her English was very bad. He himself if he had to speak to anyone at all would always use the Gaelic, and it was the Gaelic he would always speak in the house, while she, the daughter of a bitch, would reply in her English. It was a grotesque situation. A woman going about his house speaking in the language of a sixpenny love-story written by some amadan of a Sasunnach. All her little phrases were learned out of that. She spoke about her father as " My Dad " or " Poor Dad." Imagine Mr. John MacIver as " My Dad! " As if a fat little pig should up on its hind legs and speak about " My Dad " in the English, instead of " The Old Boar " in its own language. It was in the Beurla she spoke to the child too, cooing and mooing over him in the manner of a sixpenny heroine and saying " The little darlingums! " and " Mother's lovely pet! " So that the first words the brat had attempted were English words.

He leant over and spat violently into the fire.

The noise startled the child, and caused him to drop the sticky matter he had been holding to his mouth. He opened his eyes wide and gazed round him for a moment in an uncertain way. Then he began to howl. Of all noises Murdo could not abide this. It caused him to lose control of himself at once, set every nerve in his body jumping and jangling. He sat in his chair with his hands in his pockets, looking helplessly at the child, hissing desperately through his teeth in an effort to quiet him. But he only howled the more. He opened his mouth very wide and *bawled*, birsing the noise out of him with all his strength until his eyes were screwed up out of sight and his face was a shapeless pink thing on which the veins of his brow stood out a dark blue. The noise of his bawling rose up from him and twined about in the corners of the room. Then it came trickling down out of the air on to a spot on the top of Murdo's head. Finally it was like thin, red-hot wires jerking about among his brains. He moved about on his chair and glanced despairingly at the clock. Half-past eight. The woman had said she would be back by eight. She must be on her road by now. He waited another moment, until he could stand it no longer and got up to his feet.

At the door he turned round. "You'll be all right there until your mother will come," said he.

The child stopped his crying suddenly and looked round at him, the tears running on his cheeks. Then, as if he had understood what was said, his under-lip began to quiver and he burst out roaring again, if anything louder than before.

Murdo contracted his brows as if in pain and went out of the room, shutting the door behind him. He looked up the road to see if the woman was coming but the mist was so low that he could not see the length of the bridge. He set off walking, intending to meet her and hasten her on her way, at the same time escaping the more quickly himself.

But when he reached the end of the path that led up to Mr. John MacIver's house she had not yet appeared and he decided that since he was so near he would just go into Mexico's and give himself a drink.

Usually he stood alone at his end of the counter paying no heed to what the rest of the men in the room were doing and not even giving an ear to their conversation. And no doubt he would have done the same on this night had he not thought he heard a familiar name mentioned among them. They were standing not far from him and one of them had been reading a bit out of a paper which he was now putting down on the counter. Murdo recognised the *North Star*.

" That's true," said one of them, in reply to what another had said. " They're telling me it's a clever lad that's in him."

" Clever indeed," says another. " It's a fine head that he has."

" A fine head," says a third. " It's a long time since this place sent his like down yonder."

That was all there was of it. One of them took his pipe out of his mouth and spat on the floor, and then began to speak on another subject. But Murdo had seen him glance quickly in his direction as he was bending down to spit and he was in a fever to know if they had really been talking about the man whose name he thought he had heard, and if so what was in that paper.

He called for another glass of whisky and stood before it, shuffling from foot to foot. After a time the men moved to the door, leaving him alone in the room with Mexico, who plunged their glasses into a tank of water below the counter and began to polish them with a cloth. Then a voice shouted in the back room and Mexico went out to see what was wanted. The paper was still lying on the counter where the men had put it down and Murdo went immediately over to it.

It was not difficult to find what he wanted. In the column of local news was a heading:

"—— MAN'S SUCCESS"

He ran his eye rapidly over it in fear lest someone should come in and catch him there.

> "In the recent examinations in —— in Glasgow University, Roderick Urquhart has passed with distinction in ——. Mr. Urquhart is a native of ——, and is one of the most distinguished students of his year. He intends to ——."

Mexico's step sounded outside the door. Murdo went quickly back to his place, and when the man came in he was standing there drinking his whisky. He called for another glass, and after that another. He was there until it was time to shut the door, drinking steadily, and when anyone picked up that paper the muscles of his neck tightened suddenly and he looked the other way. When he got outside he was drunk, a rare thing with him, for usually he only drank enough for his purpose and then went away.

To-night he took a long time to get home, wandering about the sides of the road muttering to himself, " I am a native of——I am a native of ——."

He had forgotten, however, why he was drunk.

When he got near his house he stopped in the road to listen. There seemed to be some sort of a commotion going on in there. There was a sound of women's voices and one of them appeared to be screaming. He staggered up to the house and took a step into the kitchen. He had an impression that the whole room was full of women's faces and suddenly one of them, Annie MacIver's, broke from the rest and rushed at him, claws outstretched, her mouth wide open and she screaming in a way he thought at the time was insane. Before she could reach him some of them caught her and pulled her back, but she still struggled to be at him, screeching out " There he is! He did it! Look at him! He's drunk! "

" I may be drunk," mouthed Murdo, in her own English, swaying dangerously in the doorway, " I may be drunk, but I am not so drunk that I cannot see you are behaving yourself in a manner not compatible with the dignity that should belong to a human being."

"And remember," says he, attempting to draw himself up, "always remember that I am a native of—of Hell."

He turned and went stumbling up the creaking stairs into his room, where he threw himself down heavily on top of the bed.

The noise continued to come up from below, women's voices speaking all at once, and one voice above them all, screaming. He put the pillow over his ear and tried to shut it out. Then, suddenly, there was a change. The screaming stopped and was followed by a loud scuffling of feet. The jabbering of the other voices, all together, grew louder. A chair crashed over on to the floor. Then of a sudden the feet and the voices were outside and retreating rapidly up the road.

He raised himself on his elbow and listened, looking stupid and bewildered. Then he shrugged his shoulders and fell back again on the bed.

VI

MURDO put up a weary hand and pushed back the long black hair that was falling over his eyes. Several times he had done the same thing, unconsciously, during the hours he had been sitting there, unmoving, by the empty fireplace. Without looking up he put out a hand towards the glass that sat on the corner of the table beside him. His knuckles came against it and it fell over on its side with a faint clink. He looked up at it dully, without interest. Once or twice in short jerks it rolled to and fro on the surface of the table, and then after a slight pause fell over the edge and smashed to pieces on the floor. He stared down sideways at the fragments lying here and there. It had not occurred to him to stop it before it fell.

He turned round towards the fireplace and his chin sank as if he were about to fall again into the dull stupor he had been in for hours, but almost immediately he raised his head and gazed with a sodden eye round the room in which, thanks to the heavy clouds that covered the sky, the shadows were already beginning to gather. For a time his eyes rested on the table on which the dishes were still sitting as they had been for the last ten days. He looked particularly at the piece of soaked bread in the saucer on which a thick mould was growing, and at the bright spot on the shoulder of the black bottle that was reflecting the light from the window at his back. Then his gaze travelled to the bed, where the side-curtains were drawn back and the blankets were in disorder. He thought that he could see among the disorder of the blankets a slight depression, as if the body of a child had been lying there. Suddenly he looked across at the high chair sitting opposite him. It seemed that for the first time he noticed it was empty. On the floor beside it lay a child's shoe from which the button was missing, and beside that a piece of hard biscuit on one end of which, where it had been chewed and sodden, a mould was also growing. He shuddered violently. Ten days ago he had sat in that very chair looking across at the child sitting opposite by the side of the fire, in which the peats were smouldering redly. The child was crying and the sound that was coming out of its open mouth had annoyed him in such a way that he had got up to go out. He remembered he had turned at the door and said something. What he could not remember, what he would have given anything to remember, was whether he had noticed at that moment, he turning round at the door to say something, that the child was wearing round his shoulders a long white shawl which was trailing over the edge of the chair. Suddenly it seemed to him that he remembered having noticed it, that in fact he had particularly looked at it. He had a clear vision of himself walking up the road that night with that knowledge at the back of his mind. He shuddered violently again. Then he lifted his head and for some minutes remained like that, listening intently. Not a sound. Over the whole place was a stillness, as of death. Not in the house anywhere was there a single noise to remind one that human beings lived or had lived here. It was like a place that humanity had deserted, even to taking their echoes with them. And this silence had brooded there, unbroken, since that night the woman rushed out of the house with her bundle in her arms. After a minute the silence became more than he could endure. Not a board creaked. Not even outside was there any noise to be heard. It began to seem a very long time since he had heard anyone going past upon the road. He wished with fervour that someone would. Suddenly he felt as one might feel who is left behind after the rest of the world is called away to its last judgment. The stir and noise, the friendly noise of men, and then, suddenly, silence, always silence. He could not imagine anything more awful than the situation of that man. Not the company of one human being in his solitude, not one to look him friendly in the eyes, not even one to hate, always silence—a horror! Better a thousand times to share in the condemnation of his fellows, better to roast in hell along with them. But to be cut off alike from their salvation and their damnation—that is the real damnation. What crime could a man have committed to deserve such a doom? He began to feel a prickling at the back of his head, and to tremble again all over. Suddenly he thought he heard a noise. He listened intently. There it was, unmistakably, the sound of a foot on the road, coming his way. He got to his feet and went over to the window. He pushed his head against the side of it and looked up the road as far as he could see. A woman's skirt came in sight. Immediately he thought she might be coming into the shop. He hurried through and set the door ajar so that as she passed she might see it open. Then he went back to his standing-place by the window to watch her. He could see her plainly now. It was Morag Nic Coinnich, an old cailleach with a club-foot and a little less than her share of sense. He used to be a little revolted by that club-foot, but now it seemed to him almost a beautiful deformity. He watched the cailleach hirpling along the road, watched her almost with eagerness. When she was almost opposite the house he was holding his breath with excitement. When she was opposite the door of the shop he was getting ready to go there in order to serve her. Now, he thought, now she will turn! But the woman went hirpling past without pausing in her irregular gait. He was almost sure, however, that she had quickened her step the slightest bit and that he had seen her shoot a flickering glance at the house in the by-going.

For a few minutes after she was out of sight he remained staring out of the window with the shadow of his expectant look still upon his face. Then he turned again into the room. He saw that the bottle on the table was still half full and went slowly over to the back place to get another glass. He was about to take it off the shelf when he stopped and began looking at the floor. Several times he drew the back of his hand, wearily, across his eyes and then as if he had forgotten what he had come for he turned and went back again to the window.

He stood there a while looking out in a befuddled sort of way and then turned and went towards the door, walking like a man in his sleep. When he reached it, however, something seemed to strike him. He turned and looked for a long time at the high chair by the side of the dead fire, blinking his bleared eyes as if he were trying to call something to mind. Finally he shook his head sadly to and fro as if in grievous doubt and went out to the door of the shop where he stood looking up the road towards the town.

He was there maybe a quarter of an hour, standing motionless with his eyes turned towards the houses he could dimly see through the falling dusk. The people seemed all to be asleep, but once he saw a man pass like a shadow across a gable-end. He started to walk slowly up the road, seeming to forget he had left the door open behind him, and although in fact the rain had ceased for some time he absently turned up the neck of his jacket and buttoned it across his chest.

As he was crossing the bridge the willows suddenly began to rustle loudly and a cool wind blew in his face. He walked up the slight ascent and slowly along the street, between the houses. At one point he noticed a group of men talking together and immediately his step became brisker.

" It's soft," said he as he came up to them.

" It is soft," said one of them, and the way he looked round and quickly turned away again struck like a blow on his heart.

He wandered listlessly along until he came to the end of the street, the one street that was in it. All the time the wind was freshening out of the north, and by the time he got to the last houses it was blowing a half-breeze. Outside the last house of all Lovat's van was standing at the side of the road, and the door at one side was hanging open. As the wind blew it waved slowly to and fro, creaking dismally. For some reason a lump gathered in his throat at this point and he felt he wanted to burst into tears.

He turned back along the street, his hands in his pockets, his jacket buttoned, his shoulders hunched up and his collar round his ears, walking very slowly as if reluctant to leave the neighbourhood of the houses. Only in one window was there a light. He stood a long time leaning against the wall of the house opposite looking at the yellow square; it seemed to fascinate him. Twice a shadow was thrown on the blind. Then at last the light flickered and went out, and the street was plunged in darkness. He turned and walked rapidly away, with bent head, his heavy footsteps thrown back from the walls with an empty sound.

When he got back to the house it was quite dark and the wind had increased into what threatened to become a gale. He closed the door behind him and went into the kitchen. For a while he stood just inside the door, in the dark. Then he began to move round the room, feeling before him with his hands, seeking matches in order to light the lamp. In his fumbling he happened to stumble against the high chair. Immediately he leapt backwards, letting a grunt as if of terror out of his throat, and for some minutes he stood there staring before him into the darkness, afraid to move, and the knees trembling under him. In jumping back he had put up an arm before his face as if to shield himself from a blow.

When he came to himself he went over to the door and opened it as if to go out. Then he had another idea. He closed the door and felt his way carefully through to the back place where he took a glass from the shelf and returning to the kitchen poured out and drank half a tumbler of the neat whisky. Then he re-filled the glass and sat down in his chair.

When the thin pale light of dawn came hesitating through the window it fell on the back of the man sitting hunched up there, his arms hanging by his sides, his chin on his breast, his black hair hanging over his eyes. And beyond him it fell also on the other chair, facing now into the room, and on the patches on its side where the paint had swollen up in blisters.

This state of affairs continued for several days more. Most of that time he spent in the kitchen, sitting with the bottle before him, for the most part in a kind of stupor. Not once did he go upstairs to his bed; the room downstairs seemed to fascinate him in some way, so that whenever he came into the house he must needs go there. Occasionally, at irregular intervals, he remembered to eat, and after the first day he regularly performed certain daily tasks such as feeding the hens and attending to the cow. He could not himself understand why he should do this; it appeared to him strange at the time.

If he was not sitting there in the kitchen he would be rambling about on the moor at the back of the town, and every day about night he would go up to the street. He stood about between the houses, looking at the windows, and when the last lamp had been extinguished he turned and came home. He would never return home while there was one light burning in the street.

2

One afternoon he had been rambling about on the moor and came about evening near some houses at the back of the town. There were some children playing there and he stood to watch them. This was a thing he had done several times recently. For some reason children seemed to attract him, and he would draw as near to them as he could in order to watch them unobserved and they at their play. He was quite near to these but so intent were they upon their game, running about and laughing, that they did not see him. For some minutes he stood watching them, a smile upon his face. Then suddenly in the course of the game two of them broke from the others and rushed headlong in his direction. They were almost upon him, about to run against him, when one of them raised his head and saw him standing there. He let a shriek out of his mouth as if he had seen a taibhse and rushed away in the opposite direction, and the other, looking up, screamed also and ran after him. The rest as they passed joined in the running and the whole company careered round the corner shouting.

After they were gone out of sight and hearing Murdo still stood where he was. The smile slowly ebbed from his face and his shoulders and his hands began to droop. At last he began walking forward, his chin on his breast and a look of sadness and suffering in the sunken eyes.

He went past the houses and up the north road. At a certain point there for some reason or other he quitted the road and turned to the left along the track that led round Strongorm to the four crofts of Cladach. He seemed to do this naturally, without looking up, and as he stumbled along the stony track his eyes were still fixed on the ground. Just before he reached the crofts he turned again to the left and scrambled down to the shore. There he stood where the after-wave washed up almost to the toes of his boots; whispering among the pebbles it was with a pleasant, rhythmic sound. The sheen of the sun-sparkle on the sea before him glittered in his eye, blinding him, and he suddenly realised that for a long time he had been conscious of the sun's heat lying on him with a sense of oppression.

Near by the *Faoileag* was drawn up and lying on her side, Iain Sisealach's boat, he that was mother's-brother to Annie MacIver. He went across to an overhanging bank behind him and drew from under it the oars. Then he pushed out the boat and began to row out in the direction of Eilean Sona,* the sun striking warm over his left shoulder. When he had rowed a bit he happened to raise his eyes and saw a woman standing on the green braes above Cladach looking at him under her hand. He gave an exclamation of annoyance and pulled the harder on the oars.

Twice before he reached the island he had to stop rowing on account of fatigue. For about two weeks he had eaten only irregularly, and

* Eilean Sona is a green, rocky islet in the Minch, frequented by great numbers of sea-birds.

then but little, and now the exertion of rowing put a sort of nervous trembling on him.

When he had got out of the boat he stood a while with the rope in his hand as if in some perplexity, looking first at the rocks and then at the sea. Finally, as if he had come to a decision, he anchored the *Faoileag* in the little inlet that was there, the only landing-place on the island, and set off up the rocks and over the grassy banks. At almost every step the sea-birds rose up about him screaming, and some of the young ones running swiftly away over the grass.

Eventually he took his stand with his elbow leaning on a ledge of rock that overhung the mouth of a deep cleft running into the land. At regular intervals some black rocks beyond him reared their fearsome, dripping heads above the green water and swiftly withdrew again under the advancing wave. The water struck the face of the rock he stood on with a force that made it tremble, and each time the gouts of spray rose high above his head glancing silver as they sparkled in the rays of the westering sun. A long time he stood looking fixedly down into the cleft below him. Fifty times he saw it fill with seething, foam-flecked water, but particularly he watched it when, swift and smooth, terribly smooth and swift and relentless, that water ran back, pulling the loose rocks with it into the heaving sea. He stood there looking over, braced and rigid and motionless, like a piece of stone, while the silence settled round him and no sound was to hear but the boom and crash of waves and ever and again that terrible sucking noise beneath him as the water ran glass-smooth out of the gullet.

Gradually he became aware in his intentness of a white speck in the corner of his eye, just outside his vision, a white speck that moved occasionally. Without moving his head he slowly raised his eyes and there, just under the curve of his eyebrows, was a seagull standing alone on the top of a rock, watching him. He regarded it a while with bloodshot eyes that had had a queer, fixed look in them when he raised them from the cleft below. Then he lifted his head and a very strange sight met his gaze. The place where he was standing was below the general level of the island and everywhere he looked, from within twenty yards of where he was right up to the jagged sky-line, was a great company of seagulls, each standing motionless on the top of a rock, tier on tier, a seagull to a rock, and all looking steadily at him—as if they knew what was passing in his head and were waiting expectantly to see what his next step would be. Above him to his right great cliffs towered high over his head and there also, along the line of the sky, sat the seagulls in a ragged row, looking down at him. He began to feel self-conscious at suddenly finding himself observed by so many pairs of knowing eyes, and turned again to look where the water was running out below him. But while his eyes had been turned away a huge wave had been advancing, rising out of the middle of the sea and heaving itself towards the shore. Even as he looked round it crashed against the rock beneath him and the spray from it rising high in the air fell down upon him in a drenching cataract. When the cold spray splashed suddenly on his face, unexpected, he leapt back several paces, letting out an exclamation, and stood there shaking at the knees. The seagulls rose in a white cloud. But if they rose it was not far, each one rose about a yard above his rock, crying out with derisive laughter and flapping his wings, then they all settled back in their places again. There was a flutter of feathers and a low sardonic chuckling among them as they settled down to watch him, ringing him round. Looking round upon them Murdo could not but believe they had actually been laughing at his expense, because he, *he*, had been afraid of only a splash or two of the water. They seemed determined to watch the thing out. Having got one of their two-legged enemies alone, cut off from his fellows and defenceless, they seemed determined to make the most of the game. For some reason the cold hardness there had been in his breast seemed to melt at this point. He felt a lump in his throat and the warm tears gathered behind his tired eyes. He was suddenly overcome with fatigue and leant back against the rocky ledge. The gulls were now standing motionless in their places again, each on his rock, but all at once he was aware of one, much nearer than the rest, that seemed to be moving about. He looked at it and saw that it had a broken leg. Now deformity of any kind had always affected him very strongly. With a deformity, he had always thought, life would indeed not be worth living. He suddenly felt a wave of pity for the gull, so that it seemed that in a moment he must burst into tears. But the gull was walking about opposite him, and because it limped and flapped its wings occasionally it looked happier than the others in a grotesque, one-legged kind of way. He looked again and saw that this particular bird was apart from the rest, by itself. They did not seem to concern themselves with it at all and he supposed that because of the broken leg it had they had cut it off and no longer considered it one of themselves; he knew that animals did that. But the gull itself was limping back and fore and seemingly unconcerned, and because of its hirple and the way it flapped its wings as it walked it even looked happier than the others in its own grotesque way, pleased with itself, almost gay. A while he watched it, drawing his brows together as if in thought. Then he looked up at the blue sky, and the white clouds hanging in it, and at the fountains of glittering spray spurting up in the face of the westering sun, and at the grassy banks of Eilean Sona that are of a particular bright green colour. Finally he got to his feet with a weary gesture and walked away from that place, the gulls screaming and wheeling over his head. And if he was not smiling as he rowed home the strained look had at least passed from the sunken eyes of him and the lines about the face had relaxed their tension.

He pulled up the boat without being observed and scrambled on to the road. However, twice before he reached home he had to stop and rest himself, and he was staggering with fatigue when he sat down in the kitchen to resume his vigil.

But for some reason his heart was lighter, or at least less heavy than it had been before, not so heavy now that it could not be borne. His feet trod the earth, under the same sky for all, and every day with its own share of things to do.

3

On a day, in the middle of an early harvest, that Murdo came home about the greying of evening, and he tired and the feet of him heavy and a dull pain behind the shoulders of him from working all the day in his strips of field. But it was the pleasant, healthy fatigue that was on him, and the great hunger in his belly. The veins that spread and branched in his body, net-meshing through his trunk and limbs, throbbed with a regular rhythm, and the warm blood running its circuit through him distended those on his arms and hands that had been swinging about, and on the calves and the inside of his legs that had been standing and stepping. As he came up to the house he still felt along the soles of his feet the sharp-pointed yellow stubble breaking and crunching under the stiff leather of his boots.

He threw his jacket on the bed and sat down in his chair to rest himself a moment before he would get up and prepare his evening meal. The veins showed big and full on his wrists, which he rested on his knees, and on the backs of his hands when he turned them over. Through the little vessels in his brain went the blood to the thrusting rhythm of the òran buana, the reaping song that the muscles at the back of his tongue had been singing all the afternoon, interminably. He wondered, it seemed to him very seriously, how he was ever going to prepare and eat his supper to that rhythm. He might put the spoon round his teacup to it, but his jaws would not chew to it. He tried to stop that song going through his head by starting up another, but to his surprise he found he could not remember another. All the tunes he ever knew eluded him. Odd phrases came to his mind of the words of other songs and he found himself trying to fit them to the tune of the òran buana. He was exasperated to find he could not do it. Then he remembered that was not what he was trying to do at all, but to get that tune out of his head. He decided to get up and prepare his food but discovered a difficulty he could not get over—he could not rise out of the chair to the time of the swish-swish of the swinging scythe. Then he surrendered himself to the rhythm of it and the song went loud through his head, a forward push and a backward swing, a forward push and a backward swing, with energy in the forward thrust and the cutting edge meeting the crisp oat-stalks with a sound like the twang of a bow-string. Finally he began to sing the words softly, yielding his nerves and muscles gladly to its rhythm, smiling a little smile to himself because the song was a very beautiful song. His shoulders swayed slightly so that their movement was almost perceptible. He must really have been very tired that evening.

At the last it was not his own will that broke the spell but the thing that saved him from sitting there for the rest of his life singing a reaping song was her step that he heard on the road outside.

He did not look round when she came softly into the room but when she sat down on a low chair at the other side of the fire, the chair that had been his mother's, he looked across at her. She had not taken off her things and under the brim of her hat the eyes looked out with a very sad expression. There were deep dark lines under them and there were lines, too, drawn at the sides of the mouth. A look in the eyes as of suffering, a hunted look almost, put him in mind of what two women had been saying to each other in the shop a few weeks before, and he with his ear to the half-open door upstairs.

" If she had not lost her head entirely," says

Sìne Ruairidh, " and gone dancing round the room, and she screaming at the top of her voice. . . ."

He got to his feet and stepped across the room to go into the back place, but when he was just behind her he stopped and put his hand down with a firm grip on her left shoulder. She put up her right hand and grasped it, pressing it suddenly to her cheek, and he could tell by the warm wetness that came over the back of it that she was weeping. There was no play-acting with her now. That was not the action of a sixpenny Sasunnach heroine but a plainly sincere gesture, graceful and from the heart. For the first time in her life maybe, she was herself. He took pity to her.

He stood in the back place and drank a glass of water and when he came into the kitchen again she had already taken off her things and was busying herself about the room.

" An d'ith thu fhathast, a Mhurchaidh ? " said she.

" I did not eat," said Murdo, stepping over to make a fire.

During the meal nothing was said between them. She indeed scarcely so much as lifted her eyes from her plate but he looked up at her occasionally, and as he looked at her sitting there at the other side of his table the expression in his eyes might have been of gratitude.

When he had taken a short turn on the road to assure himself the good weather was to last at least another day he came back into the house. A while he stood at the foot of the stairs as if undecided. Then he sighed and shrugging his shoulders went into the kitchen and closed the door behind him.

VII

AFTER a notable hard winter the spring broke early.

When it was but a few days old Murdo went up one day as was his custom to the fang where his sheep were. Leaning his elbows on the bar of the fang he fell to regarding the creatures, looking with solemn eyes under the snout of his bonnet. It afforded him some quiet pleasure. One of them that would raise its head would include him in the mild look it cast around, and go back to its browsing as if assured that everything was as it should be and in place. Not with the sheep's acceptance, however, his mind went through the days, but walking leisurely, looked with even eyes at the gone things it saw there.

When he had been standing yonder for a time, he began to be aware of the day around him. He raised his head and looked before him towards the hills. He drew breath, and sighed. "Nach i tha blàth!" he said aloud.

There was a thin gauze of mist over the hills and the mountain moors that came right down to within a yard or two of where he was, a light flimsy thing that might have been of the air or from the earth itself. Still and silent it lay, this mist, but now and again it would be drawn aside to reveal a hill shoulder or a patch of moorland and suddenly he was feeling a great desire to walk off into it, towards the hills. His second thought was to resist the impulse, but he thought better of that again and yielded to it.

When he began to walk his dog ran out before him, barking over his shoulder and running along waving in the air his feathery tail. Murdo, falling into his stride, regarded the animal thoughtfully and began to knit his brows. There had been two young dogs that Domhnull Bàn offered him. One that sprang about and barked was of a light brown colour that instantly took his fancy. The other sat on the ground with his head on one side, drawing his paw along his nose. He was black all over except for a brown dot above each eye. Murdo looked at him, snapped his fingers and called him, " Lachie! " It was only this moment that he understood why he had done so. The dog was in fact almost an exact copy of that other Lachie, an old, dignified fellow, that had allowed him to embrace him, he remembered, when he was a little child. He frowned, wondering if he would choose so again if he had the choosing now.

Meanwhile he did not observe how far he was going or in what direction. The open weather had come but a few days before and the moor was seeping. The mist retreated before him and closed again behind, leaving always a circle of black sodden peat and brown heather tufts, himself leaping in the middle of it. At last of a sudden he found himself over the ankles in a bog, and saw bog-water gleaming before him. That brought him to himself. He realised that for what seemed a very long time he had been leaping and louping and splashing his way across the moor at a great rate, as if he were really going somewhere. He glanced round and saw that just beyond him, to his left, the ground appeared to rise into the mist. He made for that, jumping from ploc to ploc, and when he had scrambled up on to a rock turned round to consider his position. He was daubed with wet soil to above the knees so that it would be absurd to return by the way he had come, across the moor. But he had come across it more or less in a straight line, or so he thought, and therefore if he kept along the high ground, going towards the right, he ought to come out above Torr where he would strike the road. If he had gauged his position right there ought to be a path somewhere above him used by the Sasunnaich when they came up to shoot at the deer. He turned and began to clamber up among the rocks and heather, the dog panting at his heels.

But when he had been climbing for a time and no path appeared he began to wonder if perchance he had not been mistaken as to his position.

Eventually he did come on a path, but it was coming from the left and running straight ahead, rising all the time. He followed it, hoping only that before long the mist would lift and reveal the country.

When he had been going along that stony path for a time, taking to the heather at the side now and again to avoid the pools of water that lay in the middle of it, and always rising in the thickening mist, he noticed all at once that the dog was acting in a peculiar manner. He had stiffened himself up and was sniffing suspiciously round, and the hair along the back of him standing up on end. He chirruped to the animal, patted his head, and walked on. But suddenly he himself had the feeling he was not alone up there, and, as if he wanted proof, almost immediately there came, loud and clear, out of the mist above him, the clink of an iron heel striking against a rock. He wheeled right about in his tracks and there on the path, only a few yards from him, looming large out of a sudden lightening of the mist, was the figure of a man. So silent and motionless was he that he had the air of having been there a long time, and yet Murdo himself must have passed that spot less than a moment before. For the space of several seconds they stared in silence at each other; then the mist drifted slowly between them. Murdo turned at once and walked off up the path, and as he did so there came again from above him the same clinking noise as of an iron heel striking against a rock.

He had recognised the man; at least he thought he had. He was a big fair man from Baile na Creige that he had seen now and then in the town and once or twice at the Sacraments—when he still went to them; and the man, or men, up on the hill were doubtless from the same place. He had no need to ask either what they were doing there. He knew well enough it would be the whisky, and he had walked away at once because he did not wish to seem to be prying. It was no affair of his. He was aware too that it might be unpleasant if not indeed dangerous itself to let the Baile na Creige men think he was prying. If instead of himself it had been Mr. Billingstink, the Sasunnach exciseman, that had come upon them he would have run the risk of at least a broken head.

But it was not the meeting of the man in the mist that made him draw his brows together as he strode up the path, the dog at his heels, growling still; it was the fact that the path was taking him steadily higher and he knew by the glimpses he got of the chasm below him on his right that he did not know at all where he was. Then the mist lifted a little again and snow appeared a short distance above him. This was more than he had expected, although he knew the snow was still low on the hills. He was on the point of turning back the way he had come at the risk of offending the Baile na Creige men when the path suddenly dipped down and vanished into the mist below.

For about a mile he strode rapidly along the track that wound steeply down the hillside.

Then he passed through a little wood of birch and hazel, crossed a plank bridge over a roaring cataract of brown, foaming water, and came to a stand on a level place where the green grass was soft under his feet. He knew where he was now. He was at the mouth of a glen they called Gleann Dà Loch.

This glen is about six miles long and has in it two lochs. The first, about three miles long, has level grassy banks of fertile land; the second, higher up and about a mile in length, has rocky shores all covered with trees. Once there had been twenty or thirty families living in the glen, but they had all been driven out about his grandfather's time.

Even as that thought was in his head the mist began to lift again and a great black structure loomed suddenly beside him. He looked at it and saw that it was not such a terrible big structure at all, but that merely, unknown to himself, he had been standing near the stone gable of the last house in the glen. The one gable was all there was of it. The mist continued to thin itself, until the near end of the big loch came in sight, and the sun must have been shining above it because there was a sheen as of silver on the face of the water and a gleaming gauze of mist also over the grassy banks. Only at one other place was there sign of habitation and that was a foot of crumbling wall on a little knoll by the loch side. No sound was to hear but the dull rumbling noise of the torrent to the left. No sound at all.

On a sudden he became very sad because of the people of the glen. He saw it there as it had been, a little world in itself, savouring its own joys, tholing its own peculiar sorrows. There had been old people in it, old men and women with a lifetime's memories and the full of their heads of old songs and sgeulachd—what talk and what singing on winter evenings by the lamplight while the moon shone outside. There had been young men and lasses, and they at the courting on summer evenings in the woods of lapping water. There had been little children running about the grassy braes and knolls, shouting to each other in their play. The voices of little children calling in the musical Gaelic tongue. But that day was no more. Instead was the light on the loch face, the moss-grown mounds among the braes, and silence.

For some reason he kept coming back to the thought of the children. It was painful the way his throat swelled when he thought of them running about there, the bare legs twinkling.

Suddenly it seemed to him that *there* if you want it is an ordering for the world. How else should the world be ordered but that little children should run barelegged about the braes and the grassy knolls shouting out of the gladness of their hearts ? What else is there that should take first place to that in the ruling of men's affairs ? What else, in the name of God ?

He felt that he could not bear to stand longer

there, therefore he turned and strode off along the path that led away to the right up into the mist, five miles across the hills to Torr. He walked rapidly up the winding path, his chin on his breast, and when he had gone three miles, to the top of the ridge they call the Saddle, he had a sudden impulse to sit down on the cairn of stones that marks the summit. He did not know why he wished to sit down there but the feeling was strong on him, and the strange feeling it was, as if for the time his limbs were not for walking, but only for feeling. For a long time as he walked his senses had been terribly acute. The thaw had come suddenly and a thousand little streams were running through the bogs and down the hill slopes, and it had seemed to him that in the murmuring noise they made, the toraman, he could hear as it were voices talking together, the voices of the people of that place, old men talking together in low tones about some secret matter. Then the sounds grew more distinct so that he thought he could distinguish between them, one here and another there. He thought he heard a freshet start its running on a mountain side ten miles away. Finally it was as if he heard the faint noise of the snows melting on all the bens of Alba. Sitting there he began to think he could distinguish yet another sound, above the loud breathing of the dog at his feet, the little prickling noise of brittle heather points tearing the silky surface of the mist.

It was at that moment that the voice spoke

in his ear out of the mist that ringed him round. It was a voice, very faint and very loud, and a flash of light before his eyes. He sitting there on a cairn of grey, hard, moss-grown stones, his shoulders jutted out broad on either side and the slope of his body inwards to the narrow of his waist, running melodious fire through his limbs and they twanging like string of harp; heart at him bounded in his breast and the rising note of its throb to the pinnacle where the sorrow met gladness in snow heat of inner fire, but outside everything aloft, and his dog looking round at him, it seemed, out of his own eyes. . . .

It was but a flash, and shortly he got to his feet. It occurred to him to say aloud, he standing there (a phrase he had heard with Iain Mór when speaking about a man): *Cha teid rud sam bith a steach ach an rud a bhitheas a stigh cheana; Nothing will go in but the thing that is in.*

As he went stepping down the mountain side, the heart leaping in his breast, there passed through his mind in strange procession a number of pictures out of his own life. He did not seem himself to have anything to do with the calling up or the choosing of these, but simply they seemed to arrange themselves and unroll before his eyes.

First it was Mac Ailein Iain in a pair of yellow boots telling to Iain Mór how that things marched in America in a way that shortly for the satisfying of all his bodily needs man would not require but to press a button or pull a lever. Iain Mór, greatly pleased, nodding his head and saying: *Good for man that the machine will take the toil of labour out of his hands.* And adding: *And well for man also if he will not go but where he may take his soul scatheless.*

Then it was himself standing by an open grave, a cold wind blowing, snowflakes drifting. The black hair of him blew about his eyes. And the first thought in his head was of a million people in Glasgow and the dust flying off them in the tearing haste they were in to put past another piece of life and leaping head first into their graves with arms and legs splayed to the four airts of heaven. And the second thought was of a long column of men marching with rhythmic pace, slowly, over the shoulder of Càrn Bàn, the wind piping a coronach among the trees. And he thinking the beauty of the phrase was of no value because maybe it had none except to the man that would be reading it.

Then it was a winter evening in Glasgow, a book of poems between them, and the priest looking him suddenly in the eyes, a look half scornful and half questioning, and he not knowing how to reply. Remembering now the sad look that was on the priest when he got up and went out the door, and thinking he knew now the cause of his sorrow, he found himself loving that worthy man.

The thought that he had not known how to reply, and he with his eyes turned at that time in the wrong direction altogether, put a stern look on his face for a moment. But by and by, he walking down the hill, he began to smile, then to chuckle, and finally he burst out into loud laughter so that the young dog turned round on the path and looked at him with his head on one side and his tail wagging.

There had come into his head a picture of one million and more of people hanging on to each other's tails and tearing breathlessly round and round in circles gesticulating wildly and shouting to each other: *This is Civilisation! This is Progress! We are getting on!*—That was it! The fools were rushing round and round in circles and did not know it; with the great speed they were going and the terrible intentness that was on them they were even under the impression they were getting somewhere. That for you your Glasgow! Noise there was a-plenty, noise gu leòir, loud and unending and meaningless like the speeches a man will be making when he is drunk. And smoke there was too, nobody would deny them smoke, coming into it at evening the place was as like Hell as any hell on this earth could well be. But the full tale of all the " progress " that was in it was a tale to put a laugh on a man walking with himself on a mountain side in the first warm mist of spring.

So he came down out of the mist and past the pine woods, and Niall Torr, brother of Calum Beag, pausing in the low doorway of his house to watch the splendid figure of a man striding rapidly along the road, his face to the town and a dog trotting at his heels.

2

The promise of an early and open spring was one that was not kept. The day after the day that was mentioned a wind came out of the north, snarling and showing its teeth. Heavy clouds mounted scowling up the sky, drooping and dribbling on the flanks into the flapping blanket of mist that wrapped the bens. Men that had been for the spring work came and stood at their doors and regarded the seeping fields and the rocks and trees looming like their own grey shadows through the sleety rain, and retired, shaking their heads, into the interior of their dwellings. In the street women went to the shops in short dashes from door to door, or rushed out gesticulating and shouting to clusters of damp bairns dawdling home from school with their coats over their heads.

Iain Beag laid down his hammer and turned round into the room. He put his hands into the pockets of his trousers and frowned suddenly.

" Matà," he said, " It was only the spirit of him that was keeping him alive—and when he saw the kind of winter it was like to be—he seemed to think it would not be worth his while to be fighting on."

Kenny Mhurchaidh Bhig glanced at the chair standing empty by the fire, and turning his head aside began fumbling in his pockets for his pipe. Old Coinneach Mac Dhonnchaidh 'Ic Alasdair Ruaidh suddenly made a noise in his throat, and nodded his head. Iain Beag threw a sideways glance at him, but in the lamplight the shining snout of his fisherman's cap was casting a black shadow over his face. Only the end of his tongue could be seen quivering on the floor of his toothless mouth. No one could say whether he had merely made an involuntary, old-man's noise, or had really begun to say something and immediately forgotten what it was.

Kenny Mhurchaidh Bhig cleared his throat. "God is merciful," says he. And added, "'Tis a cold world and a friendless that's in it to-day for the men of his generation."

He lifted his eyes and let them rest on old Coinneach, who sat by his side in a stiff, upright position. His head was bowed and a gnarled hand rested on each knee, and in the shadow cast by his bonnet snout it could not be seen whether his eyes were open or closed.

Iain Beag made a movement of his shoulders and looked away at the fire.

Iain Mór had died at the beginning of winter. Once his had been a great place and a namely for the singing and the dancing and the piping and the telling of tales. Great had been the coming and the going about that place at one time and many the notable gatherings on winter evenings, and the fame of some of the men that would be piping there on evenings of the summer was no small thing. But that was in Iain Mór's day. At that time the plough ran in many an acre now unenclosed and heather grown. At that time many of the glens were full of men. Iain Mór lived to see another day. The day of bracken and the wild creatures of the earth. The march of the years swept them away, by families, townships, glens. The old people looked at the question in each other's eyes, and each man feared to utter what was in his heart; the young looked at the wide moors and the sky, they looked at the falling rain, and kicked their heels and wished themselves out of it. Iain Mór went to his resting grave and the handful that had been around him to the last were broken up. Certain people in the town were heard to rejoice at that same thing.

Kenny Mhurchaidh Bhig cleared his throat loudly in the silence.

"Iain Bhig!" said he, softly.

"*What!*" said Iain, without lifting his eyes from the fire.

"Iain Bhig! *When* will come the end?"

Iain Beag turned as if reluctantly and for a space they looked straight into each other's eyes. Then Iain turned away and looked on the floor. "I'm not understanding you, a Choinnich."

"You're understanding me right enough," said Kenny after a little, with a hint of reproach. Then, lowering his voice, "Iain, little hero, 'tis the curse! The curse that lies on Alba! Will God lift it off us at the last, or will He wipe our tongue and people from the face of the world?"

Iain Beag continued to look on the ground. " What curse are you speaking about ? " he said at last, almost as it were resentfully. " I'm not understanding you." He drew in a breath. " 'Tis that matters take their own course, a Choinnich," he said.

Kenny Mhurchaidh Bhig looked at him intently the space of half a minute, drawing in his lips and lifting his bushy eyebrows. But Iain Beag refused to meet his eye. Kenny looked at the fire, drew up his shoulder and let it fall again. Then he cast a sideways glance at the man leaning against the bench. Finally he stuck his pipe between his short, black teeth and stooped and struck a match against his boot, passing his hand with a forward movement along the sole.

" I'm after—meeting—Donald Mitchell," says he between puffs, in an altered, careless tone. " It seems he's back."

" Domhnull Ailein Camustrolivaig ? " says Iain.

" Hmm—Camustrolivaig."

" What's his news ? " says Iain indifferently, for something to say.

Kenny jerked his wrist and sent the match flying across the room. " Oh, news ! He hadn't any. The poor lad can't speak."

" He can't *speak* ? " said Iain, looking at Kenny and as he said the last word frowning suddenly.

" 'Seadh," says Kenny, looking under his lids at his pipe bowl and throwing off his words with a casual, indifferent air. " 'Seadh—No Gaelic at him—no Gaelic at all at him—It fell out of the mail-car."

Iain Beag turned away with a wearied air and shrugged his shoulders, as if to say he was in no mood for jests. Kenny Mhurchaidh Bhig paid no attention to him. Still looking down from under his lids he leaned back against the wall, uncrossed his legs and crossed them again, and folded his engrained and ragged hands over his waistcoat, settling himself at his ease.

" 'Seadh," says he, when at last it seemed he was comfortable. " 'I am sorry,' says Domhnull. 'I'll have to trouble you to be speaking in the English, Mr. MacKenzie,' says he." He puffed rapidly at his pipe. " 'No trouble at all,' says I, my hand to my bonnet at once. 'That's soon done. And very welcome, to be sure!' " The pipe sang loudly. "A big black hat like a minister's hat he had on his head, and a thin stick under his oxter, and 'spataichean' on the feet at him—quite the Gaelic gentleman."

He got up and stepped across to the fire with the intent look of a man about to spit. He held the pipe aside at the end of his arm, worked his jaws up and down with a chewing motion and made a tube of his pushed-out lips. The spittle went "poof" into the red peats.

He returned to his seat beside old Coinneach. " 'Seadh," says he. " 'Seadh dìreach. It's a dead language that's in the Gaelic. The young people of to-day will see it under the ground."

He spoke in a light tone, as if he were glad of it. And in fact at that moment a sly smile lurked about under his moustache. When he had paused a moment in vain for Iain Beag to raise his eyes or make reply, he looked straight before him and continued in an absent, meditative tone. " There was a man of them in it—however—Murchadh Iain Ruaidh——"

" Murchadh Iain Ruaidh," interrupted Iain Beag, coming to himself.

His stump made a scraping noise on the floor as he drew himself up, shifting his weight. He wrinkled his brows and seemed about to speak.

The door opened. He turned his head, and remained some seconds staring with an amazed face at the man that stood there. Suddenly the pipe slipped from Kenny Mhurchaidh Bhig's fingers and clattered on to the floor. Iain Beag lifted his arm and passed his hand across his bald crown. " Thig a stigh, a Mhurchaidh," he said, uncertainly. He turned to his bench and began tapping with his hammer, stooping over his work.

Murdo came into the room and at the first step the drops flew off the edges of his bonnet. He glanced at the face of Kenny Mhurchaidh Bhig, and it was dark with anger.

" Hail to you, Kenneth," he said, and when the words were still in his mouth he already knew the tone was altogether too jocular.

" Hail to the stranger," replied Kenny, staring rather impudently right into his face and at the last word twisting his mouth.

His hostile eyes followed Murdo as he moved slowly across the floor, affecting not to notice the uneasy silence he had caused to fall. The thick coat that covered him from his ears to his calves made him seem surprisingly bulky, and gave a look almost of the grotesque to the smallish feet and puttee-bound legs appearing below it. He kept a broad back to the company and dawdled across the room. Finally he picked up a feadan from where it lay and idly turned it over in his hand. Bending his head he blew some dust off it. With a sudden vigorous movement he twisted it under his hands, then looking thoughtfully took the naked reed between his lips. The reed squealed startlingly a high-pitched, vulgar defiance. Kenny Mhurchaidh Bhig paused in the act of striking a match and glanced up under his lifted eyebrows at the stooping, glistening shoulders. Murdo took a long step across to the fireplace. He pushed the snout of his bonnet right up off his brow, which gave him a somewhat jaunty, careless air. Leaning his elbow on the mantelpiece he put the feadan to his mouth, seeming to caress it with his lips. The reed giggled. Finally, very softly, he played a little tune. At one part he played it wrong. Iain Beag at once lifted his head and half turned his face, but after cocking an attentive ear a moment turned again and stooped over his work. Murdo looked sideways at the feadan and frowned, as if doubtful if he had it right. When he had played the air a second time—and wrong—he paused again.

Kenny Mhurchaidh Bhig puffed slowly at his pipe and looked with curious, unwinking eyes at Murdo, as if to express that he was prepared for anything. From the bench came the heedless, swish-swishing noise of a plane. At last Murdo seemed to decide he had it right. He played the tune a third time, strongly and confidently, and he marked the accents with unnecessary vigour by slapping the wet sole of his boot against the floor.

Kenny Mhurchaidh Bhig cleared his throat. " What tune is at you there ? "

Murdo put the name on it.

" O-ho," says Kenny, in a mocking tone. " There now! That's *just* what it will be, right enough. And who taught you it like that ? " he added with something like venom.

" It was my mother taught me," replied Murdo, smiling with a corner of his mouth.

" Well, it was a worthy woman that was in your mother," says Iain Beag, turning himself round and if anything smiling a little too. " But she had it wrong. Here to me the feadan."

Kenny Murchaidh Bhig snorted and rammed his thumb into the bowl of his pipe.

Iain Beag was on the point of putting the feadan to his mouth when the door opened a little and the face of Duncan Lachlan Iain appeared squinting round the edge of it.

" It was with me that I was hearing the birds of spring and they singing in winter," says he, coming in. " In the name of God what have I here ? "

"Were you not thinking it was MacCruimein himself you were hearing?" says Kenny Mhurchaidh Bhig.

He got up wearing his spitting face. Murdo stepped hastily aside from the vicinity of the fire.

"Indeed, I was thinking it was MacCruimein," says Duncan. "And if I thought I thought also that it was the rheumatics that were in the finger-joints of the worthy man." He winked his good eye at Murdo.

"Well, apart from yon trifling error about MacCruimein you were nearly right, for it was the rheumatics the woman had that taught him the tune." Kenny ran his eye with lingering scorn down Murdo's person.

"God about us!" exclaimed Duncan Lachlan Iain, as if in the greatest consternation. "A woman piper! I won't believe it. The day I see a man bear a child that day I'll see a woman tune the pipes, and that day I'll know I am dead. Man, man, they have not the wind nor the trick of the fingers nor the musician's ear nor the poet's heart."

Iain Beag smiled a little at the man's fervour and Murdo had difficulty in keeping back the grin that came natural to the face of one that would be conversing with Duncan Lachlan Iain.

"Ah, women!" says he. "God forgive you, a Dhonnchaidh, for reminding a man of his troubles. I'll be bidding you good night, men," he said, moving to the door.

Iain Beag and Duncan bade him good night.

Old Coinneach Mac Dhonnchaidh 'Ic Alasdair Ruaidh raised his head and looked round about him. " Dé ? " says he, clearly thinking he had been addressed by someone. He saw a man moving to go out. " Oidhche mhath leibh, a laochain," he said. He sighed and his head drooped and he returned to his old man's dovering.

At the door Murdo paused. " Oidhche mhath leibh, a Choinnich," he said to Kenny Mhurchaidh Bhig, and pulled out his face into a ludicrously pleading expression.

Kenny looked up, glaring ferociously. Suddenly something strange happened to him; the expression seemed to melt and slip down his face. He turned aside and clutched his mouth in his hand.

" Oidhche mhath leat, a Mhurchaidh," he said between his fingers in a strange, choked voice.

His shoulders shook.

3

Outside the noise of water filled the darkness with its various sound. It kept up everywhere a rapid dripping from invisible projecting roofs and eaves, and ran as it seemed under his feet with distressful melancholy, gluc-gluc-ing in innumerable runnels it had worn for itself. Even the occasional voice of the sea rose overlaid and muffled in its insistency.

This noise falling distractingly in his ears

caused him to hesitate at corners and splash about uncertainly on the familiar road. At the bridge in particular he screwed up his face and went feeling before him with his hands in fear of stepping into the swollen torrent whose roaring rose up solidly before him like a wall. Having touched the parapet he struck at once into a brisk pace and went confidently up the brae, because in darkness a man will always take the face of a hill more quickly and with less scathe than he will descend the other side.

The bleared light of his own window emerged from behind the wall of what had been the house of the cailleach Beitidh Mhór, and jumped along like a frog in the corner of his left eye. Behind, the torrent lifted an incessant clamouring and suddenly there seemed to rise in front of him a similar roar. Lights flashed a moment above his head, then he was staring amazed into two round eyes of lights flying towards him through a veritable blanket of rain. Something resembling a huge black shadow rose out of the middle of the road and leaped sideways at him. He grunted as the wind was knocked out of his chest, and threw out his arms.

When the car had rushed past and away, with its diminishing swishing, he came to himself and found he was clasping round the waist with all his might some tall, thin man—he could feel the extreme thinness of him through the thick coat he was wearing—and the other, for his part, was clutching himself round the neck as if he meant never to let him go.

Murdo gasped a mouthful of breath.

"Who's in it?"

His voice came muffled and indistinct because his mouth was pressed into the man's shoulder. By the coolness that ran over his foot and slid along his sole he knew he was standing in a pool and the water had at last gotten into his boot.

The arms about his neck began to relax a little.

"Oh—I—Iss it——" stammered a once familiar voice in his ear.

Murdo shook his head free and laughed.

"Rory Urquhart! Is it *you* that's in it really?"

He twitched his arms tight about the man's waist so that the word he was about to say broke off short and flew across Murdo's shoulder. At last they took their arms off each other.

When they got inside Murdo went immediately to the table and with a twist of his fingers caused the lamplight to leap upon the room. He threw off his coat and crossed over to the fire and got down on one knee before it. He first pushed a poker vigorously between the bars, causing a thick layer of grey, velvety peat ash to melt away swiftly through the bottom of the grate, leaving only a number of red hearts of peats. Those he took carefully between the tongs, and built them up into a glowing cone. Round this he erected the dry, black slabs, setting them on end with the tops touching, and when some of them were too big for his purpose he pressed them across his knee and tore them apart. He did all this with smooth unhurried movements, with an air of concentration, so that his voice sounded vaguely when he said over his shoulder to Roderick Urquhart, " Put your coat off you."

Urquhart had been but half willing to come in. He was standing by the door and the water drip-dripping from the edges of his coat. He took it off now and came and sat before the fire, his back to the lamp. And he peered about him at the room and at Murdo sitting in it.

Murdo did not look up. He was stooping and unwinding the puttees from his legs, passing the rolled-up end from hand to hand with a rapid circling motion. By the time he had finished the flames were already bursting through and licking the backs of the peats.

" Are not you the stranger ? " he said, straightening himself.

He looked at Urquhart, and stopped. Rory was disappearing behind the cloud of steam that was rising from the fronts of his legs. Through this cloud his head appeared dimly and his glasses glimmered a questioning puzzlement.

Murdo rose.

" There's two miles before you yet. You'll get your death. I'm going to give you dry clothes."

Urquhart rose also. He was to be refusing. But his protesting, bony hand wavered and fell to his side. He had opened his mouth to speak, but instead of speaking he opened it wider, and yet wider. His nose went up in a series of jerks as his head went backwards. He screwed up his eyes tight. His head of hair seemed to slip forward to meet his rising eyebrows. The sneeze he gave nearly threw the spectacles off his face.

"Yonder now," says Murdo at the door. "There's a cold on you already."

He lifted a finger and pointed to the ponderous press between the bed and the door to the back place.

"You'll get the whisky yonder."

A moment later he re-entered the room with his swift, even movement, seeming to push the air with his chest.

"Trousers," says he, laying the articles over Urquhart's chair, "and socks."

The whisky had put irregular patches of dull red on Urquhart's sallow cheeks and brow. He was standing before the fire preparing to take off the wet garments. Little wisps of steam came out and licked about his knees.

Murdo swung the kettle over the blazing peats and sat down to remove his boot. He surveyed the wet foot a moment and stuck it out before the fire, twiddling his toes and feeling a desire to laugh as the comforting warmth played like a feathery caress along his sole.

A moment later he did in fact laugh out loud. Urquhart, out of his trousers, resembled nothing so much as a dejected stork. He was in difficulties. One large, red, knotted knee jerked up and down as he prodded about with his unbelievably slender leg in the leg of Murdo's trousers. He gave to the proddings of his skinny shank the same absorbed attention he was wont to give to the problems in his books—a dogged, unrelenting attention, and flushing dully if it taxed him more than usual, as if he feared the thing would get over him and prove him stupid; and when he succeeded it was not by any caper of the over-leaping mind, but by dint of doggedness, and seemed always to surprise himself a little. Murdo's laughter at his present predicament could not have been restrained. It arose as it seemed in some well of pure, impersonal goodwill and bubbled richly. Round and mellow, with a pulse of hidden vigour. An excellent laugh.

Urquhart glanced up over the rims of his glasses. Mild surprise tinged his immense gravity.

"I envy you your unaffected laughter, Murdo," says he, and prodded, and at last successfully. His eyes looked vaguely before him into space. His right shoulder sagged and his right hand was busy behind him thrusting down the tail of his shirt. His left shoulder lifted and his left hand held up the trousers in front of him. Murdo looked quickly away at the fire. The smile left his face and retreated behind the eyes and sparkled there as with a private amusement. His eye happened to fall on Urquhart's boots. He stooped down and made a work of setting them on their sides where a slow warmth would reach them.

He did not look up when Urquhart's feet appeared near his hand, but straightened his body with a sudden unsupple movement, and sat sideways to him. The amusement went out of his eyes.

The even, groaning sound of rain rose over the silence that had fallen in the room. A tiny noise wheezed occasionally inside the kettle. In the spout a thin steam slowly formed into puffs which floated out at intervals and vanished upwards. Murdo watched them grimly. His face began to harden into a surface, without expression. In his eyes the reflection of the fire flickered before a deadening wall. His body tightened. A faint ticking began to emerge from some pocket of Urquhart's clothes. On its rhythm the tension mounted upon the room. The groaning rain packed like a dense wadding round the thickening air. The hand that lay on Murdo's knee moved together and drew itself up into a taut fist.

" It's a loud noise that."

Urquhart's voice crackled in the silence. The sound of rain fled backwards on the instant into an inconsiderable grumbling.

Murdo started slightly. He unclenched his hand, and his eyes looked idly into the palm.

" You're right," says he, easing his shoulders and letting out of him with relief the air he had unconsciously been holding in his chest. " It's wet."

His eyes rested a moment on the lusty flames tonguing upwards and then, as if the moment had come, and could no longer be delayed, he slowly turned his head. The look that lurked in his eyes, as if he feared a little what he would see, vanished at once at sight of the profound unquiet in Urquhart's peering face. In that look, which startled both a little, they were seeing each other for the first time for years; maybe even it was the first time ever that they saw each other. Murdo need have had no fear for the bases of his sureness, but the nakedness of Urquhart's questioning was a something more intimate than he expected to stumble on. He drew back hastily upon himself with the sensitive man's horror of intrusion.

Urquhart had in fact in the end been caught at unawares and he attempted to retreat and shroud himself, an attempt half-hearted and only half successful. The revelation had been too complete. He had been surprised outside his defences. He put up an uncertain hand to his spectacles and with the other fumbled at his breast pocket for his handkerchief.

Without his glasses he was defenceless entirely. An intentness seemed to come forward in his face. He seemed to *look* with his face. But it was his eyes were surprising, strangely blue, pale as the sky. He looked straight at Murdo and could only dimly see him. He gave a little self-conscious smile, polishing at his glasses, and after all he smiled somewhat to one side of him. A sudden tenderness swelled in Murdo's throat, a warmth came up about his eyes. Urquhart was like a bewildered kitten.

" You'll not be hearing the sea, of course—up here," said Urquhart, picking up the phrase where he thought it had dropped. " It's the sea we will always be hearing—at home yonder."

He settled the spectacles on his nose. To slip the leg over his ear he moved his head once, slowly, from side to side, a movement which at another time would have expressed a hopelessness of doubt.

" True. But we'll be hearing it, though."

Murdo made a slight, gathered motion of leaning towards him. His face held a secret.

" On nights of frost the shouting of it will rise up and come walking over the land."

Urquhart glanced quickly at him, disturbed a little at how the intensity vibrated in his voice. In Murdo's eyes a flame leapt up and died. He was all at once aware of his words echoing faintly across the silence that followed, and flushed. He turned away his eyes to the fire and bending over thrust his arm into the box of peats. Unbelievably the rain increased in intensity, drumming upon the earth, and a dull roaring rose and ran round the house. At the same moment the lid jigged on the kettle.

" Now," says Murdo, rising. " Tea! "

Urquhart had always been a man to measure out his words, a dour, careful fellow, pondering every syllable that would be said to him, and very sparing of reply. To-night he chattered. About sundry nothings. Sometimes he could not wait till Murdo answered his latest triviality before his brittle voice went on again. His odds and ends of phrases were without conviction; he had no interest in the reply and could not wait for it. Most of all he seemed to fear a silence. When such occurred he hastened to fill it, even if it was only to repeat something he had said before. The sea, for instance—the sound of it, the nearness or distance of it—he seemed to think that a good subject, for he kept returning to it whenever he was at a loss. He was at pains to maintain a light and careless tone, but more than once Murdo caught him, thinking he was unobserved, regarding him with a serious puzzlement and concern that were in strange contrast to the lightness of his words. The impression grew on Murdo that Urquhart had other questions of a very different nature that he wished, and feared, to put.

Otherwise, the man was little changed. Perhaps he stooped a trifle more, with the weight of a distinguished academic career and the post that followed quickly, but he still shambled through life, awkward and out of place, his long narrow head thrust forward from his narrow shoulders, the look of ponderous gravity scarcely lifting from his sombre face, and maybe he peered about even more from side to side as if in doubt as to his way. The moustache he had let to grow was not a success either, an irregular, feathery thing, a line of tufts along his lip, the colour of a mouse. Another man would have taken it off. Slow and ungainly, Urquhart; but what he had he held.

The nervousness that fluttered from him to-night beat against Murdo in vain. He seemed as it were to sit at home within himself, looking out. The way the long hair fell back, and the slight thinning of it about the temples, gave to the smooth brow a look of breadth and massiveness. Some light was always in his deep eyes, but it was the varying glow of something from within that filled them, not, like Urquhart's, the pale and still reflection of lights that passed without. But chiefly Urquhart was impelled to watch unquietly and by stealth the smallish, nervous hands. They were not agitated, nor were they still either, but when they moved it was with an even, unhurried motion, full of a confident roundness.

"And how is your wife, Murdo?" Urquhart hastened to avoid a silence.

"My wife? If I'm not mistaken she'll be peeping out between the curtains there."

Murdo's face filled with laughter. He looked towards the bed and seemed to listen. Urquhart glanced and moved uneasily.

"But—but maybe Mrs. Anderson will be in her sleep."

Murdo seemed on the point of laughing out loud. The title was almost too much.

"Mrs. Anderson? O no! If Mrs. Anderson were in her sleep Mrs. Anderson would be snoring!"

Still no movement from the bed. Murdo's eyes twinkled. He looked as if he were about to do something mischievous.

"Anyway, she's there," says he. "Those are her clothes on the chair yonder."

That did it. A feminine squeaking got up, "O Murdo! O Murdo!" A plump arm came out and hurriedly dragged some of the clothes out of sight. Urquhart peered in solemn consternation at the size of the sudden upheaval billowing the curtain. Murdo laughed.

"Nach d'thuirt mi riut!" says he, and added "You can come out now, Annag. Ruairidh has seen plenty of women in bed."

Urquhart's concern was serious, for his dry virginity.

"O indeed, no, Murdo! Indeed I haven't seen!"

He blushed furiously in blotches over his cheeks and brow, moving on his chair and glancing from Murdo to the bed and back again. In the bed a tittering was going on.

The uneasiness that had been on him during the meal became still more marked when, put at her ease by the mention of her special kind of conversation, she was like to question him.

". . . They're saying you'll be in England now. It's you that's lucky. You'll be liking that I'm sure?"

But he could not avoid taking seriously everything that would be said to him. And his reply gave him serious thought, to make it completely truthful.

"I'm not sure, Mrs. Anderson. I don't think I would effer be feeling at home among the English. Decent men, you know, O worthy men, some of them, but somehow—somehow you neffer seem to make contact with anything deep down in them. They don't seem—*interested* at all. But decent men, O yess, fery worthy men."

He hastened to address Murdo—" Have you seen Murdo MacKenzie lately, Murdo ? "

But she had not understood his reply anyway.

Urquhart's language was peculiar. With scrupulous politeness he attempted to speak to Murdo in the Gaelic, but it was poor Gaelic he had, with self-conscious patches of the English Beurla over it so that it resembled his own sallow face when he blushed, and as often as not there was more English than Gaelic in it. And to Annie MacIver he replied in his careful, aerated English. But whatever he said, the thought sat as ungainly in his mixture of speech as himself was ill-fitted in the crofter's trousers.

After Annie MacIver's question there was no disguising his discomfort and anxiety to be gone. He looked gravely at Murdo while she spoke and the fact that the clearness in his face did not cloud or vary seemed to perplex him more. Murdo looked at him labouring to hide his eagerness for the road and was more convinced than ever that Urquhart dearly wished to stay, and really speak. But for some reason dared not.

At the door he thanked Murdo—for the daily neighbourliness of fire and meat, over-profusely—and hurried into the night buttoning up his coat. Murdo remembered what it was he had been going to ask.

"How does your post suit you in—in Sheffield?"

But maybe Urquhart had not heard the question for there came back to Murdo's ears only the splashing of his boots among the pools.

4

Grey skies will not drop forever, even in the days of sorrows in a wet country. To be sure the mist lay long over the land, but it was an enchanted mist, drenched in the perfume of fresh, growing things, full of a soundless chasing of lights and shadows, shot through with the sudden songs of birds churling among unseen branches. A breeze blew up out of the south, and the mist rolled northwards. The land appeared, drifting out against the breeze, and it was already covered between the moorland and the sea with a bold patchwork of oblongs of new-turned soil. Yet a while of fresh days and the young shoots had greened them over. On hot noons the mounting sun burned the necks of men who stooped, cutting black, glistening gashes in the face of lonely moors. One evening when the summer dusk stood hazily and pink along the street a group of men that were standing yonder stopped suddenly in their conversation and raised their heads to listen. From the edge of the moor, away behind the houses, rose suddenly a sound, the sound of pipes. It mounted roaring on the air, and wavered, broke into a cluster of throaty, chuckling notes, died away, then mounted again in a steady roaring. The men looked into each other's faces, surprised and listening. The pipes had not been heard since Iain Mór's day ended. Now the tune was plain to hear, the clear, lusty notes dropping out richly, forming a slow pattern against the wall of drones.

" That's Kenny," says one man softly, in a listening voice.

There was no wind that evening, but an indefinite flitting about of light, soft airs. The sound of piping came sometimes from a distance, from the moor; sometimes it came down out of the sky and the notes dropped about them clearly, roundly; sometimes it was inside their own heads that the piping was. The drones approached, and receded, behind the pattern of notes; they rose, and fell, against each other.

" That's not Kenny," says Murdo the Flea. " Kenny never had that amount of skill in the fingers at him. It's himself, yon."

But the Flea was mistaken. When they reached the place it was not Kenny or Iain Beag but it was Murdo Anderson that was playing. Kenny Mhurchaidh Bhig was sitting on a rock with his eyes screwed up looking at Càrn Mór. Iain Beag stood with his back against the wall of his shop, his brows drawn together in a look of concentration. Now and then the piper looked at him, turning the eyes in his strenuous face, and Iain shook his head or nodded.

Murdo stopped at the end of his pacing and broke into the crunluath. His toe tapped rapidly on the ground. His fingers bounded off the notes so nimbly that they seemed to describe short ripples along the chanter. The virile, slotted notes flew about, throwing a mesh of sound over the hearers, a contracting net that caught and drew the throats and breasts. And left them strangely numb and vibrant when, at last, the music ceased.

"O, he'll learn!"

Kenny Mhurchaidh Bhig's flat tone dashed brutally to fragments the flimsy edifice of rhythms and faint echoes remaining upright in the air, supported as it were upon the pulses. Everyone felt a little uncomfortable. Only Murdo looked affectionately at dark Kenny and smiled as with some secret knowledge.

The piping recommenced that evening began to attract its own. Sometimes on those long summer nights when the air was still and warm and the light fading from the bens there would be as many as twenty men standing about or squatting on the grass at the side of Iain Beag's workshop, and one stepping up and down in the middle of them, stepping and turning, with his arm round the bag of the pipes. The stricter folk began to look sideways and to lift up their hands. . . .

In laborious days there will be healing and

accord. At the approach of harvest the men drew closer to the earth and to each other. A simple rhythm governed their existences, a unity expressed in swingings of the arms, slow steppings, bowings to the earth. The sun shone brilliantly, swinging down into the south. In her slanting rays at evening the purple bens advanced across the moor. Dry winds blew strongly, with a sharpening tooth. Now it was by the light of his window that a man went home at evening to his meal.

The return of the young people from hotels brought for a time, as usual, a faint and colourless excitement into the surface of existence. One would be aware of formless agitations dying perpetually on the casual air; their wantings stirred without shape in the darkening edges of afternoons. At evenings the shops were full of a sifting of them, blown in there by this headless wind of vagueness. They spoke, while the subject lasted, about the harvest of the "season," the pot-bellied rabble of Englishry, and spent with an easy hand the wages of obsequiousness. Later they spoke of dullness and the likelihood of rain, and when the end of all forbearance turned them out at last into the street they stood in knots at corners, blowing upon their hands, cursing the place and wishing for they knew not what.

This winter, however, it became a habit with many of them in search of amusement and distraction to take themselves on evenings to Iain Beag's. Much of what went on there was certainly beyond their interest—*Ach*, they had been in the habit of saying, looking superior, *they'll only be singing Gaylic songs whatever*—but recently the place had begun to get a name for high spirits, one or two excellent jests were traced there that had caused the neighbourhood to titter, so that it came to be said among them: *There will always be some fun going at Iain Beag's.*

Whether he knew or suspected something Duncan Lachlan Iain was certainly very persistent this evening in urging Murdo to sing.

" Siuthad, a Mhurchaidh," he would be saying. " You've been making another song surely."

Murdo did not for a time consent, but he denied nothing.

" Matà," he said at last, " I don't believe I haven't one you didn't hear before."

" Out with it, then! Sing it! " shouted a number of those that were there.

Finally Iain Beag turned round from his bench.

" Siuthad, a laochain! " says he.

He put his hands in his pockets and stood as if waiting.

Murdo fixed his eyes on a point in the opposite wall. He seemed to have difficulty in not smiling at what he was seeing there.

" Here you have it then," says he, preparing to sing.

It happened that near a month before Mr. John MacIver had stopped him one day on the road and reproved him for his way of life.

" I hear you will be going every day to the house of ungodly men," says he, looking on the ground and sighing. " And there you will be spending your time in vain singing and jesting."

His greasy voice dripped slowly.

Murdo heard him out, looking at the lowered lids, that lacked lashes almost entirely.

" Och," says he, " there's no harm at all in it."

He had no wish to anger or defy the man, more particularly as he had the misfortune to be related to him.

" Feumaidh tu cunntas a thoirt—You must give account," Mr. John MacIver paused—" of every vain word you speak."

He put the tips of his fingers together over his belly and without lifting his eyes from the ground stepped away straight before him down the road.

Murdo watched with a faint smile the fat man moving away from him, bulging his seams. There came into his head some of the tales that passed about the missionary, his fervent loins. He was trying to imagine him at his gallantries. Near the bend of the road some men met him and greeted him. He could see the bonnets come off and the faces turning. Mr. John held on his lordly way with barely an inclination of the head. Murdo frowned, and remained looking very seriously at the spot where the missionary's self-righteous buttocks had gone out of sight round the bend. Then his brow cleared.

He smiled, as if some private thought had pleased him, and turning sharply on his heel walked away with a purposeful air. And as he walked from time to time he chuckled. For a week thereafter Annie MacIver was distracted with curiosity as to what Murdo would always be scribbling in a little book, rubbing out and scribbling again, stopping from time to time to shake his head and chuckle.

He had scarcely begun to sing when Duncan Lachlan Iain lifted his round head and gazed about the room, looking cross-eyed with a wildly ludicrous expression of surprise, as if he had just thought of something terribly funny. His face became distorted with the effort to restrain a bellow. His mouth fell open. He gave a thin, helpless bleat of a laugh and collapsed over his knees and began to shake with internal mirth, pressing his knees together and his hands against his thighs. One after the other the men looked up with a sudden illumination and went off into a fit of laughter. Murdo did not dare to look at them. His nostrils and the corners of his mouth twitched. He continued to fix his eyes on the point in the opposite wall. But he had to stop several times before he got to the end of the fifteen verses there were of it, because of the way the audience screamed and yelled, every man of them wheezing and snorting and rocking to and fro. Even Iain Beag himself, and he a man not much given to laughter, was hanging on to his bench with both hands and scarlet in the face. For long after he had gotten to the end they were unable to subside. They sighed and panted, pressing their hands against their sides and bellies, the tears running out of their eyes, and several times when quiet was about to be restored someone started a ripple of laughter and set them off again.

Not without reason. The song is humorous beyond belief, sly and outrageous, half affectionate. Anyone that knew Mr. John MacIver, his person and reputed gallantries, was bound to be convulsed. It went to the tune of "Ho-ro Bhodachain" which as everybody knows that has heard it is a chuckle from the heart. A terrible catchy tune it is.

He sang it again, and then a third time he had to sing it, and the men that were there, near a score of them, swaying in time and joining lustily in the chorus, two short stamping refrains to each verse. But whereas in the original song that refrain was " Ho-ro Bhodachain," now it was " Ho-ro Chullachain."

That song went through the place like a fire and set two parishes a-laughing. For many a day the mere appearance of Mr. John MacIver on the road at a distance was the signal for laughing and chuckling, and the first Sabbath he could hardly get through his sermon in peace for the giggling there was among the young people and they stuffing their handkerchiefs into their mouths. It was no use to cough angrily and glare at the congregation. From that evening his sway over the younger people was gone forever. They had seen him once in too ridiculous a light. Ever after he was doomed to seem only preposterous. It is as " Cullachan "* he is known to this day.

And not he only was aware of the change. The godly woke up to find their authority shattered and the fashion of constipation and the long face fallen into perpetual disrepute. They were at their wits' end, but not the godliest among them dared say a word openly for fear Murchadh Iain Ruaidh would make a song about him.

The great-share of the people trembled no longer to go their own way. At Iain Beag's there was scarcely room to stand. The evenings were spent in singing, and if you had been outside sometimes when the men were there and the yellow light streamed from the window it would have seemed to you that the shop rocked to and fro with the laughter that was going on inside it. And on nights of frost when the moon shone down on a white world, bens under snow and the sea roaring overhead in the middle of the heavens, there would come from the end of the house the continuous skirl of pipes.

5

The piper stretched his right hand above his head, feeling backwards, and touched tenderly with a finger the drones. His hand remained a

* Cullachan—a little male pig, but may also mean a little impotent man.

moment in the air and a listening came into his puckered face as he leant a careful ear to their roaring. Then he took off the high note he had been holding on the chanter and, still listening, broke a handful of chattering notes, preliminary. Someone burst into merry laughter and clapped his palms together, making a noise that flew upwards and exploded under the roof like a ball of hollow sound. The loud noise of many people talking, moving about, guffawing and laughing, fell suddenly to a sibilant ripple round the walls. Attention became fixed on the erect figures in the middle of the room, poised, waiting. With a movement of his right hand the piper pressed the bag upwards under his oxter, and fell at once into the tune. Twenty-four young men and girls, as one person, began to dance.

The hall had been built four years before, on a hillock beside the road, a half-mile north of the street end. The young people were to be dancing there on winter nights. But when it was already completed, wanting only the floor, the godly stepped in and put an end on the project. Old Angus MacDonald, he of the iron beard, distinguished above all elders of the Free Kirk for his ferocious holiness and the profundity and resonance of his religious groans, carried away the key, and to make doubly sure the place would never be put to vain and unsanctified use he let two iron bars into the stones of the doorposts and fixed them with two padlocks and two chains. The keys he tied together and hung on his wall, above the fireplace, so that his eyes could daily rest on them with pride. He refused to give them up, and swore he would have them with him on the Day of Judgment to testify against the lewdness of the place and to his own surpassing uprightness. It was no use to try to seize them in his absence, for then Ceit Mhurrach was on guard, a woman with a tongue to sear the liver. But it happened that Shonny Eachainn Charavi was uncommonly good at making a noise like a cow. In the middle of the night he got into the Elder's byre and hid himself in the rafters. At the end of five minutes a noise was coming out like a herd of cows in labour. A light sprang up in the Elder's window and shortly himself emerged and hurried round the end of the house carrying a lantern. Calum Mac Dhonnchaidh Odhair with a red handkerchief round his jaws darted in at the open door and lifted the keys off their nail. Ceit Mhurrach screamed like a fury and rose in the bed to be at him. " My shame on you, woman! " shouted Calum. " 'Tis your nakedness I'm seeing yonder! " And used the odd seconds to make good his escape from under her claws.

This night since the dropping of dark the sound of dancing and merriment had come from the lighted building above the high road. The sense of accustomed restraints so lately loosened brought an edge and an abandon. The pipes roared through the room, buffeting the ears. An excitement gripped the breasts and mounting upward like a heady vapour looked out in shining eyes. Not only the dancers whirled and danced but the blood throbbed in time in wrists and temples and glowing cheeks. Nothing went that was not in time. Even through the minds the long thoughts did not pass nor the odd-shaped fellows, and but the half-thoughts tripped it, sharply pleasant, on the feet of the reel. They were yonder in a kind of intoxication, drunken with sound and a wild defiance of the music. In the meekest breast an ancient affirmation raised its head; the dullest understood an antique something, stirred obscurely at the core.

"Nach tu an t-eun!"

A man near the entrance turned his head quickly to see who it was had spoken in his ear. Murdo was standing close behind his shoulder. His eyes were fixed on the whirling figures in the middle of the room, smiling, approving. Apparently he had addressed one of them, speaking softly to himself. He had placed his left hand across his chest. The man noticed particularly the little finger, which was tied up in a white cloth.

A series of wild yells got up behind them and flying forms were seen flashing past the open door. Unable to restrain themselves for high spirits some of the young men were dancing a dance of their own on the level space outside.

A hundred yards below, a single house sat on

the edge of the black shadow it cast across the road. There was a coming and going, a trickle of figures that disappeared into the shadow or emerged into the light of the rising moon. Inside were merry voices and a reflection of the gaiety unrestrained above. Mór Ruadh, the Flea's wife, stood with her hands on her great hips, presiding in her own house. Her broad, red face was covered with smiles; she was happy and concerned at the same time like all her kind when bellies are at their filling. A grunting of old bodachs clustered round the fire, wagging their heads. There came a noise of smacking of lips on pipe stems and puffs of smoke ascended. Mór Ruadh ran a cold eye over them slowly and looking at Murdo shook her head to and fro with a motion of despair. She grinned. Murdo smiled back at her and although he did not know what it was, he felt that they were sharing some amusing matter. Mór Ruadh's face suddenly fell quite serious. She called out in a startlingly loud and unexpected tone, " Sit out, sluggards, and let see the fire! *Out* of there! " And added in a sighing voice expressing the last degree of exasperation, " O God! " She looked back at Murdo and immediately grinned again, and for some reason she blushed.

The bodachs paid no attention whatever but one or two pushed back their chairs not more than an inch or two. One of them yawned loudly—A-a-ah ha! " 'Seadh," says he, continuing the conversation where Mór Ruadh had interrupted, "The day of the old men is over, it seems."

The Flea got up in the middle of them and pushed his chair back noisily with a careless movement of his legs. He put his fists above his head and stretched his burly body lazily. "The day of old men without wisdom," says he, "is never ended too soon."

"And the day of young men without sense never begins too late."

The Flea looked at Murdo while this was said and opened his eyes wide, with the expression of a man that cannot believe what he hears. Then he winked a knowing wink and jerked his head in the direction of the owner of the querulous voice, as if to say, "Listen to yon!" A sudden grin overspread his broad, red face.

The bottles sat quite openly on the dresser; nevertheless when the Flea went over to fill a glass for Murdo he coughed loudly and kept his back to the room, and he poured with a secretive tilt of the elbow.

Eachann Ruairidh Bhàin was leaning back against the dresser, his feet placed before him close together, a glass in his hand. Murdo stepped across to him. "It's likely the weather will last a little time yet," says he.

Eachann looked up and his eyes smiled.

"It's likely."

He was a dapper man on the near edge of forty, with a black moustache curling suavely on his lip and a splendid pair of long-lashed eyes in his head, and the curve of his fine nose was a very pleasant thing. His mother had been the neatest small dark woman that was in that place ever. Not a man in her day that did not lose sleep over her, and in the end Ruairidh Bàn had her through a small accident. Eachann was her son. His small body was put together with such delicacy, so perfectly proportioned, that it made even Murdo's excellent figure look not clumsy but a shade more massive than need be to make a pretty man. They talked, and if they talked—about the weather and last year's crops and the lambs they were likely to have—it was not that either of them cared a bodle for the conversation or the words that were passing between them, but now and again they looked, friendly, into each other's eyes, two men standing together at their ease, warmth curling within them, kindness that was comprehension in their bowels. Eachann smiled easily, the smile of a kindly, quiet man. In talking Murdo frequently waved his hand; several times one or other of those present looked quickly at him because in the corner of an eye his bandaged finger seemed a small white object describing curves through the air.

At something that was said Eachann laughed —a low, melodious laugh, like a pleasant fact of nature. Almost at the same moment Eachann Caravi choked on a crumb. He coughed, and the drop that had been trembling all evening on the end of his red nose flew off at last and missing the dish of butter by a hair's breadth alighted harmlessly, thank God, on the table. Young Colin of Lobster Colin had been away somewhere drinking. He observed the accident.

"My sorrow, 'Eachainn," says he, "It seems you have sustained a slight loss."

Caravi stopped the rapid movement of his jaws, and looked up. Keeping his eyes on young Colin he lowered his head and made a snuffling with his nose along the back of his hand and part of his sleeve. Not having understood what the lad was laughing at he shrugged his thin shoulders with indifference and stuffed his mouth. Since Eachann Ruairidh Bhàn had laughed Murdo was aware of a bubbling-up sensation in his chest. It seemed to him this evening that everyone said and did cheerful, amusing things.

Footsteps sounded in the passage between the rooms and a conversation in breezy out-of-door tones dropped away suddenly just inside the entrance. Some men had come in that had walked briskly down the hill talking together with briskness and animation. The door was loudly closed by a vigorous arm.

The head of Kenny Mhurchaidh Bhig appeared round the edge of the kitchen door and his eyes looked about for Mór Ruadh.

"Tea for the fiddler!"

"For Domhnull Bàn ?" said Mór.

Kenny was already half-way ben to the room. He returned and looked round the edge of the door, casting his eyes across most horribly. Mór giggled.

"O well it's Duncan then, poor man."

But Duncan was no way sorry for himself certainly. His voice was heard at that minute shouting out as he entered the other room, and from the feminine shriek that went up it could be told he had said something outrageous. Clearly he was determined to act in no respect with dignity this evening. Catching sight of Murdo coming in he left off pursuing Annie MacIver with gestures and grimaces round a little table and amid delighted laughter slunk guiltily away to a corner, his shoulders round his ears, and squinting up occasionally as if momently expecting to be seized and beaten. A good performance, rich in a wild, demoniacal humour. Cross-eyed Duncan as a leering Presbyterian faun was in a part for which he seemed designed by Nature. Annie MacIver, stupidly intent, continued to lollop round the table, and filled the room with the ear-splitting shrieks that came out of her mouth. Murdo regarded her with the faint, indulgent smile that had become habitual with him when, as usual, she overdid it; she with the paint and the powder on her face and her hairs on the table and the mincing English at her, and every Sabbath morning all bound up and tied together and the Bible in her oxter knickering off to the kirk with that unshakable confidence in herself and in the rightness of things that her like share only with God.

In this room one was even more conscious all the time of some big excitement near. People, mostly youngish people, came in with the glow of it on their cheeks and an echo of it in their laughing voices. With all the fresh arrivals the room became more fully charged with it. They clustered round several little tables or stood about the walls, and everyone, standing or sitting, ate and drank with a look of meaning soon to go. Amid the loud continuous chatter Murdo's ear was caught by a phrase of a conversation between some young men that were standing in the passage outside the door.

" And what did you say ? " said a deep voice, and a laugh in it.

" I said, ' Even a farmer cannot always be harrowing.' "

Three or four voices guffawed. A girl that was sitting near the door cried out and bit her lip and blushing furiously immediately pressed her handkerchief to her mouth, looking aside at the floor. A moment later Murdo saw her whispering eagerly along her hand. Her neighbour was bending her head to listen and tee-heeing and tittering.

" Bring the fire over! " shouted someone in the far corner. " Kenny wants to spit."

Kenny Mhurchaidh Bhig advanced with unconcerned face from the centre of a laughing group and advanced upon the fire, pushing out his lips..

" A Mhurchaidh, they're wanting a piper."

Murdo went out, smiling without being

aware of it. But everyone smiled this evening, and smiling looked at his neighbour, discerning in him droll and lovable graces hitherto unnoticed. Every throat held a chuckle.

He was the more astonished when in the dark passage he encountered a number of men retreating from the kitchen in a loud grumble of angry tones.

"That's *that*, then!" said one, and the phrase was full of spite.

"A-ach!" said a second, snarling. "And Sasunn also! We know yon!"

He immediately bumped against Murdo who had drawn himself up against the wall. "Diaoul!" he added rudely. They went out, grumbling.

In the kitchen the silence was uneasy. No one spoke. Only looked. Iain Beag sat at the table, with a cup before him. His face was white with anger. But he kept his eyes lowered and his mouth tightly shut. It was certain *he* had said nothing during whatever had occurred, had taken no sides; however, everyone that glanced at his pale face, set and furious, felt with an uncomfortable twinge that it was himself had angered Iain. Murdo's eye travelled over those that were present and fell early upon Roderick Urquhart, sister's-son to the Flea, who was standing in almost the same place himself had occupied a short ten minutes ago. He started when he saw the man's face, full of blotchy anger. Urquhart, when he saw he was observed, backed against the wall, for all the world like a cornered rat, and bared his yellow teeth in a silent snarl. Here clearly was the culprit, in his red obstinacy, fain to bite, and Murdo was seized with amazement. The man had been so friendly, the last time. With an effort taking his eyes away from the glowering Urquhart he cast another glance over that uncomfortable silent company. He noticed Eachann Ruairidh Bhàin's dark eyes regarding him, with a strained look in them as of suffering. They were there like people under a spell of discomfort, and waited for someone to speak the word that would release them.

Murdo knit his brows and went out. The fault was surely Urquhart's, for it was too plainly against all in common that the anger that possessed him flamed.

He walked several yards up the moonlit road and immediately smiled again and forgot the unpleasant thing when he saw young Colin of Lobster Colin. This humoursome and witty lad was two years in the University of Glasgow, where he was getting a great name in the foreign languages—apparently he was devoting to those subjects a quite unusual ability. And he was namely also in the matter of the bottle for a capacity beyond his years. But Baile na Creige had a reputation too ; it was no discredit to a promising lad to be somewhat overcome. He stood astride the ditch, swaying slightly from the hips. With his head thrust forward, and screwing up his eyes, he was engaged in peering gravely at the landscape.

Murdo regarded him a moment.

"What now, Colin," says he, in the Beurla. "Trying to 'see life steadily and see it whole'?"

The student peered again at the unnatural antics of the hills and trees. A pained expression passed across his face. He frowned carefully. His tone conveyed reproof.

"Whas the use of talking like that, man? I can't even see *Scotland* steady or see it whole."

Murdo laughed, and addressed himself to the hill. From above came the sound of lusty singing, a pause in which a single voice must have sung the verse, then a crowd in vigorous chorus. Drawing nearer he could distinguish words, and the voice that sang alone, and behind the song a noise of movement, the scraping of fiddles, women's laughter. They were letting themselves go up yonder.

Inside, the hall was loudly a-hum. A reel had shortly ago come to an end. Down the middle of the floor came stumping in his heavy boots Dan Abrach, that lived with himself in the crook of Glen Fala. He looked neither to right nor to left, making his way, but for some reason came to a stand in front of Mór Ruadh.

"Hooch!" says he, and snapped his fingers over his head.

One or two that were standing near twisted their necks and smiled. Mór Ruadh looked down at the bodach with an amused glance.

"Hooch!" says she, and gave her head a toss.

Then she looked down at him again, lifting her eyebrows, as if to say, " What will he do now, the creature ? "

" Hooch! " says the creature.

He executed a step or two before her with his feet. The nearest began to laugh and stood away from them. Duncan Lachlan Iain observed the matter from his seat on the top of a barrel and immediately played a few bars on his fiddle.

" Sin a bhalaich! " says the Abrach, without looking round. " Suas e! "

Duncan was not loth, he commenced to play. Everyone stood back, laughing, and gave them the floor. Dan Abrach put up his hands on Mór Ruadh's shoulders. With a half-amused smile, as if merely she would not spoil the fun, and blushing a little, the big woman put her hands also on the shoulders of the bodachan kicking up his heels before her.

At first she merely tapped with her toes and swayed her large body in time, looking down at Dan as if doubtful whether after all the creature could or would dance. But the Abrach had no doubts at all; he both could and would. At the correct beat he swung his big partner and the two of them executed a rapid half-circle down the room. Everyone laughed, watching them. They went like this completely round the hall, dancing for a time on the spot, then at regular intervals swinging down the floor, circling rapidly round each other.

It was the figure they made that was amusing.

The empty, senseless expression never left the Abrach's hairy face. The weird-looking and to tell the truth, rather dirty old fellow " hooched " wildly and kicked up his heels in a sort of laughterless senile gaiety, an abandon of decrepitude. It could not be told whether he was a little drunk or merely very old. Mór Ruadh danced looking down at the Abrach as if surprised each minute to see what she had in her hands; her face was continually breaking into smiles. Her feet scarcely appeared to move, yet they carried her big, heavy body through the steps with the utmost smoothness and nimbleness. Whereas the bodachan capered with his legs, she was light-hearted with her head and shoulders. More massively, but equally with her light partner, she expressed the gay spirit of the dance.

Duncan Lachlan Iain mischievously increased the time. More and more wildly the Abrach skipped about and kicked up his heels; before swinging he stamped with his feet and " hooched " again. Mór Ruadh's face got redder and redder and more and more covered with smiles; she resembled a ponderous piece of furniture careering on smooth castors down the floor. They seemed to fly along the room.

At length the pace became too great to be maintained. With a final caper, seeming to leap up and click his heels behind him in the air, the Abrach returned Mór to her place. She remained laughing and gasping for breath, pressing her hand against her bosom. The

Abrach went and stood near the door. Producing out of somewhere a flaming red handkerchief he pushed up the snout of his bonnet and proceeded to mop his steaming brow. Some young people that were standing there moved away a little on account of a smell that was coming from his boots. Murdo took the pipes in his arm and walked to the end of the hall to play for the next dance. The fun continued.

At some vague time in the small hours of morning it was Murdo that locked the door and brought away the key. Slipping it into his pocket he chanced to look along the road, southwards. From time to time throughout the night, he had been conscious of a subtle lifting of the inner mind, not the surface agitation of merriment and dance, but from time to time on chancing to observe some trivial act or movement, a gesture of an arm, a posture, a simple thing that ordinarily would appear most unsignificant, his breast would fill as when one witnesses a thing heroic, an action sprung directly from the root and principle of all. He felt indeed that here, this evening, something was beginning, and those his people, stirred beyond themselves, moved with gestures symbolical, not unsignificant, across the face of the growing future. Away down the moonlit road the figure of Iain Beag, alone, hirpled into the distance. Nearer, an irregular group, and one that was Duncan Lachlan Iain, with a fiddle under his arm, hurried in his wake. Again turned in Murdo strangely the affirming gesture of the mind: *That is so; so that was and will be.* In a light unworldly, watched by unworldly eyes, the figures walked upon the road, moving of themselves in the isolation of significance.

The air around stirred only in occasional breathings, smelling of the earth. Grey bens, topped and dusted with snow, were scarcely darker than the pearly light. So clear they were, so suddenly in the turning eye, it seemed always you had caught them stealing silently up to you. At the side of the road, on a fallen dyke, sat old Coinneach Mac Dhonnchaidh 'Ic Alasdair Ruaidh, in his dovering it seemed. His fists clasping his stick were pressed against his breast, he had the air of contemplating, he the last of a generation that remained to see the day that was in it. Iain Mór and all the lusty Gaelic men that made his circle had taken the long road before him, and left himself as it were to yearn for them over another generation that cared for none of the ancestral things, but, shallow and colourless increasingly, went heedless bye down the road to noise and nothing. The ruins of a kind, big man, he sat in his own particular loneliness, his mind in a smoke of gloom.

At Murdo's approach the drooping figure stirred.

"That's you, little hero."

The voice spoke a little strangely, with an

edge of clearness unusual in these latter years, as if tardily he had come again into his full mind. Although his head was bowed it seemed certain from his tone that he made no idle greeting to a man passing on the road, but knew perfectly who was in it. Murdo understood him to have something to communicate and stopped by him, waiting. Surprisingly, Coinneach said no word. After a silent moment without moving, he slowly turned his head.

For Murdo the movement had suddenly a hidden fullness of meaning. There slipped again into his mind the strange awareness, as from a loop of the eternal falling about that place, so that they acted now in some timeless other-world, of import in which was the thing about to be revealed. Greybeard Coinneach, grown larger than himself, appeared like the symbol of a force sensed only, not apprehended, in his intentness of listening, towards the moor.

By a score of tracks and paths, out of sight, the folk were moving home. A faint noise of their going came after a little to the listening ear. The noise grew and sharpened, filling through the silence. By and by the moor was full of movement, footsteps in the heather, voices.

In the depth of his beard the dotard chuckled.

FINIS